Secrets
of Gingerbread Men

Valorie M. Taylor

Sadorian
PUBLICATIONS

Published by Sadorian Publications, LLC - Durham, NC

Cover Design: John Riddick, Jr.

Library of Congress Card Catalogue Number: 131877
ISBN 0-9700102-7-3 (pbk)

Second Printing, August, 2002
10 9 8 7 6 5 4 3 2

Published and printed in the United States of America

www.Sadorian.com

ACKNOWLEDGEMENTS

First, I give thanks and glory to the Lord for the promise of this project. It was literally spoken into existence and I have found that I'm a much better writer, mother, wife, friend and woman because of the faith and prayer required to birth this thing.

I'd also like to acknowledge four people who have been critical in my literary success. Shirley Hickman, my beloved mother, who bought paints, easels and writing pads for Christmas and birthdays and encouraged me to pursue creativity and dreams with blessed assuredness. My best friend of 20+ years, Christa Armstead, in whose eyes I saw something that I could be if I challenged myself with the truth already inside of me. Cora Hullum, in whose friendship I've found great comfort in at the crossroads of my life. Thanx, C.

And finally, to my beloved husband and life partner, Tyrone Taylor whose prayers, candor, friendship and sincerity have excited and encouraged me every step of the way. It is ironic that this first published work would be about men-to-be-admired. I'm certain that pressed between these pages is my joy of him, my admiration and my not-enough-words-to-describe-it love for him.

Secrets

of Gingerbread Men

Hand Me Downs

Chapter One
Shock Therapy

The blast of the alarm clock bit into Tuesday morning with piercing desperation. Outside was gray and damp all over Los Angeles. The rain had come unexpectedly in May like a houseguest who arrives too soon and catches his host in his underwear. Beams of sunlight ripped through the looming, gray clouds giving only a glimmer of hope. It was the kind of day for which optimists were created.

Kendrick heard a key turning in the lock of the heavy metal warehouse door that separated him from the rest of the world. "Good morning, Kendy!" echoed Margo's high-pitched voice. "Up and at'em!"

From the warmth of his custom-made sleigh bed, Kendrick turned over pulling the green satin sheet over his head.

Margo made herself comfortable at the kitchen counter and sipped coffee from a tall, paper cup. She placed her headphones on her ears and rocked her head to taped dance music. "Kendrick, you've got to wake-up sometime!"

Kendrick slammed his fist into his waterbed mumbling something about wanting to kill her some day.

After reluctantly sliding his black robe on and pushing his feet into velvet monogrammed slippers, Kendrick proceeded to drag his tired body into the kitchen.

"Well, good morning," chimed Margo over her steaming cup of coffee as Kendrick scuffed in, looking regurgitated.

"Rough night, huh?"

"You know it was rough, Margo!" he grumbled rattling the empty coffeepot.

"Huh?!" shouted Margo

Kendrick gave Margo an irritated look.

"Oh sorry," she said taking the earphones off and joining his frustrated silence. "You think you'll be able to meet with the museum directors about that piece you were consulting them on?"

Kendrick shook his head in disbelief. "What's with you, huh, Margo?! Why are you pretending that Roman is not dead?! You're a psychotherapist for cryin' out loud!" He snatched the little white bag that undoubtedly contained a sugary goody from Margo's favorite bakery off the counter.

"Hey," said Margo putting her cup down and clutching Kendrick's shoulder, "it's gonna be alright. I know Roman's death-"

"Roman's suicide, Margo!" shouted Kendrick as he pounded his fist on the counter. He clutched the bag in his other hand and whispered "Roman's suicide."

"I know Roman's suicide has deeply affected you, Kendrick," she said taking the bag from him and setting it on the counter. "But you've got to move on. Life is too-"

"Don't say it, okay?" Kendrick flopped onto the leather-topped bar stool and reached into the pocket of his black silk robe for a cigarette. He placed it between his lips and patted his pockets for a lighter. "I'm in no mood for it today, Margo. No mood. My long-time friend and roommate was found dead yesterday," Kendrick reminded Margo of the tragic news that had re-shaped his life. He opened drawers around the kitchen in desperation as he continued,"...the police won't let me see the suicide note. "He angrily mimicked the unsympathetic policeman "'*the note wasn't addressed to you, Mr. Walker*'. Is that any way to treat me?!" He slammed a few more drawers. "And why can't I find any matches around here!?"

"I told you before," said Margo not looking up from the newspaper, "smoking is bad for you anyway."

Frustrated with his search, he plucked the cigarette from his lips and tossed it onto the counter with disgust. Then he ripped opened the bag and bit into the treat.

Margo looked at Kendrick over the rim of her red-framed glasses and asked, "What time are we supposed to be down town?"

Kendrick looked at his gold watch trimmed with tiny

diamonds, "Aw, man! We've got less than an hour!"

"You better get dressed," reminded Margo as she snapped the morning paper onto the counter.

"You know, Margo," he said shaking the half-eaten pastry at her, "if you weren't my-"

"A-a-a," she warned putting her finger up but never looking up from the paper, "We've talked about that before, Kendrick. I will not allow you to project your anger toward Roman onto me." Margo adjusted her glasses on her nose before putting her headphones back on she said "I'm *here* as a friend."

Kendrick threw his danish onto the counter with a splat and stomped off to his bedroom.

The sounds of Margo and Kendrick's clicking heels echoed in the sterile corridor of the L.A. morgue. Pathologists and other personnel donned white lab coats. Aside from quick nods as they passed by, all of them refused to make eye contact with the couple. Kendrick figured death was their business and human pain a professional set-back; why engage in sorrow if not totally necessary?

The closer they got to office number G1539, the faster Kendrick's heart raced and his body perspired.

As they turned the final corner, Kendrick saw an assistant wearing a button that read *Forensic Science Spoken Here*.

Suddenly, Kendrick felt ill. He grabbed Margo's shoulder and shook his head.

Margo put her around him and walked him the rest of the way.

The rustling of leather against leather filled the silence as Kendrick fidgeted in his chair. Dr. Bhanduri barely looked up from his paperwork as Kendrick and Margo sat in front of him holding each other for support.

Dr. Bhanduri's well-rehearsed concern melted into unspoken wonder at first glimpse of the stiffly seated couple. His thoughts were obvious as he speculated at the relationship between the well-dressed black man and his 70's throw-back-looking white, female companion. He could only wonder what they had to do with the dead Hispanic man cooling on slab #5.

"Roman Casuga's body was discovered in a motel room on Sunset Boulevard late Friday night." spoke Dr. Bhanduri in a hushed tone scanning the paperwork through his bifocals. "According to our autopsy findings, Mr. Casuga committed-"

"Look," interrupted Kendrick leaning on the desk,

rubbing on his forehead and desperately needing a cigarette. "We know all that. Didn't Roman leave a note?"

Dr. Bhanduri returned to his paperwork for confirmation purposes. "Yes, he did." Then he produced a hastily scribbled note of only three words on Hollywood Motor Inn stationary: YOU KNOW WHY.

Kendrick's whole body shook. He wanted to run out of the office screaming into the corridor. He felt Margo's warm, concerned hands squeeze his firmly. But nothing comforted him.

Margo invaded the silence and spoke with the doctor quite professionally and void of emotion. To Kendrick, they may as well have been discussing some lab specimen.

Roman's words burned in Kendrick's mind. They were addressed to him, to the motel attendant who found him, to the police, Dr. Bhanduri; everybody and anybody who ever speculated that Roman Casuga might be gay.

As the shock of Roman's last words grinded to a halt, Kendrick found himself staring at a TV screen that framed Roman's sleeping face. The carnage of his massive head wound was tastefully concealed with a mound of white towels. Dr. Bhanduri continued to divulge the details of Roman's last hours.

"When was the last time you saw Mr. Casuga?" inquired the doctor.

"About 4 p.m. Thursday."

Dr. Bhanduri scribbled notes. He stooped and looked over his glasses. "Did the two of you argue?"

"What?!" shouted Kendrick. "No! What are trying to say, doctor?"

Margo grabbed Kendrick's arm and whispered "these are routine questions, Kendy. Just cool off."

"Mr. Casuga was your er-uh friend, Mr. Walker?" asked Dr. Bhanduri, uneasy with his prejudices.

"Yes," answered Kendrick turning away from the horror on the screen as he buffeted the doctor's obviously probing question. "Roman Casuga *was* my friend."

Dr. Bhanduri's suspicions gave way to his own prejudices. The matter was settled in his mind; he was dealing with people he had no respect for nor did he care to understand them. He turned off the monitor. He returned to his paper work letting the moment pass to comfort Kendrick through his display of feminine sorrow.

"Mr. Walker," he asked, "did Mr. Casuga have any next of

kin?"

"No," said Kendrick as he gripped the back of his neck to relieve his tension. "Just me." Kendrick sighed and produced a black business card with raised red letters from the pocket of his leather jacket. He laid it down on the desk in front of the doctor with a snap. "Jezebel's out on Santa Monica," said Kendrick as he stood to leave the coroner's office. "I'm the owner. Every phone number you need is on that card. If there are any papers I need to sign, just call me."

Inside the bustle of a trendy cafe nestled on the strip of boulevard in Los Angeles, Kendrick sat quietly and still. The volume of clinking tableware and mid day conversation did little to raise him from his slump.

"Hey, Kendy, you-"

"You know, Margo," he said cutting her off, "I really hate it when you call me Kendy!" He pushed his bowl of untouched curry soup across the table. He patted his jacket pocket for the comfort of a cigarette.

"Not gonna eat that?" asked Margo around a mouthful of her lunch.

"No," said Kendrick as he looked at his friend's dizzying spiral blond curls, floppy hat and the red lipstick that framed her big, white smile. "Margo! You really frustrate me!" He put the unlit cigarette to his lips. "I don't even know why we're friends."

The waitress passed by and whispered, "I'm sorry, but this is a smoke-free restaurant, sir."

"It's just danglin' here, honey," shot Kendrick shooing her away, "it's no threat to anybody."

Margo bit into her sandwich again and stretched her arm across the table to spoon a taste of soup from Kendrick's abandoned bowl. "I've got the solution to your problem, Kendrick."

"Well, the psychotherapist actually has a solution for a hurting friend," spat Kendrick as the cigarette waved at her.

"That was rude, Kendrick," reprimanded Margo spooning more of his soup.

"Look at you, *Ms. Manners!*" he said.

"Kendrick, you've got to let go of all this," she said flatly gobbling up his soup. "You've got to put this anger thing in perspective."

"And just how do I do that?" he asked with a doubtful smirk.

"Roman killed himself," she said consuming the soup.

"He didn't kill you."

Kendrick sat back in his chair. "Your little fancy flip-flop on words is not gonna do it for me this time, Margo. Why should I expect you to understand...Roman was like a brother to me!"

Margo swallowed hard and asked, "You have three brothers, don't you?"

"Technically, they're my brothers," said Kendrick nodding. "But I haven't spoken to any of them in what, eight, ten years?"

"Well, your brothers *are* alive, aren't they?" interrogated Margo.

"Yeah, I guess they're alive," said Kendrick annoyed with Margo's obvious direction of probing. He leaned forward plucking the unlit cigarette from his mouth. He fired at her in a whisper "Now wait a minute. Are you telling me that I should get in touch with my brothers about my anger over my dead roommate and friend who happened to be gay?"

Margo sat back in her chair. "I'm just saying that right now you have some real needs; some things you need to get off your chest." Margo turned on her clinically diagnostic demeanor and said "The best way to begin the healing process is to first be honest with yourself."

"I am being honest with myself!"

"Oh, yeah? When you came to me three years ago, you said your life had no clarity."

"That was because Andy walked out on me. He walked out on a three-year relationship. And if I remember correctly, your professional advice to me *was 'Kendrick, celebrate yourself and discover your identity without him.'* Let me tell ya', honey, loneliness is no picnic. I've been celibate for two years!"

Kendrick's broadcasted intimacy brought the clinking tableware and mid-day conversation to a sudden stop. Everyone stared at Kendrick and Margo for one embarrassing moment.

"Margo," whispered Kendrick, "you really bring out the worst in me."

"I don't think so, Kendrick," said Margo shaking her head. "I think the worst in you comes out when I'm not even around."

Margo threw her hand in to the air to get the waitress' attention.

Kendrick reached forward and slowly brought her hand to the table. "Wait," he said, "I'm sorry. You've been trying to help me...in your own strange little way."

Margo smiled.

"Okay...." said Kendrick as he took a deep breath. "Tell me, Dr. Day," he asked sincerely, "how do I begin to heal? I mean, really heal."

Margo smiled and leaned forward on her elbows. "Kendrick, for the last couple of years, you've been holding too much inside yourself. For as long as I've known you, you've held this deep anger toward your family; especially your brothers. What's with that, huh?"

Kendrick twiddled his well-manicured fingers. "...Hand me downs," he mumbled.

"What did you say?" asked Margo leaning in even closer

"Nothing...nothing."

"See there," said Margo sitting back in her chair, "you never want to talk about it. And it's eating you alive," she told him as she shook her head hopelessly. "Your homosexuality and now the loss of Roman seem to keep pushing you closer and closer to the edge. I can't save you, Kendrick. But if you're willing to be totally honest with yourself, well, maybe there is some hope out there for you."

Kendrick looked at Margo a long time, "Funny you should mention the edge. There's one more thing that's pushing me there, Margo."

"What?" she asked ready to resolve every one of his concerns. "We can work that out, too, huh?"

"Maybe..." Kendrick dropped his head as he tried to fight the tears that wanted to flow. He took a deep breath and began "...I got a letter the other day. Just like Roman's, my HIV test came back positive, too"

All the color drained from Margo's face leaving her white as a ghost. Her whole body trembled. She tried to smile. Her witty comebacks eluded her. Her eyes darted around the café for inspiration; anything to cushion the blow.

The noise of the café seemed to grow intensely and it competed with Margo's thoughts.

She snatched her hat off and ran her hand through her hair. The tears fell from her eyes in huge droplets.

She reached for Kendrick's hands and held them tightly in her own. "I'm so sorry, Kendrick. So sorry."

Kendrick drummed his fingers slowly on the table. "Me too."

"Have you seen a doctor?" asked Margo trying to sound brave.

"Yeah," sighed Kendrick looking at the table. "He confirmed it. He said no length of time could be determined. I could live another 50 years," said Kendrick smiling, "or die tomorrow."

Margo stared blankly ahead. "...All the more reason why you need to re-establish contact with your family," she said as if reading the future. "You've gotta let them know about this."

"Why?" asked Kendrick now appalled. "Why would they even care?! Didn't you hear me? They haven't talked to me in almost ten years!"

The waitress laid the check face down between them and left quietly.

"This is the time, Kendrick," whispered Margo leaning forward.

"Time?" laughed Kendrick. "Time for what? Margo, I understand the news must be a terrible blow right now, but-"

"Kendrick," she said closing her eyes, intent on making her point, "you've still gotta let it go."

"Let *what* go?" he asked sarcastically and folding his arms.

"Whatever's been hurting you all these years," explained Margo. "You can't just let your family find out one day that you're dead." Margo grabbed Kendrick's hand and his attention. "It would be like doing the same thing Roman did to you. Remember Roman's note...'YOU KNOW WHY.'"

Kendrick snatched his hand away from his friend. Then he turned the check over and pulled his platinum credit card from his wallet. He put the unlit cigarette back to his lips and stood up from his chair.

"...Write letters to your brothers, Kendrick," persisted Margo grabbing his hand.

Kendrick laughed and shook his head. "I can't believe people actually pay you money, Dr. Day."

"Put everything you've felt–the resentment, the pain, the years of hiding and trying to create an identity for yourself–put everything on paper!" spoke Margo quickly as she hurried to keep up with Kendrick who was headed for the cashier.

Kendrick greeted the hostess obviously ignoring Margo.

"Don't worry about being polite," Margo added throwing her body between Kendrick and the cash register, "just write it down even if you don't send the letters. Once it's out, Kendrick, it's gone!"

Kendrick stopped short of handing the bill to the hostess. He thought for a moment tapping his credit card on the bill from the restaurant. "...Then what?" he asked looking her squarely in the eyes. "What happens after that?"

Margo breathed a sigh of relief. "I can't guarantee the outcome, okay? But, Kendrick, you will feel a great burden has been lifted from your shoulders." Margo straightened his coat collar and fought her tears. "...You'll live the rest of your life with peace of mind, Kendrick. You owe this to yourself."

Kendrick pulled gently away from Margo and proceeded to pay the check. "I'll give it some thought."

Chapter Two
Confessions in Black

For 72 laborious hours, Kendrick locked himself away unshaven, fatigued and surviving on cigarettes and Grand Marnier.

According to Margo's instructions, he angrily spilled his thoughts and history onto personal stationary with pensively chewed-up pens that often ran out of ink.

The warehouse was littered with used tissues, half-empty liquor bottles, and cigarette butts and old photos. Kendrick diligently plowed through his past, surrounded by the dim seclusion of his home.

When his anger would reach its boiling point, he literally stabbed at the paper with his confession. Moments of compassion would gently sweep his heart. Regret for the hard words would follow. Loathing would give way to tears. The roller coaster of love and hate proved to be exhausting.

He slept stiffly in the purple canvas and metal chair waking often to the aches and soreness in his back. He remained fully dressed in his faded blue jeans and gray sweatshirt protesting any form of hygiene until the gut-wrenching job was done. He reeked of cigarette smoke and funk.

At times he'd awake from a sound sleep amongst the clutter of his letters ready to rip them to shreds. But he couldn't destroy them. For Kendrick, the letters were his proof of passage on a journey called *inner peace*. A destination he wanted more than anything to reach.

Besides, he told himself, Margo promised that things would be better. Much better.

While pressing past impulses of indecision, resentment and anxiety, Kendrick hastily folded the letters, wrapped the video and sealed them in black envelopes from Jezebel's. He addressed them to Ethan Walker at the Sacramento Kings headquarters, to Darryl Walker of Chicago, Illinois and to Pastor Moses Walker of the Holy Grace Worship Center in Little Rock, Arkansas.

He rested his chin on his hand and stared at the packages for a few hours contemplating his next move. He didn't feel lighter as Margo had promised. He felt worse than ever before. Out of desperation, he placed a frantic call to Margo. "Well, I did it," he said into the receiver.

"You've got to mail them, Kendrick," said Margo hurriedly from her office telephone.

"Isn't it enough that I put all my secrets on paper?" asked Kendrick puffing on the cigarette he held in his shaking hands. "...I mean, why do I have to let my brothers know all of this stuff?"

"It's how healing begins, Kendrick," said Margo reassuringly. "Besides, you made a video for Moses. That saved you a lot of writing, huh?"

Kendrick didn't answer.

"I've got a feeling things are gonna be good, Kendrick. But you've gotta go all the way with this."

Kendrick lent no evidence that he concurred with her optimism.

"Look," said Margo with a sigh, "I've got a 2 o'clock starting in exactly four minutes. It's Mrs. Ronkowski," she huffed, "talk about one floor short of the penthouse."

Kendrick didn't respond to Margo's attempt at lightheartedness. "Well, I'll talk to ya' later. Mail the letters *and* the video. Bye!"

Totally exhausted with the effort, Kendrick showered in the warm glitter of his gold metal and glass shower for the first time in three days.

The steamy water anointed him from head to toe as he washed the smoke and funk from his body. The fear of what his brothers' reactions might be melted from him and swirled down the drain. He dressed in a pair of casual slacks and a snug knit shirt that accentuated his modest build.

He avoided the 17th century mirror that hung in his

living room. But something made him stop and look himself squarely in the eyes.

What significance did he play in this thing called life, he wondered. He could breathe on his own, feed himself. The man staring back at him in the mirror, for all intents and purposes, appeared perfectly healthy; same brown face, short wavy hair cut and blunt side burns. He had the same thick eyebrows and fused together mustache and beard framing a chiseled jaw.

"...Same dead man," whispered Kendrick despairingly. He opened the warehouse door and allowed sunshine to pour in on him.

He tilted his head and closed his eyes as the sun bathed him in warmth. It was short-lived encouragement.

Venice Boulevard traffic whizzed by. Pedestrians strolled the street talking, laughing and enjoying the break from the rain. Kendrick hastened to the mailbox clutching the parcels tightly in his hands afraid that if he slowed his pace, he'd lose his nerve.

An elderly woman hobbled forward and reached for the blue handle. She put her letters in the mailbox just before Kendrick could.

The door squeaked, slammed and startled Kendrick into fidgety second thoughts.

The old woman nodded at him politely and offered a tight-lipped grin. Kendrick shoved the letters and video into the mailbox not allowing himself to change his mind.

Then he backed away from the mailbox, turned and walked the streets of West Los Angeles for hours until dusk.

***

Ethan Walker boarded his basketball club's chartered jet in Sacramento, California shaking the hands of a few of his team members as he made his way down the aisle. He settled his neatly dressed, slim 6'8" frame into a seat near the aisle and closed his eyes.

A fellow teammate unfashionably wearing his Sacramento Kings jersey asked Ethan for the window seat.

Ethan looked up and offered the greenhorn passage.

The young man settled his 200 lb. frame into the seat and offered his hand. "Armstead. Armond Armstead."

Ethan opened his eyes and sighed. He obliged him reluctantly and shook his hand "Ethan Walker."

The obviously excited rookie said, "Aw, man, you don't need no introduction. I know all your-"

"Say, uh listen, Armstead," said Ethan as politely as possible, "I'm meditating here. Can we talk later?"

"Oh, sure, sure...guess I should meditate, too." Armond pulled a small Bible from his duffel bag and began to read it quietly.

Ethan closed his eyes and sought his center of peace.

Just then a frazzled office assistant rushed onto the plane squeezing past the boarding players and waved a black envelope.

"What's this?" asked Ethan as she put it in his hand.

"It came in the evening's mail, Mr. Walker," huffed the young woman exhausted from sprinting. "It was marked urgent. It was in the wrong mail slot. Sorry."

Ethan took the hastily scribbled envelope penned in white ink and opened it.

The first few words tore at his heart. Ethan laid his head on the seat and quickly wiped a tear from his eyes. But his tears continued to fall quietly in the soft echo of the airplane cabin filled with the distant whisper of voices.

"Walker," asked Armond with quiet concern, "what's up with you, E?"

Ethan said nothing as he inadvertently let the letter fall open to his teammate. Armond scanned it speedily as Ethan mumbled "my brother. My little brother..."

Dear Ethan,

This is one of the hardest things I have ever done. Still it must be done. I need closure to some issues in my life that have spun wildly out of control. I find myself grasping for pieces of knowledge and understanding. Somehow they fade into nothingness before I'm able to apply them.

I am angry at you, Ethan. I have been angry at you a long time. Of all my brothers, I thought you'd be the one to stick by me. The one who would understand me. The one who would support the decision I've made for my life.

The longer I write, the harder it is to admit the truth to you; to spill the entire ugly truth about my homosexuality. Even now, seeing the word on paper does me some good, although be it very little.

But now the cat is out of the bag. The last

shoe has dropped. I feel like I've stepped out of the closet and into traffic!

I have AIDS, Ethan. And deep down inside my heart I blame you! Right or wrong, I've got to let go of the boiling anger that's been inside me for so long. I figure at this point, what have I got to lose?

When we were growing up you had such power, such foresight. I wanted to be just like you. Stupid and childish of me but I always thought that since you had so much, surely there was some to spare.

For a long time, I liked it when people thought we were twins. Truth is, I felt pretty bad since I was just eleven months younger than you, I felt like I took your rightful place as the baby of the family.

But then, you got taller and I stayed the same height.

You became a disciplined athlete. I stayed the artist Pops never took seriously. I'll bet you don't know that every teacher you had through grade school was thoroughly overtaken with your passion for learning and perfecting the things that interested you.

I had no passion to speak of. No talents that would propel me through life on a silver platter. I couldn't wait to be grown and do my own thing. But your teachers were handed down to me. Your teachers and their prejudiced expectations of the Walker boys. And I disappointed them time and time again. I was no Ethan Walker.

I don't know how long I have. I'm not making any promises. I don't expect any either.

Kendrick."

"Ethan, man..." whispered Armond, "I'm sorry, but I couldn't help but read about your younger–"

Just then, two team members seated behind them comparing the wealthy details of their off-season antics bellowed with laughter.

"This is the proof," began Ethan solemnly. "We act like

we are so far above most people...my little brother is dying. He's dying, man!"

Armond touched Ethan's arm to quiet him. "Hey, man, it'll be all right. Your brother is in the hands of the Lord. He–"

"How many of us have really taken the time to call family with the exception of Packowski over there, huh?!" shouted Ethan quieting the passengers with his overwhelming emotion.

"Do we keep in touch?!" he shouted loud enough to rouse the two behind him. "Or are we satisfied with the fact that people are always trying to get in touch with us? We tell ourselves we're right for pullin' away from them cause we think they just want our money!"

"Sound like you talkin' 'bout yourself, man!" said one of the team members behind Ethan. "I always keep in touch wit' my *peeps*! Bought my mama and my sister a house! I share the wealth!"

Ethan sheepishly took his seat not wanting to battle with his teammates. The battle in his heart was more than he could stand right then.

"...Look, E.," quietly ventured Armond, "people die everyday, man. Callin' your brother wouldn't have kept him from gettin' AIDS."

Flickering memories of Ethan and Kendrick's childhood played in his mind like a tattered black and white film. Ethan saw himself as a driven and disciplined youngster. *How could I have overlooked Kendrick's introverted insecurities*, he wondered.

"You know what, Armstead, you're right..." said Ethan wanting the embarrassing conversation to end with this stranger. "I'll be alright," He said as he folded the letter carefully and put it in the breast pocket of his sport coat. *But even the slightest effort*, considered Ethan behind closed eyes, *it might've kept him from feelin' like he's dyin' all alone.*

***

Across the U.S. in Chicago, Illinois, Darryl Walker opened his front door, threw his gym bag on the floor and began to sift through his mail.

"Oh, Darryl..." called a lady's voice from the kitchen.

"Regina?" answered Darryl perking up as he took his sweat jacket off revealing his muscular physique. "Is that you?"

"It's Tammy, you ignorant buffoon!" she said playfully as she opened the kitchen door. Then she slinked over to him, swaying her hips to an ancient feminine rhythm. She stood dangerously close to him and rubbed the top of his head. Her earthy perfume filled his nostrils while her height advantage over him thoroughly turned him on.

"Don't you remember me from the aerobics competition this past summer?" she cooed.

"Oh yeah!" said Darryl as he nuzzled his face against the nape of her neck. "Tammy from the team Xcess, right?"

"Good memory, Darryl Walker, Mr. Chicago 1999!" She walked over to his black leather sofa and sprawled herself shamelessly on top of it. "And do you remember offering me a place to let me lay my head if I was ever in the Windy City again?"

Darryl threw his jacket on the floor and closed the apartment door. He consumed the eye candy that was Tammy with her long auburn tresses and black spandex mini dress. "...Yeah, I remember. But how did you get in here, girl?"

She smiled and said, "I told your neighbor I was your sister just in from out of town. He let me in."

"With that dress on," said Darryl as his eyes covered her from top to bottom, "anybody would have to be crazy not to let you in, girl!"

Tammy smiled seductively and beckoned Darryl with her feminine wiles. "I know we haven't seen each other in a while, but to forget my voice, Darryl; it hurts, you know."

"Oh, my sister," laughed Darryl joining his lovely guest on the couch intent on correcting his mistake with her, "I'll just have to show you some brotherly love, girl. Chicago style."

The next morning Tammy strolled into the bedroom carrying the mail, a cup of coffee and allowed Darryl's oversized work shirt to fall from her shoulders. "Wake-up, sleepy head!" she teased slapping his shoulder playfully with the envelopes.

"It's a really bad habit," whispered Tammy mischievously, "but I can't help but flip through other people's mail" she said sipping her coffee. "Bills. Bills. Another-hey!" she said nudging her sleeping companion. "Look, Darryl, a black envelope." She turned it over and held it up to the light. "Hmm, and not just any black envelope but a black envelope from Jezebel's in Santa Monica! That's one wild place. D., who do you know on the West coast?"

"Huh," said Darryl sleepily rousing enough to notice the mail in her hands. "Tammy," he said snatching the mail, "you're a sneaky little-"

She kissed him passionately before he could finish his

thought. Then she waved the black envelope enticingly just beyond his reach.

"Let me see that!" he said reaching for it.

Tammy snatched it out of his reach and scampered playfully across the bed.

Darryl overpowered her. He tore into the envelope and read the sobering words in silence:

Dear Darryl,

> *You are the biggest culprit of all! You've been a walking 16 year-old hormone with ears since you were five! You never had any respect for women yet women have adored you beyond comprehension!*
>
> *I want to apologize for that. I really want to but I can't! I'm angry that I'm dying of AIDS. That's right, I'm lashing out and Margo says it's good for me to let go of the things that have plagued me for so many years.*
>
> *Who's Margo? She's my best friend. She's my only friend. She's also a psychotherapist.*
>
> *Margo helped me straighten out some things about my childhood. So the thing she helped me understand is that one major set back in my life was having you as an older brother.*

"What is it, Darryl?" asked Tammy trying to get a better look at the letter.

"Hold-up!" shouted Darryl blocking her view with his shoulder.

> *The turning point for me was when Mama insisted that I use your letterman jacket as a winter coat my first year of high school.*
>
> *It didn't keep the snow off my back. And besides that, it was too big for me! In more ways than one, it just didn't fit!*
>
> *Girls were attracted to you. I could have been wearing the jacket and nothing else! It wouldn't make anybody notice me! All those fancy, embroidered letters and awards on that jacket!*
>
> *Maybe it should've made me feel good. But it didn't. I'm no good at sports!*
>
> *The letterman jacket, that hand me down,*

it was a slap in the face to all that I knew I was, Darryl! Everybody knew!

So why be mad at you and not Mama? Because I told you how I felt always having to wear hand-me-downs. You promised me you'd buy me a winter coat of my own. Brand new! You never did. Some female, if I recall correctly.

How could you ignore me? I was desperate. I was 15 years-old?! Your own brother, man!

Maybe you have questions about my disease.

Maybe you don't.

Maybe you'll just crumple this letter, toss it in the garbage and say "serves the little faggot right."

I'm having a difficult time closing this letter. So just consider it closed.

Kendrick

"Darryl?" asked Tammy stroking his naked chest with her hands. "Darryl, baby? What's got you lookin' so guilty?"

"...My little brother has AIDS," confessed Darryl as his hands began to shake.

Tammy slid her hands from him and for lack of a better phrase said "You never told me you had a brother."

Darryl turned around and took a serious look at his date whom he had only met once. Her unwashed face traced dark circles under her eyes and mere specks of her lipstick remained. In the daylight, she was a stranger.

Their unfettered passion jumped to mind as he said, "You know, Tammy, you never told me your last name."

Chapter Three
The Fabric of Brotherhood

Big-hipped Sister Isabella Frenchette stormed into Pastor Moses Walker's office with a fierce almost crazed look in her eyes. "Why wasn't my brother Thomas chosen as the junior boys' Sunday school teacher?!" she thundered from under her fuchsia straw hat.

Moses looked up from studying his Bible and gripped the nape of his neck. He motioned for Sister Frenchette to take a seat across from him.

She slammed the door shaking the inspirational pictures on the walls. Then she stepped forward, plunged her wide hips into the chair and shoved her purse into her lap.

"...There were a lot of brothers applying, Sister Frenchette," began Pastor Walker.

"I know *that!*" she said leaning forward and pounding her fist on the desk. "And how is that that jail bird Deacon Brisbaine got the position instead of Thomas? Thomas is a school teacher you know, Pastor Walker!"

Moses took a deep breath. "...I know, Sister Frenchette."

"Oh, I see," she said in a tone that confirmed her suspicions. She readied herself to walk out the door. "I thought you were different, Pastor Walker!"

Moses stood and rounded the desk to retrieve her. "Wait, wait, Sister Frenchette-"

"No! You wait!" she said turning around to face him. "Now Thomas has always been a little effeminate. But *I* have

29

always accepted him. This is not the first church we've come up against that discriminates-"

"Discriminates?" asked Pastor Walker.

"Yes, Pastor Walker," said Sister Frenchette grimacing. "Discrimination! You want me to spell it out for you?"

A look of righteous indignation came across Moses' neatly bearded, chiseled face. "And do you always run to his rescue, Sister Frenchette?" he asked positioning himself on the edge of the desk. "Whenever your brother Thomas comes up against something that doesn't cater to or acknowledge favorably his chosen life style, do you always take up for him?"

"You got your nerve, Pastor Walker!" she hissed. "I am *his* sister. I have given most my life to make sure that boy had everything!" Her voice cracked as the lump of sorrow arose in her throat. Tears stung at her eyes. "My Mama entrusted that boy to me when she died and-"

"I know Thomas is dear to your heart, Sister Frenchette. He's family, I understand that." Moses handed her his handkerchief. "Making the ultimate sacrifice for family is extremely difficult for most people. You have to understand my position."

Moses led Sister Frenchette back to the chair and sat her down. He adjusted himself on the edge of the desk and began gently "...one of the parents got wind of Thomas' application for Sunday School teacher. She complained to me that she felt her son was already vulnerable growing up without a father. She had nothing personal against Brother Frenchette but she didn't want what she called *the wrong signals* communicated to her boy. Other parents voiced their opinions, too, Sister Frenchette."

Sister Frenchette kept a stiff upper lip and kept her eyes glued to Pastor Walker.

"For the sake of the membership," said Moses shaking his head slowly, "I couldn't appoint Thomas to Sunday school teacher."

"All right," said Sister Frenchette taking a deep breath, "I can understand the politics." Then she hissed venomously. "But how do you justify an ex-con as Sunday School teacher for such vulnerable young minds, Pastor Walker?"

"I believe Deacon Brisbaine loves the Lord, Sister Frenchette," defended Pastor Walker. "He can at least teach the boys to avoid a life on the streets."

"And what about my brother Thomas, huh?" asked Sister Frenchette with a raised eyebrow, "Doesn't his love for the Lord account for anything?"

"Of course, it does, Sister Frenchette," said Pastor Walker, "but you have to-"

"What's your opinion, Pastor Walker?" asked Sister Frenchette batting her eyes nervously now annoyed by the rigmarole. "What do you think of my brother Thomas?"

Moses took a deep breath and admitted, "I don't think the lifestyle that Brother Thomas leads is right. It's an ugly thing to even imagine two men..." Moses shuddered at the thought of it. "...Sister Frenchette, get him to agree to some counseling with me. I can show him in the Bible where-"

"He needs no counseling, Pastor Walker," said Sister Frenchette as she went for the door.

"...He's still welcomed here at Holy Grace, Sister Frenchette...."

"Thomas is an excellent school teacher!" she declared. "He's won awards. The students *voted* him the school's favorite teacher even. They don't seem to care that he's..."

"You can't say it, can you, Sister Frenchette?"

"You know, Pastor," she asked never turning from the door, "from the pulpit, you preach love, acceptance and forgiveness. But behind closed doors you're just like all the rest."

Moses folded his arms across his chest and sighed. "I'm sorry you feel that way, Sister Frenchette. But parents don't often get to choose their child's teacher or school for that matter. In an institution like the church where we have some say-so, our children are the only guaranteed resource we have for the future spiritually. Frankly, they are too precious to risk."

Sister Frenchette turned the knob and opened the door to leave, "...no matter now. *We* will be looking for another church, Pastor Walker."

Moses returned to his desk chair and leaned back wearily in it.

He tried to pray but his thoughts were jumbled. He rubbed the tidy edges of his salt-and-pepper beard.

Just then he heard a light tapping on his office door.

"Come in."

Lisa, Moses' volunteer office assistant, poked her head in. "Pastor, I've been holding onto the mail most of the morning. Can I bring it in now?"

"Yes, yes," smiled Moses waving his hand trying not to let the affects of his previous conversation show.

He gathered his books and Bibles in front of him and read the pages with a jumbled mind and an uneasy heart. "I'm sorry. I've got to prepare for this annual Family Consortium banquet day after tomorrow..."

"I understand," said the college co-ed. "Well, if there's nothing more, I've got to get to my class."

"Thank you, Lisa, for holding all the calls this morning," said Pastor Walker trying to lighten the residue of war that lingered in the office.

"Too bad I couldn't hold Sister Frenchette," Lisa joked. "If you ask me, I think you did the right thing not letting that flaming faggot teach the boys."

Moses looked at Lisa careful not to agree or disagree.

She placed the mail on the desk and left.

Moses picked up the black, video-sized envelope addressed in white ink to his church in Little Rock, Arkansas.

He noticed the Los Angeles return address and his heart started to beat out of control. Sweat beads popped onto his brow. He could sense the bad news that lay ahead. And although he didn't want it confirmed, the experienced preacher knew he had to view the tape.

Alone in his study, he turned his back to the door and popped the video into the VCR the congregation blessed him with during the last appreciation service.

His breath escaped him at the sight of Kendrick's face. Time had taken its toll on Moses' memories of his sweet-faced little brother. And the angry way Kendrick looked into the camera lens laid the groundwork in Moses' heart that his little brother's news would be earth shattering.

"Hello, Moses," said Kendrick wearing his gray sweatshirt and looking quite dirty. "You're the only one of the Walker brothers who's receiving a video instead of a letter." Kendrick rubbed his prickly hair.

"This is hard for me, Moses. Really hard. I suspect you've known that I'm a homosexual for some time now." Kendrick chewed his lip and looked nervously at the floor. "And yet, you, the preacher man, you haven't wanted anything to do with me!" Kendrick turned away and laughed privately.

He twisted in his chair uncomfortably and said "you claim to have the answers but what is the answer for me, huh?"

"I'll bet you're wondering how I can do such a horrible, low down, unholy thing as having sex with another man, huh? Well," he said with certainty, "I don't just go speeding through life letting people touch me, you know. I'm no table dancer and I don't march in any parades. I've had relationships. Real relationships. Not so different from what you have with your wife, you know."

Kendrick rubbed his face miserably as he looked into the camera. "I've been diagnosed with AIDS, Moses. This video may very well be the last time anyone sees me while I at least look healthy.

"Margo, my friend, she says this confession thing is good for me but I don't know about that. Mentally, I don't feel any better. I'm depressed. And physically," Kendrick sighed, "there is no more me; I feel like something is eating away at me from the inside out."

Kendrick looked strangely beyond the lens.

"But Margo says once I start talking about it, I can't stop until I'm purged and not a moment sooner." He laughed with a degree of anger. "That Margo is one for the books."

Kendrick lit up a cigarette. "You know the last time I saw you was at Mama's funeral?

That's right, twelve years ago....too long for brothers not to talk," needled Kendrick.

"Oh, and I blame you, Moses," said Kendrick sarcastically. "Yup. I figure you should have made the first move by now. Like Mama always said *'Moses, you're the oldest, you oughta know better!'*" Kendrick blew smoke at the lens.

The camera jiggled a bit as a muffled voice asked a question.

"What?" asked Kendrick frustratedly looking beyond the lens.

"What do you blame Moses for?" whispered the off-camera voice.

Kendrick settled back into his chair and looked straight into the camera. "His shoes," he said shaking his head. "His shoes. Always the first one to wear the brand new leather shoes. By the time I got them, they had been stretched out by Darryl and scuffed up by Ethan while he went sneaking off to play basketball in them instead of going to church." Kendrick laughed and puffed on his cigarette.

Then Kendrick pointed at the camera lens with this smoking cigarette and said "You always got the best, Moses. You were the first one out the chute and you always got the best." Kendrick shook his head at the irony.

He became enraged as he took a moment to reflect. "I guess Mama and Daddy forgot how to use a camera by the time I was born!" His nostrils flared. He stood from his seat. "But that's just one of the things I'm mad about!"

"Wait, Kendrick!" said the off-camera voice again. "You're gonna-"

"Turn it off, Margo!" shouted Kendrick as he walked toward the camera filling the screen with the gray of his sweatshirt.

The camera swirled to the floor. "...But, Kendrick I-"

"Turn it off!!"

The screen faded to black. Electric snow followed.

"You never once told me Kendrick was a homosexual, Moses" said Stella, Moses' wife of twenty years.

"I couldn't, babe," he said sweating nervously and unable to take his eyes off the screen as his anger grew. "This is just the kind of thing I preach against!" he said pointing at the screen. "I don't want to have anything to do with this!"

"Then you're not fulfilling your duty for the Lord if you don't want to win your own brother to Christ. Your ministry is no more than him, Moses." She said softly and pointed at the TV screen. "It's no more than him..."

"But I didn't make him this way!" said Moses ejecting the tape and shoving it into the envelope in which it arrived. He pushed it across the desk and thumbed his beard.

"You are probably the only one who can help him, honey," said Stella pushing the package back toward him. "He's hurting, can't you see that?"

"What can I do about it now, huh?!" Moses got up from his desk and went to the window to stare out of it. "...I just don't know what I would do if one of my own sons came home and told me something like that."

"Pretend for a moment that Kendrick *is* your son, Moses," said Stella in a non-offensive way. "What would you tell him? What would you want him to know before he dies?"

He shuddered at the challenge feeling the cold emptiness only a parent feels when forced to deal with the notion of losing a child.

Moses turned to Stella's loving face with the sting of tears in his eyes. "I'd want him to know how much I love him, Stell. And how much the Lord loves him, too."

Moses and Stella quietly sat down together on the sofa.

"...When I was sixteen," Moses told Stella, "I decided to save up some money to buy myself a football. That's all I wanted. The football cost $12.95 plus tax at Baxter's Sporting Goods. It was all I could think about," he smiled reminiscently.

"I wanted that football more than I wanted to date you, Stell."

Hand Me Downs

Stella smiled the warm smile that Moses had fallen in love with at first sight.

"...I always knew one day I'd be a preacher. But first a football player, you know? It was all that mattered. I used to keep my money in an old jelly jar with a rusted top. It was marked *football*.

"One day when I was countin' the money I'd saved up from doin' odd jobs around town, I heard my mama outside talkin' to Kendrick.

"But, Mama," he said almost cryin', *"I don't wanna wear Ethan's old shoes anymore. They hurt my feet. I want new shoes like Moses has."*

"Kendrick," Mama said, *"You're only seven. Mama can't afford to buy you brand new shoes you're gonna grow out of in just a month or so. Hand me downs ain't so bad."*

"Well what about a new winter coat? The one Darryl gave me-"

"What's wrong with it? It fits, doesn't it?"

"I just don't like it." Kendrick insisted.

"Well now, Kendrick, that's just silly. You complainin' about somethin' that there's nothing even wrong with."

"'I hate hand me downs!'" screamed Kendrick at my mother. *'When will I ever get anything brand spankin' new!?"*

Mama told him, *"Boy, you betta' watch yo' mouth!"* That's how Mama was with us boys.

Then Kendrick screamed *'why I always gotta wear somebody else's junk!?"*

"Stella," Moses continued, rubbing his forehead, "those words ring so clearly in my head, even today. Kendrick said *'You'll see one day I'm gonna have everything I ever wanted brand new! And ain't nobody gonna tell me I'm wrong for wantin' the things I like!'"*

"I watched Kendrick run across the poppy fields away from Mama and something struck me like a ton of bricks; *I knew Kendrick would have everything he ever wanted, Stella,"* said Moses to his wife peering despairingly into her eyes. "And a few things he never bargained for."

"The $11.58 you saved from working, Moses?" asked Stella curiously. "What did you do with it?"

Moses dropped his head in shame. "I-I hid it in my drawer. I figured if I couldn't see it, God couldn't tell me what do with it." He shook his head miserably "I could've bought Kendrick some shoes of his own, Stella. Don't you see? That one act of unselfishness, well...maybe I could've changed things."

Stella shook her head slowly as she absorbed Moses' story. "You know what you've got to do, Moses, don't you?"

"I'm not goin' to L.A., if that's what you're thinkin', Stella," said Moses bolting from the sofa, shoving his hands in his pockets and walking to his office window. "You can forget that!" he said over his shoulder.

"Moses," asked Stella with steel-like composure, "how many broken and desperate souls have we received at the church recently? What, two maybe three?"

Moses didn't answer.

"The majority of the members know God's love, Moses," told Stella to Moses' uncompromising glare. "But Kendrick doesn't know the way." Stella stared at the video hopelessly. "That video proves it."

"Stella, Kendrick is there all the way on the West coast 'cause he wanted to be there!" shouted Moses. "He's a homosexual 'cause he wants to live that way!" Moses walked over to his desk and slammed the videotape package into the trash. "He had options just like the rest of us! Same upbringin', too! He knows the difference between right and wrong!"

Stella's expression of concern didn't change.

"How could you miss the manipulation of this video, Stella!?" asked Moses pointing at the garbage. "Nothing is ever Kendrick's fault! It's always somebody else's!"

Stella shook her head slowly but silently maintained her position. "You're right, Moses," Stella said as she arose and took the video from the trash. "This is his fault. But did you ever read in the Bible where Jesus started a church, opened the doors and said '*c'mon in and let me change your life.*" She placed the package on the desk and waited for Moses to answer.

He shook his head knowing exactly where she was going with this. "...No, Stella."

"No is right, Moses," she continued. "He *went* to the hurting people; prostitutes, thieves, even the diseased folks. Jesus didn't remind them they were unworthy of God's love as he was trying to heal them and save them."

Moses looked quickly at Stella as she said lovingly, "and that's not your job either, Moses." Moses hung his head.

"Jesus wasn't afraid to touch their lives," said Stella encouragingly. "And you shouldn't be afraid either, Moses. You're a minister of the gospel," reminded Stella. "A chosen vessel. A-"

"But none of those people were related to Jesus, Stella," said Moses putting a finger up to signify his revelation. "Kendrick is my brother. This whole thing is too close of an issue for me."

Stella placed her hands on her husband's shoulders. "Even more of a reason to go to him, Moses."

"No!" growled Moses.

Stella stood still.

"Besides, I can't guarantee that I'll be able to get through to that bullheaded brother of mine with love of Christ before he dies. I didn't make him the way he is."

"Okay, man of God," she said starting for the door. "You pray for your own direction."

"Wait, Stella."

She turned to her husband and offered the beauty of her patient nature.

"You know what bothers me most about all this? Darryl, Ethan and Kendrick, we're all cut from the same cloth," Moses sat down at his desk. "I mean, we all had the same mother and father–God rest their souls–yet some how, we're all so different.

"I mean, look at us," continued Moses. "Ethan is a pro basketball player. He's good, too. He just plays for a lousy team. And Darryl is a bus driver. I never understood why he prefers the windy city and wild women to his hometown. And Kendrick," Moses shook his head proudly, "do you know that kid went to Paris to study art right here from Little Rock, for Pete's sake. So different..."

"Yes," smiled Stella clasping her hands in front of herself, "and you were chosen to preach God's Word. That's the fabric of brotherhood, Moses. It's made up of your memories of good times and bad. The cloth you were all cut from is strong. It has nothing to do with where your brothers live or even how they live. Because the fabric of brotherhood, Moses, it's weaved in your heart."

Stella kissed her husband gently on his shoulder and closed the door of his study leaving him alone with the company of his conscience and his God.

Moments later Moses walked into the Sunday School classroom where Stella was arranging some of the supplies and said, "my plane leaves for L.A. at 9:40 tonight."

Chapter Four
Born This Way

Kendrick dressed himself eagerly sliding the cool of his silk cobalt blue shirt over his well-defined arms and chest. He preferred to leave the top buttons undone so that his chest hairs could tease the imagination. It was part of his owner's mystique at Jezebel's.

Although he didn't feel festive, completing the uniform that put Jezebel's on the map was a priority.

On went Kendrick's gold watch that whispered understated elegance.

His black, lightweight slacks complemented his slender build. Finally, he tossed on his favorite navy blue frock coat and gave himself an approving nod in the mirror.

He walked into the living room where Margo sat patiently dressed in her party clothes swirling the last sips of her third glass of wine around in her glass.

Margo hopped happily from the couch and smiled at Kendrick. "Lookin' good," she said with a thumbs-up noticing the return of his graceful style. She set her wine glass down, straightened Kendrick's collar and said "well, don't you feel lighter since writing the letters?"

"Yes, I do, actually," smiled Kendrick as he breathed a sigh of relief. "It's all out now."

"Good," said Margo hugging him. "Better get your trench coat. It's raining pretty hard out there."

Margo downed the rest of her port in a gulp. "Let's get ready to party!" she said throwing her hands into the air and snapping her fingers while she cut a few dance moves. "You've been held up in this warehouse too long; almost a whole week!"

"Yeah," said Kendrick heading for his bedroom to retrieve his rain coat, "I kinda' miss Jezebel's."

There was a knock on the warehouse door.

"Now who could that be?" asked Kendrick checking his watch.

"I'll get it," said Margo heading for the door. "Go get your coat. It's probably somebody with a wrong address."

Kendrick disappeared behind the huge Ilia Olun painting to his bedroom.

Margo swung the door open. Three black men stared at her as rain and wind beat at their backs.

Her mouth fell open.

One of the men, dressed in a forest green warm-up suit stepped forward, looked her up and down and smiled insatiably. He licked his lips and said "You must be Margo."

She smiled and put her hand on her hip. "And you *must be* Darryl."

Kendrick's footsteps were heard from around the corner as he called out "Who is it, Margo!? Who could be visiting at this-" Kendrick stared into the faces of his estranged brothers. He froze as his lungs refused to breathe for a moment.

"Well," said Moses elegantly suited in a taupe overcoat with the hint of a neolithic black and gold tie, "aren't you going to ask us in?" Rain trickled from his hat into his face.

A cold shiver went through Kendrick as the blood rushed from his face. "Come in...come in."

The four brothers stood awkwardly darting glances at each other and the exotically converted warehouse that Kendrick called home.

Ominous and colorful mobiles plunged dramatically from the ceiling. Huge black statues separated whole rooms. Eclectic furniture pieces created artsy, interesting little conversation areas.

"..Isn't this the part where you guys hug each other or something?" asked Margo in her groovy, upbeat fashion. "C'mon, you guys," she said snapping her fingers and stumbling under the weight of her buzz, "earth to the Walker brothers. Earth to the Walker brothers."

No one moved. And no one dared give voice to their obvious disinclinations.

"I didn't expect any of you to come here," said Kendrick

as he looked at Margo for an answer. "That's not why I wrote you the letters," he told his brothers borderline apologetically. "I never thought you'd show-up at *my* door."

"Well," said Darryl hanging his duffel bag around the neck of a bronze replica of the Venus de Milo in the foyer. "I came here to see you one more time before you, you know, kick the bucket."

"Wow," said Margo as she snickered now feeling quite tipsy. She folded her arms and watched them as if they were lab rats in a maze.

Kendrick scratched his head in amazement. "You guys traveled all this way? And you mean to tell me, you're not mad at what I said in the letters?"

No one said a word.

"Alright, I'm mad!" volunteered Darryl getting in Kendrick's face. "You called me a walkin', 16 year-old hormone who has no respect for women!"

Darryl raised an eyebrow and flashed his winning smile at Margo. "...present company excluded."

"And," demanded Ethan wearing his business casual look from the airplane, "what's this mess about how my teachers liked me better!?"

Kendrick was speechless.

All eyes fell on Moses who shoved his hands in his pockets and said "You're a sinner, Kendrick. But God loves you," he said unconvincingly. "And He can save you."

"Look, Moses," shouted Kendrick, "don't come up in here talkin' that-"

"Alright!" shouted Margo holding her hand up and grabbing her purse. "You guys are at least talking to one another." She tried unsuccessfully to hide her incessant laughter. "And that's my cue to leave."

"Wait, Margo!" shouted Kendrick as they played tug-o-war with the door. "What are they doin' here?" he asked through clenched teeth. You never said I would get a visit from the people I've just told off!"

"Sorry," said Margo yanking the door.

Kendrick snarled as he pulled harder, "I should've never listened to you!"

"Well, Kendy," said Margo pulling as hard as she could, "the future cannot accurately be determined by us mere mortals. Call me. Bye." She slammed the door.

"Okay," said Kendrick turning to his brothers slightly embarrassed by his and Margo's theatrics. "You guys ought to come in and sit down." He lifted Darryl's duffel bag from Venus' neck and dropped it on the floor. "Can I get anybody a drink?"

"A soda for me, Kendrick," said Moses trying to get comfortable on the more-for-show-than-sitting aqua colored sofa. "No caffeine."

"Do you have carrot juice?" asked Ethan studying the purple metal and canvas chair.

"No, Ethan," said Kendrick sarcastically. "Fresh out."

Ethan shrugged his shoulders. "Then I'll have a mineral water."

"Okay," said Kendrick. "And Darryl, what will you have?"

"Scotch," he replied rubbing his hands together in anticipation.

Darryl, Moses and Ethan made themselves as comfortable as possible without saying a word to each other.

Kendrick placed their drinks in front of them on the coffee table. "I don't get it," he said pausing to shake his head. "How did all of you happen to show up at the same time? Did you guys plan this or something?"

"No," answered Moses looking at Darryl and Ethan. "I took a cab here from the airport. These guys were walkin' up to the door when I got here."

"Yeah," said Ethan reaching for his mineral water, "the limo driver said the address I gave him wasn't a residential one." Ethan chuckled and looked around. "Who'd have thought, a warehouse? Man, I thought I was at the wrong place until I saw Darryl."

Kendrick scratched his head pensively. He turned to Darryl who was downing his scotch and asked "and how did you get here, Darryl?"

"Bus," answered Darryl with a satisfied sigh and burp.

"So, Kendrick" said Moses trying to make his hefty frame comfortable on the weirdly shaped sofa, "you looked like you were on your way out."

"Yeah, Moses," said Kendrick. "I was going to my club," he said arrogantly. "Jezebel's in Santa Monica."

"Oh," said Moses catching the subtle innuendo, "I see."

Darryl snickered as he observed the look of shocking disapproval on Moses' face.

Kendrick's cellular phone rang cutting into the awkward silence. He pulled the small device from his belt and answered with an irked "Yeah."

"No!" Kendrick scrubbed his brow with his fingers and paced the floor. "Look, Nolan, I won't be there tonight-

"No," reprimanded Kendrick, "I said I'm *not* coming to the club tonight...then tell her that!"

Moses, Darryl and Ethan scanned the floor in front of themselves imagining how Nolan fit into this enigma.

"Look, Nolan, you're in charge, alright?" shouted Kendrick pointing into the phone. "I've got family in town." Kendrick sighed. "Unexpectedly..."

He rubbed his temples. "Yeah, family. Nolan, I wasn't born in a cabbage patch, you know!"

"Okay! Bye!" Kendrick hung up the phone and stood stiffly next to the couch where Moses sat.

"Kendrick," asked Moses pleasantly, "why don't you sit down, man?"

"Can't," he answered rubbing his fingers rigidly against his forehead. "Why'd all of you come here, man? You talked to each other about the letters, didn't you?" accused Kendrick sharply. "I know you did!"

"Nope." said Darryl leaning forward and placing his glass on the table empty. "Didn't even know these guys got letters."

"I figured I owed it to you, Kendrick," offered Ethan now relaxing comfortably in the purple canvas chair.

"Me too." said Moses.

"So, you guys haven't been visiting one another all these years barbecuing and stuff like that?" asked Kendrick pointing at them.

"Nope," said Darryl. "Haven't seen Moses here in about seven years. And Ethan, only time I see him is when his sorry team is losin' on T.V. to the Bulls! Yeah, baby! Chicago!"

Ethan bit his tongue and said, "I'm way above your little, childish insults, Darryl."

"Not what you expected to hear, huh, Kendrick," asked Moses watching his youngest brother's reactions.

"No, Moses," admitted Kendrick. "Not what I expected at all."

"Yep," said Moses taking a sip from his soda, "the more things change, the more they stay the same."

"Is that some clever little church way to stick it to gays, Moses?" asked Kendrick vehemently.

Moses choked on his soda. "No, Kendrick! Why would you think–"

"So, Kendrick," asked Darryl blatantly, "how did you find out you had AIDS?"

"Man, D.!" shouted Ethan, "Do you have to run rough-shot over a brother like that? You haven't changed one bit! You're still-"

"It's okay, Ethan," assured Kendrick trying to get a grip on himself. He turned to Darryl, "a friend of mine encouraged me to take a test anonymously...I've known for about two weeks. I've been trying to work through it ever-"

"When did you know you were gay?" Darryl blurted out.

"Aw c'mon, you guys!" shouted Kendrick looking at all of them as if a foul was committed. "You've known! Don't deny it! When I saw you at Mama's funeral, I was there with my partner, Gino!"

"Don't remind me," sighed Moses putting his hand over his face. "You were cryin' all over him, fallin' all in his lap. It was embarrassing...."

Darryl sat back and crossed his arms. "I guess you're gonna try and convince us that you were born that way, huh, Kendrick?"

Kendrick stood square-footed. "As a matter of fact, Darryl, yes. I *was* born this way!"

"Come off it, Kendrick!" returned Darryl waving his hand.

Kendrick crossed his arms and sighed. "I always knew I was different," he explained reflectively. "There was *something* that made me different from all of you!"

"But why different, Kendrick?" asked Moses. "Why not just unique or special? Why does being different always have to bring humiliation to the family?"

"Humiliation?" asked Ethan looking Moses up and down. "Who's? Yours or Kendrick's?"

Moses didn't answer.

"Why am I a homosexual and not any of you!?" argued Kendrick.

"Yeah," laughed Darryl running his fingers across his mustache and eyebrows narcissistically, "like *that's* gonna happen!"

"For the record," shouted Kendrick angrily, "I am unique and special and gay!"

"Hey," said Ethan standing to his feet and putting a supportive arm around Kendrick's tense shoulders, "I don't think you two are giving Kendrick a fair shot here. Now I've read about this kind of stuff. It's no secret Mama always wanted a girl. Maybe somehow in the mysteries of life, the girl element, that was missing in our family, found its home in Kendrick's life."

Kendrick shook his head miserably at Ethan's logic and

pulled away from his embrace.

"Girl element?!" asked Moses turning around on the sofa. "Ethan," he said pointing a convicting finger at him, "I'm gonna pray for you."

"Let me get this straight," said Darryl his tongue now quite slippery from untold measure of scotch. "Are you saying that you knew you were a homo from when you were a little kid?"

"Yes," answered Kendrick matter-of-factly.

"Well, I beg to differ!" said Darryl shaking his head. "How can a little kid be a homosexual when he hasn't even had sex before?"

The Walker brothers were silent.

Although bound to their individual opinions, there was a profound significance to the echo of those words that lingered in the air. Even if they were first conceived in Darryl's slightly buzzed state of mind.

Darryl bolted from his seat and went into the kitchen mumbling.

"Were you molested or something like that, Kendrick?" asked Ethan. "Just tell me who it is and I'll kick their-"

"No, Ethan," sighed Kendrick his defenses now spent, "I wasn't molested."

"C'mon, Ethan," said Moses, "stop trying to define immoral behavior with physiological mumbo-jumbo!"

"You live in a box, Moses," said Kendrick insultingly and shaking his head. "You live in a box."

"Then tell us once and for all, Kendrick," asked Moses, "what got you here, huh?"

Kendrick paced the floor removing his frock coat and trying to fit his explanation into words. "...Okay, Moses, you were the football star and aspiring preacher, right?" asked Kendrick as he perspired. "That preacher thing; Mama liked that. And, and Darryl, the good-looking one with girls calling all the time...and Ethan, you were Little Rock's first method 3-point shooter. Pops liked that!"

Kendrick stopped and dropped his head, "what was I but the reminder of dashed hopes for Mama and another mouth to feed for Pops?" He held his head in his hands, "all I was good for was passing your old hand-me-downs to. Nothing more. Nothing less...."

"You know," said Moses stunned as he watched Kendrick draw Ethan into a pool of sympathy, "I wish I could bottle your command of sympathy and global imposition!

Unrewarded genius is almost a proverb!"

"What?" asked Kendrick.

"Yeah," continued Moses with his biting observation, "if I could market your manipulative way of getting the world to see things like you do, my church could build the youth center in record time!"

"If you could see your way to let people like me be involved in your little congregation, maybe you'd *have* enough money to build your youth center!"

Moses was taken aback for a moment as he remembered his conversation with Sister Frenchettte. Then he shook his head and said "...I wish to God it were so easy, Kendrick."

"Man, K.," expressed Ethan "I never knew you felt that way; so down on yourself."

"Well, well, well," said Darryl returning from the kitchen with his shot glass scotched to the rim and obviously scotched himself. "Down on himself?! Isn't all this emotionalism so sweet? *And* so lady-like?" he teased throwing a bent wrist up. He took a sip of scotch and began "Kendrick, you little-"

"Wait a minute, Darryl!" said Moses loosening his tie. "Now, Kendrick, you can't live the rest of your life retreating from manhood."

"Yeah, man," added Ethan, "you can beat this!"

"Beat what?" challenged Kendrick, "A.I.D.S. or homosexuality?"

Neither Moses nor Ethan answered.

"What good am I to anybody now, huh?!" shouted Kendrick as his voice echoed back from the metal ceiling. "How can all of you just walk in here and try to tell me how to live my life!? Well, what's left of my life."

Kendrick gave each of them a dirty look and mumbled some obscenities. "Look at my life!" said Kendrick pointing to the pieces of his collection. "Look around at what I've got! Originals! Everything you see is mine!" He pointed to himself and hollered "First!"

Kendrick circled his brothers shouting, "You guys never had to wear somebody else's junk and like it! You never had to be left behind because you were too small or too young to participate!"

"Kendrick, let go of the past, man!" said Ethan. "Mom and Pops did the best they could."

"Finish that statement, Ethan," said Kendrick pointing at his brother, "they did the best they could for the three of you!"

"Everybody has a place in a family, Kendrick," began Moses. "We don't get to pick and choose the order."

Kendrick looked at his brothers' faces as he tired of his own campaign. He flopped onto the sofa next to Moses and held his head in his hands. "Why did you all come here?!"

"We came for you, Kendrick." said Moses. "Different reasons, but" he said looking at Ethan and Darryl's faces, "we came here for you."

"Alright," said Kendrick finally taking his hands from his face, "Moses, tell me *your* reason? Come on, tell me."

"Honestly?" asked Moses ready to throw caution to the wind. "Guilt."

Kendrick was impressed with Moses' candor but turned to Darryl quickly. "And yours, Darryl?"

"Mmm," thought Darryl thoroughly enjoying warmth of his numbed senses. "To get you to start likin' chicks," he said with a big smile.

Kendrick resented the answers so far but felt he should complete the damage. "...And you, Ethan?"

"Curiosity," replied Ethan without any fanfare.

"Well," said Moses catching a glimpse of Kendrick's sober state, "I guess we all know where we stand. Don't we?"

Kendrick shook his head in disbelief. "I suppose we do."

Chapter Five
Last Rites & Dying Wishes

Ethan stood up, stretched his 6'8" frame and yawned. He decided to take a break from the nonexistent conversation in the living room. The rest of the warehouse tickled his natural curiosity.

He found that the same eclectic feel of the living room continued in theme throughout the cleverly divided span of space. Colors jumped out at him. Statues and bold works of art stood guard at every turn.

"Pretty interesting, huh?" asked Kendrick startling Ethan.

"Oh yeah," said Ethan surveying the showplace with an approving nod. "It's a nice place, Kendrick. It's really somethin' else," he said looking up and around himself at all the creative and interpretive wonders.

"Say, uh, Kendrick?" asked Ethan gravitating slowly toward a boldly stroked canvas of red, orange and gray. "Don't tell me that's an original Olun hanging over there?"

"It's an original," confirmed Kendrick proudly as he sided up to it. "I know Ilia."

Ethan's mouth fell open. "You know Ilia Olun?"

Kendrick nodded imperiously.

"Did he charge you the same twenty grand that that piece is worth?" asked Ethan.

"Not quite," snickered Kendrick as if he had a secret.

Ethan continued to gaze around at Kendrick's exorbitant possessions in utter amazement.

"You want this Olun, Ethan?" asked Kendrick stroking it

longingly. "Just say the word and it's yours."

"Yeah, man!" said Ethan happily. "I'd be a fool not to...," Ethan took one look at Kendrick's desolate eyes and said "well, I don't know."

"It's okay, E," said Kendrick looking around sadly. "All this stuff has to go somewhere."

"Kendrick, I've been thinkin'," said Ethan taking a look over his shoulder to insure their privacy. "I've been negotiating with this herbal health research firm called Vitalia for a few TV spots and maybe the herbs could help you with your disease. Hey, man, it might even cure it. Who knows?"

Kendrick shook his head, "I can see it now." He mimicked a radio announcer and said "Ethan Walker's brother has AIDS and Vitalia Herbs saved his life!" Kendrick snarled, "no thanks, man. I'm not a test case!"

"You're takin' it the wrong way," said Ethan. "Don't misunderstand me, Kendrick."

"I understand alright-"

"Kendrick, man, it's not like that!"

Ethan's little brother didn't budge from his fury.

"You know, Kendrick," began Ethan apologetically, "it's been a long time since we've talked, man. Nobody can just pick up where they left off when there's so much time between them. Funny, I never realized how much havin' a brother meant when we were growin' up."

Ethan dropped his head and admitted, "I miss it a lot." He laughed and shook his head. "No other like a brother. Remember Pops used to say that?"

Kendrick remembered a simple pleasantry from his childhood that was soon overshadowed by the gloom of his present circumstances.

"This Vitalia thing," continued Ethan, "I guess I'm just tryin' to make up for 12 years of bench warmin'."

Kendrick stopped fuming for a moment to appreciate the sincerity of his older brother. "...I'm sorry, too, Ethan. It's just that nobody really knows how to deal with this A.I.D.S. thing. Including me." Kendrick walked back toward the living room.

Just as Ethan turned the corner to follow him, he spotted a dusty, black bass guitar in a darkened corner of the warehouse. He walked over, picked it up and noticed that the garage-like space housed a drum set, keyboard and a saxophone.

"Kendrick," he asked entering the living room and holding up the bass guitar, "got a band you never told us about?"

"No," said Kendrick, "those instruments were left here when I bought this place."

"Darryl," asked Ethan shaking the bass guitar in his face, "you still play?"

Darryl hopped to his feet and challenged, "can you still beat a drum?"

"Yes, sir," answered Ethan as if tossing his hat into the ring, "I can."

"Then *I* can still pluck a bass guitar!" Darryl snatched his sweat jacket off and shouted, "It's on!"

"Wow," said Kendrick popping happily from the sofa and heading for the music room, "I never thought I'd see the day the Walker brothers would play music-" Kendrick noticed Moses didn't move from the sofa. "What's wrong now, Moses? Aren't you going to join us?"

"Everybody knows I never played an instrument. Besides, that's what the three of you were into."

"For a moment there I thought you were gonna tell us it's a sin to play a little funk," said Kendrick.

"I wasn't going to say anything," said Moses.

"You could croon for us," said Kendrick trying to insult him into cooperating. "I mean, you do sing at your church, don't you?"

"Of course, I sing at my church," defended Moses sensing the subtle insult. "But that's not *all* we do."

"That's right," said Kendrick sarcastically, "you get souls saved."

Moses took a deep breath and stood up so that he was eye to eye with his baby brother. "If nobody has the guts to say it," he breathed, "I do. You need to realize that the gay lifestyle is demonic."

"You're so out of touch, Moses!" laughed Kendrick viciously. "What? Now I'm a spawn of the devil because I'm gay?"

"Kendrick, you-"

"Look at yourself, Moses!" said Kendrick. "You, in all your holiness, can't condemn me to hell 'cause this is my hell, Moses!"

"C'mon, man-"

Kendrick pointed directly at Moses' face. "We come from the same womb, Moses. You can't deny it; a little bit of me is in you."

Moses smiled and returned "and a little bit of *me* is in

you."

Kendrick turned to leave.

"Wait, man," said Moses, "I'm not trying to condemn you, Kendrick."

"One thing, big brother," asked Kendrick, "Let me ask you one thing. Have *I* hurt anybody?!" he demanded. "Because of the lifestyle I have chosen, have *I* hurt anybody?"

Moses stood nose-to-nose with Kendrick. He wanted to reach out to him but feared he wouldn't be received. "You have hurt one important man," began Moses. "His name is Kendrick Walker."

"Touché," said Kendrick as the thump and bump of the bass guitar sounded from the rear of the warehouse. Kendrick fought his tears as he maintained intense eye contact with Moses. ".....They're gonna be callin' for us in a minute," said Kendrick wiping a tear quickly from his eyes. "You gonna sing for us?"

Moses put his hands up and said "no, no I don't-"

"It's a dying man's wish, Moses," said Kendrick dryly. "How can you possibly deny it?"

Moses shook his head slowly and said, "You've got me over a barrel, Kendrick."

"It's my specialty, remember?"

Moses and Kendrick smiled at each other for the first time in almost twelve years.

Echoing throughout the warehouse was the sound of Darryl and Ethan in a heated debate.

"Aw c'mon, Ethan. You were right there with me smokin' weed in the attic and chasin' skirts behind the barn. Now all of sudden you this big health guru who's never done one dirty little deed in his life!"

"That was then, man! We were kids!" said Ethan as he began to feel the rhythm of his drum beat. "*I've* changed!"

"Changed? You mean you *got* some change when Best Bev Bottling Company gave you that little penny-anny endorsement for that sewer water they market!"

"That did it!" shouted Ethan as he came off the drummer's stool and readied himself to pounce on his brother, "I'm gonna bust you up, man!"

"Hey!" shouted Kendrick as he and Moses ran in and held onto Ethan.

"Let him go!" hollered Darryl dropping the black bass on the floor sending twings and twangs into the air. "Mr. Chicago'll just have to whip-up on his tall, lanky-"

"We're here to play music!" reminded Kendrick.

"Oh yeah!?" exclaimed Ethan calming himself and straightening his clothes, "well, what's Moses gonna do?"

"Play the tambourine," quipped Darryl as all of the brothers including Moses bellowed with laughter.

"Hey remember when we had that gig down at Jo-Jo's bar?" asked Kendrick.

"Yeah," said Moses glad to join in the laughter. "I also remember Darryl almost got Jo-Jo's place shut down for havin' that waitress serve you those whiskey shots!"

"She was more than just a waitress, preacher man," teased Darryl reminiscently. "Her name was Desireé and she turned Darryl-the-pup into Darryl-dog-the-ladies-man!"

"You said that same thing about your third grade teacher, Darryl," said Kendrick fiddling with the keyboard.

"And Mama's hairdresser Ms. Leotha," added Ethan laughing hysterically.

"Jealous!" concluded Darryl returning his focus to the bass and mumbling. "...just jealous. All of you!"

"Moses, remember that blues song I wrote?" asked Kendrick.

Moses, breaking just long enough from his hysteria, asked Darryl "How did it go again?"

Kendrick began to play a melody on the keyboard. He stopped and started over again as the melody escaped him.

Darryl laid down his base rhythm. Ethan joined in on the drums. Moses threw caution to the wind and began to make-up silly lyrics in his untrained and untalented singing voice until all of the Walker brothers were doubled over with laughter.

"We stunk as a band," said Kendrick turning off the keyboard.

"That's for sure," agreed Ethan.

"Speak for yourself!" said Darryl still trying to master the timing of his instrument.

Kendrick and Ethan retired the thoughts of mastering their instruments until the only sound in the room was Darryl's amateur thumping.

"For years I've wondered about Aunt Alice's dentures," said Ethan as he pointed his drumstick at each of his brothers. "And now that we've got all the suspects in one room-"

"It was Kendrick's dumb cat Plato!" accused Darryl.

"What would Plato need with Aunt Alice's dentures?" laughed Kendrick.

"Well, all I know," confessed Moses, "is that when Aunt Alice came to visit that summer in '71, she took her dentures out to eat that tapioca pudding Mama made."

"And soon after that," explained Darryl, "I saw that cock-eyed Plato strollin' across the grass with those dentures in his mouth! The little fur ball was walkin' and Aunt Alice's teeth were just clackin' in his mouth!"

"You must've been drunk, D!"

"No, Ethan, man, I was sober!" said Darryl. "And I knew they were Aunt Alice's dentures because they had that same chip on the front tooth!"

"You know what's really crazy?" asked Moses.

"What?" they all asked.

"A year or so after Aunt Alice went back to Boston, I saw Brother Porter walkin' all tall and proud into the church one day with brand new dentures!"

"You lyin'!" hollered Darryl consumed with laughter.

"Naw, man," said Moses, "he even testified about how the Lord blessed him with a slightly used pair of teeth! Guess what? His dentures had that same chip in the front!"

The Walker brothers laughed relentlessly.

"Wow," said Moses glancing at his watch. "It's already one o'clock in the morning."

"What?" asked Kendrick desperately checking his watch. "You guys don't have to leave or anything, do you?"

"Not me," said Ethan.

"Nope," said Darryl as he continued to fool around with his instrument.

"...I've got a bad back," said Moses rubbing his side. "And it doesn't look like you have room for all of-"

"You could have my bed, Moses," said Kendrick graciously. "I've got sleeping bags for us! Just like when we were kids."

Darryl and Ethan made faces at each other behind Kendrick's back.

"...And my bed heats up," continued Kendrick hospitably. "It vibrates, even."

Moses shook his head. "Well, I uh...."

Darryl laughed. "Kendrick, come on, man. Snap into reality. Don't you know that preachers can't sleep in the bed of the sodomized or somethin' like that?"

"Darryl, you're an idiot!" quipped Ethan. "Man, I've been a lot of places. Slept in a lot of beds. And clean sheets are clean sheets!"

"…Kendrick," whispered Moses shaking his head. "Thank you, but-"

"Moses," interrupted Kendrick, "I know people have prejudices about homosexuals but a hotel bed has just as many secrets as my bed does."

"Okay," said Moses reluctantly realizing he was outnumbered in both logic and sincerity, "I'll stay."

"Hallelujah!" shouted Darryl, "The preacher is mixin' wit' da' sinners!"

The Walker brothers laughed except Moses and Kendrick who shared a look that silently cemented their division.

"Kinda' hungry, Kendrick," said Darryl rubbing his stomach. "Got anything to eat around here?"

"Chuck Cheesers All Night Pizza delivers," he said.

"Sounds good, Kendrick," said Darryl. "Order us a few of 'em."

"Make at least one of them a vegetarian," said Ethan as Kendrick ducked into a quiet corner to make the call.

"So, how are the boys?" asked Ethan of Moses.

"Fine, fine," said Moses. "Gettin' big. Wishin' they could meet their pro basketball player uncle Ethan Walker."

"I've just been so busy, that's all," said Ethan.

"Busy?" asked Moses. "For twelve years?!"

There was an uneasy silence that fell over the room.

"What's with us, man?" asked Darryl. "I mean this thing goes way past Kendrick and his problems." He banged his fist against his chest, "We're brothers, family! What, are we ashamed of each another? We don't speak for years. I don't get it. What has happened to the family?"

"Mama died," said Moses pulling pictures of his sons from his wallet. "She was the glue that held all of us together." He passed the pictures to Darryl and Ethan.

"Yeah, but how long can we use that excuse?" asked Darryl. "Hey," he chuckled holding up the photo, "this boy of yours has my ears!"

"Let's hope that's all he's got of yours," laughed Kendrick hanging up the phone. "Let me see" he said reaching for the photos, "now this must be Paul and he's got to be David. And of course, Samuel."

"You knew their names," said Moses puzzled.

Kendrick handed the photos back to him, "Stella sent birth announcements. And she's been sending pictures of the boys for years."

Moses shook his head in disbelief. "Well, at least somebody still believes in the family."

"You live in this big place all alone, Kendrick?" asked Ethan.

"I did up until about a week ago," said Kendrick. "My roommate died."

"Died?" asked Darryl picking up his bass. "Of what?"

"Gun shot," said Kendrick dispirited. "Roman was a good friend."

"Gunshot!?" asked Ethan. "Like a real drive-by L.A. is famous for?"

"No," answered Kendrick. "Nothing like that."

"Then who shot him?" asked Ethan.

Kendrick couldn't bring himself to answer.

"Was he your lover?" fired Darryl to Ethan and Moses' shock.

"No!" said Kendrick exasperated. "My roommate. My friend."

Darryl unstrapped his bass and set it down. "You mean, you two shared this place and you weren't lovers?"

Kendrick crossed his arms across his chest and sighed. "...We slept together once...just one time."

"It's never easy to lose a friend," said Ethan softly.

Kendrick stared into space as if reading lines from a script. "Last Friday, I stood over Roman's unmarked grave..." A hush fell over the room. "Roman was the unencumbered free-spirit who never took his life quite seriously. He hungered for a family, a sense of identity. Roman starved for acceptance.

"But Roman was never particularly careful with himself, you know? Never quite protective. And in this life you gotta know how to defend yourself or run really fast...matter of fact, he was a little too trusting of people." Kendrick shook his head miserably. "Time and time again he'd come home with his butt kicked and licking the wounds inflicted by some lover that was no lover at all.

"Somehow life had failed Roman. The good stuff was unattainable to him. The American dream with all its golden promises of happiness, prosperity and longevity were just slightly out of his reach." He spoke from the depths of his baritone. "I suppose the American dream never anticipated the Roman's of the world.

"Did you love him?" asked Ethan as Moses' and Darryl's stomachs turned with disgust.

Kendrick laughed and shook his head. "You can't love in

someone else what you hate in yourself! He was my friend. My keeper of secrets. We journeyed the forbidden road few men dare to venture. We understood one another."

Kendrick closed his eyes and continued. "In his own funny little way, Roman cheated life; the life that eluded him, taunted him. He turned his back and took the final flying leap in a race to end himself before something ended him. He died bound to his convictions and his movie star good looks." Kendrick lit up a cigarette.

"I couldn't help but admire him for his incredible bravery," he smiled. Then he said flatly, "But I hate him for the same reason. He put a bullet through his head and left an unfulfilled hole in who I am."

The Walker brothers were left cold and empty.

Darryl stared at Kendrick in disbelief.

Ethan twiddled his fingers nervously.

Moses kept his eyes closed tightly teetering on his preacher's duties and his brotherly ones.

"...Moses," asked Kendrick, "can't you give Roman last rites or somethin'?"

"Naw," Darryl interrupted, "Moses can't do that. Suicide is an unforgivable sin."

"How do you figure?" asked Kendrick now thoroughly upset with Darryl's contemptuous remarks.

"Thou shall not kill, right?" confirmed Darryl. "Well, if you're dead, how do you apologize to God for killin' yourself from Hell?"

The Walker brothers remained frozen in their individual interpretations.

Chapter Six
Man

"Hey, Moses!" shouted Darryl as he bulleted an old football down the hall at him from the music room.

Moses caught the ball with a thud instinctively holding his hands to receive the pass.

"You still got it, Moses!" shouted Darryl.

"Darryl," reprimand Kendrick as he grabbed the football from Moses and threw it back. "Put that ball back in there, man! You're so drunk, you might break somethin'!"

"Drunk?!" he asked catching the ball and throwing back at Kendrick. "I'm not drunk. Just havin' a little fun!"

Kendrick threw the football to Ethan who was rounding the corner and ended up getting hit in the head.

The Walker brothers howled with laughter as they found themselves going for passes and making imaginary touchdowns all over Kendrick's art gallery-like warehouse.

Kendrick got into the fun of going out for a pass and tackling his brothers.

Soon after, they all fell onto pieces of furniture totally exhausted from the diversion.

"Getting a little old, huh, Moses?" asked Darryl resilient, flexing his muscles.

"You could say that," answered Moses completely out of breath.

"Too much time behind a pulpit," mumbled Ethan under his breath.

"Well, Kendrick," said Moses, "I guess you *are* pretty

good at sports, after all, huh, Kendrick?"

"Yeah," said Kendrick out of breath, "I guess I am."

"You're a real man now, Kendrick," said Darryl as he patted Kendrick on the shoulder and took another sip of scotch.

"What do you know about bein' a real man?" asked Ethan.

"I tell you what bein' a real man is," hiccuped Darryl, "I can make a phone call and any one of my women would hop on a plane and meet me in L.A. right now just to spend one night with me. Now that's power," slurred Darryl adjusting his crotch. "That's bein' a *real* man."

"So that's bein' a real man, Darryl?" asked Kendrick sarcastically. "Sleepin' with every woman you meet?"

"Ya'll don't understand me," said Darryl fed up with their laughter and returning to his seat. "I get pleasure," he explained simply. "I give pleasure. The women I'm involved with know that we're together for one thing and one thing only. There's no confusion about commitment." He took another sip of scotch. "Besides, I got women houndin' for Darryl-dog up and down the highway."

"Yeah, but D.," roared Ethan, "you're a bus driver; none of the women you meet even have cars!"

"Look, Ethan," returned Darryl standing to his feet, "you may be startin' for the Sacramento Kings but you're still the same poot-butt younger brother of mine who always wanted to be just like me."

"Be like *you*?" laughed Ethan. "Man, in order to be like you, I'd have to have my legs amputated at the knee!"

"Alright, alright," said Moses. "Give it a rest, you two."

"Naw, Moses!" shouted Darryl walking up on Ethan. "It's just startin' to get like old times! Now Ethan, as much as you travel, you should have a couple of women in every city. If I didn't know any better, I'd think you had a little sugar in your tank, too!"

"Here we go...." sighed Kendrick.

Ethan thought quickly for a cap of his own but to no avail.

"...Yeah," said Darryl glancing at himself in a near by mirror, "if I was as tall as you and still as good lookin' as me, and had as much money as you got, I'd put James Bond to shame!"

"Okay," said Kendrick purposely interrupting Darryl's flow, "what *is* a man, huh? Moses here said I shouldn't retreat from manhood."

"A man is one part flesh and three parts machine," answered Darryl matter-of-factly.

"So what, man is actually the Terminator or somethin'?" laughed Ethan. "D., you need to lay off Kendrick's scotch."

"Let me school ya', boy," chuckled Darryl condescendingly. "A man is bred and designed to conquer whether on the battle field, on the job, and yes, on the court of love. That's his flesh side."

"And what about women, O' wise one?" asked Moses.

"Women were created for man's pleasure. Read your Bible, brother preacher."

"Wait, wait," asked Ethan in stitches, "tell me more about this machine thing?"

"As a matter of fact," said Darryl seriously, "a man is the closest thing to a machine in existence. Think about it."

"Kendrick," said Ethan pointing to Darryl, "no more scotch for his man!"

"His basic shape doesn't change over time." continued Darryl as he flexed his muscles. "See, look at me," he said making his muscles jump, "Mr. Chicago four years running! A man thinks logically. A man functions by what he has been programmed to do."

"So does a horse!" laughed Ethan.

Ethan, Moses and Kendrick laughed at Darryl without restraint. Ethan and Kendrick threw pillows at him and flexed their muscles satirically strutting around and shouting "I'm Mr. Chicago, 1999 four years runnin'!"

"Men build machines!" shouted Darryl to get their attention. "Machines build machines! Do women build machines? No!"

"So, Darryl, let me get this straight," asked Kendrick out of breath from clowning, "you think all a woman is good for is being barefoot and pregnant, right?"

Darryl gripped Kendrick's neck in the bend of his arm and said "No, Kendrick. You've misunderstood me. A man is not a real man if he don't at least buy his woman some shoes!"

Kendrick rolled his eyes.

"C'mon now," said Darryl, " this is your first step to bein' a man. How to treat a woman 101; let me school ya', man."

Moses took a deep breath and began "Kendrick, at this crossroad of your life, maybe you should consider-"

"No! No! No!" said Darryl stomping his feet. "Now Moses, don't go fillin' Kendrick's head with all that church and religious stuff! Only a real man would instruct his young brother to take advantage of this time in his life and sow a few wild oats!" He nudged Kendrick and made a few rude moves with his pelvis, "You know, get your groove on!"

"So what, D?" asked Ethan from the purple canvas and metal chair. "You sayin' Moses here is not a real man because he wants to share hope with Kendrick?"

"I'm just sayin' anything that teaches you to suppress your instincts to conquer; well, it's not manly, that's all," explained Darryl.

"But Darryl," said Kendrick, "you forget, I've been infected with HIV. I can't-in good conscious-have sex with anybody!"

"Lil' bro," said Darryl resting his muscular arm on Kendrick's shoulders, "there's still time. Just wear protection, that's all."

Ethan shook his head and scoffed "I always suspected you were the first graduate of Neanderthal University, Darryl. And now, I'm sure of it."

Darryl spun around and shouted, "Bump you, Ethan, you 90 foot tall wannabe!"

Ethan hopped from his chair. "Wannabe?!"

"You heard me! You *wannabe* a superstar basketball player. Hey," slurred Darryl, "you *wannabe* me!"

"Wait guys," shouted Kendrick over their altercation, "I think we should define what real manhood is!"

Darryl and Ethan groaned and took their seats.

"Let's hear from Moses," said Kendrick insincerely. "What is a man, big brother?"

"Nobody wants to hear from the preacher!" whined Darryl. "Now if you want instructions in manhood, little bro." Darryl raced to the foyer and returned lugging his army-style duffel. He pulled a hastily wrapped package from his bag and handed it to Kendrick. "Here is all the instruction you'll ever need."

Kendrick reluctantly opened the package and read the title. "C'mon, Darryl! I'm not watchin' any porno flick!"

"That's not just *any* porno flick, little brother! That's D'Niesha Does Dallas!" He threw his arm around Kendrick and said intimately "the math is simple: do you wanna die with your boots on or under some flamer's bed, huh?"

"I can answer the question of manhood and I think everyone will agree," said Ethan standing to his feet.

"Okay, Ethan," said Kendrick glad to have a diversion.

"What *is* a man?"

"A man is perfection," he said emphasizing his points with his hands. "He recognizes the skill he has been gifted with in the early morning of his life."

Darryl pretended to snore loudly.

"He sets out on a course to perfect that skill," continued Ethan valiantly. "He lives by that skill. If that skill brings him money, fame, accolades; no matter. He doesn't lose sight of his dedication to that skill. That skill feeds him and makes him who he is."

"Oh brother," moaned Kendrick miserably.

"Ethan," spat Darryl, "if I didn't know better, I'd say you were hittin' the pipe, man."

"No, wait a minute," said Moses settling them down, "Ethan, I think you're on to something."

"I know I am," said Ethan quite proud of himself. "Kendrick needs to treat his body as a temple and-"

"No, no," said Moses scooting to the edge of the sofa. "I'm talkin' about when you said a man is perfection. When God created Adam, Adam was perfect because he was complete," said Moses as if talking to himself. "Spiritually, physically he was whole!"

Moses paced the floor delving further into the meaning. "...He wasn't a composite of his life experiences. And the only reason Eve was created was for social completeness."

"That's not what I meant, Moses," snarled Ethan.

"We all know what you meant, Ethan," said Darryl leaning against a statue. "You were gonna tell us about how havin' a healthy mind and keeping pure thoughts and worshipping your body like a temple is supposed to make you a god or some crap like that! Thing is, Kendrick is not auditioning to be a salad!"

"Ignore them, Kendrick," said Ethan. "And stop trying to reinvent yourself from fragments of things you've failed at or the things you're afraid of. You're already complete! Already a whole person."

"I agree," said Moses, "Adam already had intelligence, an identity, a set of duties laid out before him."

"Look, Moses," said Ethan, "it's my turn to answer the question!"

"See there, Moses," said Kendrick, "there you go with that '50's mess about havin' the little wife and sittin' in your easy chair and kids that call you Father! The problem with you Christians is that you base your idea of manhood on one person, Adam! And Adam wasn't perfect. I mean, look at his sons; Cain killed Abel!"

"All right, Kendrick," said Moses. "Adam was not perfect. He didn't even have enough guts to say no to his own wife! But his inclusion in the Word suggests that men *can* improve on the mistakes Adam made. We don't have to fall under the wheels of insecurities," explained Moses in his most animated preaching style.

"And there's one thing you cannot deny," Moses added to their resistant murmuring, "Adam didn't shy away from the hand he had been dealt and then force others to accept his self contrived image."

"Every time we get together, Moses," huffed Ethan, "you manage to twist my words around!"

"That's because you're a little twisted to begin with," said Darryl lazily.

"Alright! That's enough!" screamed Kendrick, slapping his legs and rising from his chair. "You guys talk as if there's real hope for me! I'm dying!" Kendrick chuckled madly at the fact. "Yep, I'm dying and no one night stand or vitamin juice swallowed with pure thought is gonna change that!"

The Walker brothers sat isolated and silent in the same space like four equal sections of a pie. Each had more questions than solutions to the insurmountable issue of manhood and death.

There was a rattling knock on the warehouse door. Moses got up to answer it. "Must be the pizza."

"Who is it?" Moses asked.

"Chuck Cheeser's Late Night Delivery."

He opened the door to find a young black man dressed in baggy pants, earrings in each ear, and baseball cap. "That'll be $28.92." he said toying with a toothpick in his mouth.

Moses reached for his wallet and then stopped. "Listen, my brothers and I are having a discussion. Maybe you could help us out."

"Naw, man. I ain't' into no group thangs. I'm just here to deliver your pizza. That'll be $28.92."

Kendrick came around the corner and entered the kitchen as he overheard Moses' conversation. Kendrick crept around and lingered in secret behind an Olun to hear what Moses was saying.

"Of course you're not," said Moses pulling twenties from his wallet. "Look, there's a $10 tip in it for you if you would just answer one question."

"Ten dollars?" asked the young man eyeing the money in Moses' hand and then peering beyond Moses' shoulder into the space that resembled some eclectic gallery of nude statues and disturbing paintings. "I ain't comin' in there."

"Oh no, you don't have to step foot in the door. But the ten dollars is yours if you just answer the question."

"Naw, man," he said waving his hand, "that's chump change!"

"Okay, fifteen!" said Moses reaching for the young man. "One question."

"Show me the money then."

Moses dug into his pockets and pulled out an additional $5 bill.

"Alright," said the young man snatching the money, "what's the question?"

"What is a man?"

"I don't know. That's a stupid question!" said the young man as he shoved the pizza toward Moses. "...What is a man?"

"Wait, son." Moses pushed the box back gently against the young man and continued. "In *your* opinion, what is a man?"

The young man smiled and said, "I'm liable to give you this fifteen dollars back."

"Humor an old preacher, huh, son?" persuaded Moses.

The young man thought for a moment reaching under his cap to scratch his head "......I really don't know, Preach."

"Okay, son," said Moses, "just close your eyes."

"Close my eyes?!" he asked taking a step back. "You trippin' now, ol' freaky preacher."

"Nobody's gonna hurt you," assured Moses. "Just look real deep down inside yourself, past what music tells you that you are... past what your mama says you are...way past what society and your fears say you must be."

"If you can look past all of that," continued Moses candidly, "you will see the man you want to be. The man you were created to be. Then, son, live every day of your life being that man."

The pizza guy shook his head slowly with his eyes fixed as if reading his own thoughts. "...Sounds good but it's gonna be hard to be that man, Preach."

"Why?" asked Moses.

"The man I see," said the young man pointing at his chest, "way deep down inside is fearless, respected. It's not about money with him. He's a basic kind of guy. He wants the best even if the best things are simple. He wants to make a difference in some ways," said the pizza guy shaking his head. "Problem is, that man would never be accepted by *my* crew."

"Yeah but *if he* is rejected by your crew," challenged Moses, "*is* there another crew that *will* accept him? A crew that will respect you, appreciate what you contribute to the whole even if what you contribute is basic and simple?"

"Yeah," said the young man perking up a bit. "It's a big world out there but I guess so."

"Then tell me this," pursued Moses, "you know we all gonna die one day, right?"

The young man jokingly put the pizza box up to his face and said "yeah...but you ain't about to kill me or nothin', are you?"

"No, no," Moses laughed. "But before you die, as which man do you want to have lived? The one you're trying to be or the one you see inside yourself?"

"Seriously?" asked the young man as he handed the money back to Moses. "The one I see inside me."

Chapter Seven
Once Bitten

It was 3:14 in the morning. Kendrick paced the floor restlessly chain smoking as his weary brothers sat and laid sprawled all over the living room floor.

There had been a stifling muteness among the Walker brothers for a couple of hours. Except for the occasional stomach growl, belch or other involuntary bodily function, each of them had nothing really to say. The limits of time were gaining ground with each of them.

"Kendrick," said Moses blinking sleepily on the couch, "why don't you come and sit down for a while. You must be exhausted."

"I can't right now," said Kendrick blowing smoke from his cigarette and lighting up another. "Gotta figure some things out."

"Kendrick," said Ethan, "you haven't talked much about your club Jezebel's."

"Don't be so stupid, Ethan," spat Darryl. "You know what kind of club it is. Men walkin' around in big Diana Ross wigs, fake body parts and skin tight dresses!"

"Is that what Jezebel's is like, Kendrick?" asked Ethan.

Kendrick stopped and said "Hardly."

"You know any people like that?" asked Ethan. "You know, like cross-dressers?"

Kendrick laughed, "Not really, Ethan. But I'll bet you've come across a few of 'em in your line of work. Some of them are a little more public with it than others."

"What, Ethan," quipped Darryl, "you hopin' Kendrick can get you a blind date or somethin'?"

Ethan sat up and fired back "I asked because I wanted to know what makes people change, you sawed-off–"

"Let's keep it clean, guys," said Moses.

"Well, I don't care what you guys say," said Darryl resting on his elbows, "I could never change from who I am."

"Anybody can change, Darryl," informed Moses.

"No, Moses," refuted Darryl. "A real man couldn't change! He wouldn't change! Impossible!"

"Yes, a man *could* change," said Kendrick.

Ethan added, "Extenuating circumstances could change a man."

"...Love could change a man," said Kendrick walking by. "Prison. War. Drugs."

"A dominating woman," included Moses dryly. "Fear, a great personal loss..."

"...Time," said Ethan raising his finger profoundly. "Alcohol. Money."

"Jesus," said Moses.

"Look," said Darryl standing up, "I don't care if a dominating, alcoholic woman with plenty of money was the first thing I saw walkin' after spendin' twelve years in a prison, I'm not gonna change! I'm still gonna be myself!"

"Okay," said Moses sitting up on the sofa, "for the sake of argument, what good things could change a man?"

"...Uh," thought Kendrick slowing his pace, "spiritual peace."

"A change in one's diet," said Ethan as he opened another mineral water and guzzled it down.

"Alright, alright," said Darryl, "I get the picture." He laughed pointing at each of his brothers. "Y'all tryin' to change *me*, right?"

"Darryl," said Ethan shaking his head, "you've got *some* complex."

"Good things or bad things, nothing's gonna make me different from who *I* am. Besides," continued Darryl, "those things are all choices. A man chooses to waste his life with drugs and alcohol. He chooses to eat right and take care of himself."

The Walker brothers had no recourse but to listen to Darryl's brand of wisdom.

"It's all about choices, you guys." Darryl looked at Moses' awestruck face as he said, "even accepting Jesus is a choice!"

"Well, I guess I can die happy now," said Ethan laughing at the irony, "I have lived to see the day when my brother Darryl Walker actually made sense."

Darryl mumbled some obscenity at Ethan and bumped into Kendrick as he took another trip to the bar.

"Let's theorize for a minute, guys," said Kendrick taking a seat on the glass and chrome coffee table. "Let's say I had a second chance to live my life from this point on. And let's say I decided to go straight. Now let me take a poll: do you think the rest of the world would accept *me*?"

"Naw," said Darryl from the bar. "Once bitten-well, you know the rest. Besides, no woman wants a converted homosexual for a lover. Too much competition, if you know what I mean. Except maybe that Margo Day friend of yours. Say, uh, is she seein' anybody?"

Kendrick shook his head slowly as Darryl's answer penetrated his hopes. "..Ethan?"

"You say you've been celibate for two years now, right?" asked Ethan very business-like.

"Yes," said Kendrick calmly. "Two years."

"Man, then in my opinion," said Ethan as he laid back down on the floor, "you're clean from the inside out. The question therefore is not *will* the rest of the world accept you, *but will you* accept yourself for who *you* wanna be?!"

"Moses?" asked Kendrick

"Watch him, Kendrick!" shouted Darryl. "He'll probably tell you to go dip in Venice beach seven times or somethin' crazy like that."

"Man, would you just shut-up, Darryl!" hollered Ethan.

"Kendrick," said Moses softly. "What've you been doin' for the past two years, huh? Testing your will against this thing?"

Kendrick shrugged, "...I guess you could say that."

"Then come on and do the right thing," pleaded Moses.

"What do you mean by the right thing?!" demanded Kendrick.

"He means," interjected Darryl, "buy some cheap suit and start carryin' a Bible around?!"

Moses wilted.

"No, now wait a minute!" shouted Kendrick. "I'm sorry, Moses," he said massaging his temples in desperate need of a cigarette. "...It's crazy. I'm just lashing out at you because I know I'm dying."

Hand Me Downs

Silence fell over the room.

"Well," sighed Moses slapping his thighs. "For what it's worth, I think Ethan and Darryl are both right."

"What?" shouted Ethan. "Moses, don't you have even one original thought, man?"

"Bro. Preacher," said Darryl, "you been dippin' in the communion wine!"

"Kendrick," said Moses, "when you're feeling that once bitten thing, that's your God-given signal to change. And look," Moses encouraged, "people are constantly reinventing themselves; exercise, divorce, careers, education. You name it, we all want to be accepted in some area that makes us feel good about ourselves. We're constantly doing and undoing to make *this* fit and *that* work in our favor."

"The problem with drastic changes that only affect the outer man," explained Moses with piercing genuineness, "Is that we are seldom ready for the impact those choices have on life; like loneliness and being misunderstood."

"But, Kendrick," continued Moses smiling, "if you have a made-up mind to change things, my brother, you've got an ally."

"...Jesus?" asked Kendrick in curious quietness.

Moses shook his head, "the One and Only."

"I heard what you said to the pizza delivery guy," said Kendrick nervously wiggling his fingers, "all that stuff about the man on the inside and living to be him. You didn't even know that guy, but I could tell you cared about him even though you'd just met him. There's something really special about that, Moses. I admire that in you. See?" said Kendrick chuckling, "You were always meant to be a preacher."

Moses smiled humbly.

"I've just got one question," said Kendrick, "how do you get from point A to point B? How do you slough-off one life and walk straight ahead into another? You know, like you told that kid?"

Moses reached for his baby brother and put his hands on Kendrick's shoulders. "You forget about what people will think and do what you know you have to do according to the dictates of *your* soul."

"And Jesus will accept me," Kendrick snapped his fingers, "just like that."

Moses snapped his fingers and said, "Just like that. He's more than the world against you if you decide to do things His way.

Valorie M. Taylor

"Look," said Moses rubbing his hand across his beard, "this is no hard-lined pitch at repentance and living as a monk. What I'm talkin' about is living day to day with peace of mind and hope.

"I like what you're sayin', Moses," said Kendrick shaking his head, "that is, *if* I was going to live."

Moses reached for his suit jacket and dug into the pocket. He produced a small leather-bound book tattered and worn from its constant use. He reached for Kendrick's hands and placed the book in them. "This is a book of Psalms...victories," said Moses watching Kendrick finger the rough edges of the book, "struggles, prayers. Start your life changes based on God's words, Kendrick. Not mine."

Nature called Moses at four in the morning. Moses rounded the corner and noticed a sliver of light beaming from under the bathroom door. He tapped on it and pushed it slightly.

Inside sat Kendrick curled up in the corner of the bathtub sweating and pale. He held a razor blade in his shaking hands surrounded by the warm gold glow of a bathroom often enjoyed by the super-wealthy.

Without looking around Kendrick whispered "...Courage, Moses. Roman had courage."

"Kendrick, you don't have to do-"

"I know what you're gonna to say, Moses," said Kendrick whimpering. "You're gonna say that I need Jesus again. Well, I don't know Him like you do. I don't know if I have enough time...I don't know if I ever will..."

The sight of Kendrick's shivering body burned in Moses' brain. Anger rose up in him. "Alright then, go ahead! Do it!"

Kendrick's breath came faster as he wanted to scream.

"Go ahead, Kendrick! Your last act to command sympathy! I'll come back in 15 minutes or better yet, I'll just wait 'til daylight and find you in a pool of your own blood! And I'll bring Darryl and Ethan so they can remember you like that, too!"

Kendrick breathed harder and pressed the blade against his wrist. "Moses, I-"

"What more do you want from us, Kendrick?! What question has this visit failed to answer for you?!"

"Shut-up, Moses!"

"No!" shouted Moses. "Man, I'm not gonna be silent this time!"

"What are you talkin' about?" asked Kendrick.

68

"You're gonna hear the truth!" said Moses pointing at him. "The hard questions of life-"

"My life *is* a hard question!" fired Kendrick pointing to himself with the blade.

"That it is, Kendrick," digressed Moses as tears rolled down his cheeks and got lost in his beard.

"...Just leave me to this, Moses," cried Kendrick with his mouth stretched across his face in agony. "...If you have any human decency, leave me to do this..."

"I can't leave you like this, Kendrick. The big brother in me knows I've neglected you before...it should've never gotten this far."

"What are you talkin' about, Moses?!"

"Do you want to stay in spiritual limbo?" demanded Moses.

"Limbo over your holier-than-thou fire and brimstone crap any day!" Kendrick twirled the small blade with his fingers to get a better grip on it and readied himself to end his life.

"Kendrick," hurried Moses, "you've been celibate for two years! You're sick now, but you've got a lot of living to do. What is it about this gay lifestyle that you feel you must defend until death!?"

"All I've heard since you got here is your opinion, Moses," said Kendrick wiping snot and sweat from his mouth. "What are you sellin', huh!?"

Moses grimaced. "What am I sellin'?"

"Yeah, what are *you* sellin'?" shouted Kendrick. "Darryl wants me to start dating women and watching porno. Ethan wants to cure me with vitamins. What about you, huh? What hand-me-down do you have?"

"...All right," said Moses taking a seat on the toilet. I'll be the first to admit there are some disadvantages to being the mouthpiece for the gospel. According to the Lord, I've got to love you. In my heart, Kendrick, *I* love you, man. You're my brother. But I don't love what you've done. I blame *you* for gettin' yourself sick."

"I said what are you sellin', Moses," demanded Kendrick, "not tell me how much you hate me!"

Moses sighed. "I can quote you scripture after scripture of hope and love. But you can't afford to make a quick, thoughtless purchase, Kendrick." Moses shook his head hopelessly. He stood to his feet. "So I'm gonna say it and leave you to decide." Moses took a deep breath, "God loves *you*, Kendrick."

"Is that all?!" asked Kendrick. "Is that supposed to change my life?!"

"Only if you let it, Kendrick," said Moses.

Moses prayed inwardly. *For the first time in my life, those words don't seem to be enough, Lord. But they've got to be.*

"...Mama's gone, Moses," groaned Kendrick. "She can't mourn me," he cried staring wildly at the blade in his hands. "Pops, too. I can't leave him in shame. Just let me...."

"You're right," said Moses with his hand on the doorknob to leave. "All you've got left are three brothers who, in spite of their hang-ups, really love you, Kendrick."

"That's enough!" shouted Kendrick breathing heavily and still crying. "I'll decide for myself what I want!"

"You're right, Kendrick," said Moses softly. "You're a man. And a man has to make his own decisions."

Ethan met Moses closing the bathroom door and whispered "What's goin' on back here?"

"Nothin'," said Moses blocking the way to the door.

Ethan began to press past him.

Moses stopped him and said, "Nothing's goin' on back here, Ethan."

"I'm gonna see about Kendrick," he demanded.

"No," said Moses with authority. "I've done what I should've done all along. Kendrick is in the hands of the Lord now, Ethan."

Ethan looked into Moses' blank eyes. "You crazy-"

"Ethan, I trust Someone higher than me for Kendrick's life and his choices right now."

Ethan faked to the left and then to the right. Moses couldn't keep up.

Then Ethan put his hand on the doorknob and stopped short of opening it. His body shook as he could only imagine the trauma that Moses was trusting God to handle as he heard Kendrick crying hysterically on the other side of the door.

Ethan turned and walked back toward the living room as he said, "I don't trust like you do... that's a skill I haven't perfected."

Moses pressed his head against the door and sent his prayers into the bathroom like a General commanding the last of his surviving, battle-worn troops.

Chapter Eight
Dare to Want

"One!" huffed Darryl. "Two!...Three!..."

Moses awoke abruptly to the artistic sights of Kendrick's converted warehouse and Darryl's physical challenge. His knees ached as he found himself still in his prayer posture against the aqua sofa where he petitioned God throughout the night for Kendrick's life.

Moses looked over and saw Kendrick unharmed and snoring in the purple canvas chair. He sighed, "Thank you, Lord." Then he hoisted himself onto the couch and closed his eyes again.

"...Seven!...Eight!"

Moses sat-up and asked, "Darryl, what are you doing?"

"Push-ups! Ten! And eleven!"

"Could you *do it* then a little quieter?" asked Ethan groggily who had made himself comfortable on his suitcase on the floor.

"It's 5:30 in the morning, you super health nut!" huffed Darryl as he lowed himself effortlessly to the floor and pushed up again. "This is my morning routine...that bus I drive is one big piece of equipment...I need to stay strong in order to handle it! And," said Darryl continuing to push himself, "the ladies like Darryl-dog's big muscles!

"Yep," continued Darryl, "Mr. Chicago four years running. Too late for you, Ethan," he laughed, "...there's already one me!"

"Kendrick," said Ethan ignoring Darryl's insult. He kicked

Kendrick's leg to wake him up from his snoring. "Kendrick!"
Kendrick awoke with "Hey! Who's kickin' me?!"

"It's me Ethan! Would you stop snorin' so loud?"

Kendrick adjusted himself uncomfortably in the purple canvas and metal chair. He made another attempt to go back to sleep.

"And fifty!" Darryl popped up from the floor with an extra spring in his step. He shadowboxed, danced and dodged all around his weary brothers.

"Darryl," said Moses, "give it a rest..."

"Yeah," said Ethan. "It's just a little too early to be up and so hyper!"

He ignored his brothers and continued with his brand of aerobics. "Kendrick, you got anything to eat around here?"

"There's a half eaten pizza crust on the table," said Kendrick groggily wishing for an undisturbed, few more hours of sleep.

Darryl continued his calisthenics into the kitchen. He looked in the refrigerator and poured himself a huge glass of orange juice. He guzzled it down smacking his lips and wiping his mouth on his arm.

Then he pulled additional breakfast items from the refrigerator and cabinets setting them neatly on the counter.

Darryl blasted contemporary jazz from Kendrick's kitchen radio and made up his own romantic lyrics.

Before long the entire warehouse smelled of sizzling bacon, cheesy eggs, spicy home fries, fresh brewed coffee and French toast.

Moses, Ethan and Kendrick were drawn to the kitchen on the home cooked goodness that wafted through the air.

"Sleep all right, Kendrick?"

"Had a rough spot," he said coughing. "But, life goes on." Kendrick reached into the refrigerator and turned the orange juice jug upside down into his mouth. He smacked his lips and breathed, "Aaaahh, good every morning."

Darryl stood with his mouth hanging wide open as he remembered enjoying the juice just an hour earlier.

"What's wrong, D?" asked Ethan slapping him on the back in appreciation of the meal.

"Nothing," said Darryl returning to the preparation of it. "Nothing at all."

The Walker brothers seated themselves at Kendrick's glass and stone dining table in blessed anticipation of the breakfast that beckoned them from their slumber.

"Let's offer a word of thanks," suggested Moses.

The Walker brothers all joined hands for the first time in many, many years.

There was an unexpected comfort that filled each of them as Moses prayed: "Father in Heaven, we thank You for this time of brotherhood and sharing. Thank You for this miraculous visit that has, in some ways, made the years apart inconsequential. Thank You, Father God, for Your miracle-working power and Your faithful love. Bind us together in brotherhood. Protect and bless each of us in Jesus' name. Amen."

There was a reverent silence that fell over the brothers as each of them felt the peaceful presence of God's Holy Spirit. The Walker brothers looked each other squarely in the eyes and shared unspoken appreciation for each other while lingering to hold each other's hands.

"Darryl," said Ethan wiping a tear quickly from his eyes as if it were something else. "I gotta hand it to ya'," he said spooning a mound of eggs onto his plate, "you can burn!"

Darryl rubbed his hands together "Yeah, now if I can just hit the lotto, I'd be the perfect man!"

"C'mon, Darryl," said Kendrick. "Are we supposed to believe that money and women are all you want out of life? You can cook," Kendrick complimented admiringly. "You're an award winning body builder, you *can* play the base guitar-"

"Yeah, Darryl-dog the ladies man," laughed Ethan, "You're a man of surprises. I think you're afraid to tell us what *you* really want."

"...What *I* really want, huh?" asked Darryl happy to have center stage.

"Yeah," said Moses taking a sip of coffee, "what do you *really* want."

"Alright," said Darryl hovering over his plate and chewing his food. "For once in my life, I want to fall in love."

The brothers looked at each other in utter shock.

"Of all the women you-well, you've never been in love with even one of them?!" asked Ethan.

"Nope," he said leaning back in his chair, wiping his mouth with a napkin and then tossing it on the table.

"Not even close?" asked Ethan squinting at Darryl.

"Not even close."

"I don't believe it," laughed Ethan pointing at Darryl, "my brother the stud has never-"

"Okay, you big bean pole, what about you, huh?"

charged Darryl. "What do you dare to want?"

Ethan shoveled another spoonful of potatoes into his mouth. "I just wanna win an NBA championship game, that's all," he said matter-of-factly.

Moses laughed.

Kendrick squeezed the fork in his hand and stared at his empty plate.

"C'mon, Ethan," said Darryl, "the truth."

Ethan sipped some coffee and said reluctantly "...I don't want to-"

"We're your brothers, Ethan," reminded Moses jokingly, "c'mon, we can handle it."

Ethan looked at them, took a deep breath and said, "There's this woman"

"Well, what about her?!" prompted Darryl. "Is she fine? Does she have big-"

"Her name is Bridget Landingham. She's an ad exec I met in Milwaukee a year ago. We've dated off and on. But I don't think she trusts me. She thinks I have a woman in every city," he explained looking squarely at Darryl. "I don't know how to prove to her that she's the one."

"You love her?" asked Moses ignoring his breakfast to concentrate on his brother.

"I love her," said Ethan shaking his head slowly as child-like sweetness came over his face. "She's everything I ever wanted in a woman; intelligent, funny, beautiful...I don't know if she feels the same way about me."

"Love's something you gotta declare at all costs, Ethan," said Moses sincerely. "It's usually fear that keeps a lot of people from being happy."

Ethan stopped chewing and said, "Moses, that's the first real thing I've heard you say to me all night. Thanks."

Darryl sat with his arms folded across his chest staring into his plate as he internalized his envy, yet another thing Ethan had that he himself wanted.

"Kendrick," asked Ethan, "aside from the news you just heard about your illness, did you get everything you ever wanted from life?"

"You kiddin'?" asked Kendrick trying to seem untormented. "I've got a fabulous loft in the middle of Venice Boulevard-incidentally, no one knows it exists!" Kendrick took a sip of coffee, coughed and said, "Jezebel's is turning a profit nightly."

"Yeah," said Moses soothingly, "but aside from creature

comforts, did you get your heart's desire, is what Ethan wants to know?"

Ethan slammed his coffee cup down and pointed to himself, "How you gonna speak for me, Moses?" he demanded. "And why would *you* ask Kendrick a question like that?"

"Well, I was just-"

"You always do that!" shouted Ethan. "Kendrick has a life to live! You countin' him dead already, man?"

Kendrick dropped his fork against the glass table. The rattling pitch ended Ethan and Moses' argument. "Do I dare to want the family life," said Kendrick gritting his teeth, "the successful sweet life you three so easily live day to day?"

"...Children, a home with windows," continued Kendrick as his voice rose, "friends who aren't the shame of their families." Kendrick shook his head and grumbled, "Do I dare want the simplest of things?"

Kendrick sat back in his chair and closed his eyes. "What I wouldn't do for an overdue bill and time to pay it off...

"My life right now is in a million pieces! Do you guys have any idea what I would give to be somebody, anybody else right now?! I'd be you, Moses! You, Ethan! Yes, even you, Darryl...anything to be able to look forward to a future!"

Kendrick stood abruptly from his chair knocking it over and onto the floor. He kicked over a statue and sent a vase crashing to the floor. All the while, he screamed and yelled.

The sting of the past blistered Moses' mind as he remembered Kendrick running across the poppy field.

The brothers sat uncommonly still as the rips and shatters of priceless objects slammed against the floor and each other in Kendrick's rage.

Darryl rose up from his chair intent on controlling Kendrick by any means necessary. Moses touched his arm and stood to retrieve Kendrick himself.

"Stay back, Moses!" shouted Kendrick holding a statue above his head ready to hurl it at him.

"..Kendrick," said Moses with his arms out. "It's okay, Kendrick. Really okay..."

"All this stuff means nothing! It's just like me, Moses!" shouted Kendrick looking around. "Right now, it means nothing!"

"Kendrick, I can't give you a crash course in faith, trust and manhood. I can't promise you a future that you feel you've been cheated out of. But-"

"You don't understand, Moses!" cried Kendrick, "I have no right to ask God for anything! *I* am a nothing! God has given up on me!" He beat his chest for emphasis. "I have AIDS!!"

"The only giving up I've heard since I got here is you giving up on yourself!" Moses said flatly. "...Slowly. Methodically. Calculatively giving up."

Kendrick pointed the statue at Moses and said "you can say that because-"

"No!" shouted Moses like thunder from his belly. "No more self-pity, Kendrick! Enough with the finger pointing already! Listen for a change. Open your eyes, man. Don't you see the Lord's divine work happening here?" Moses pointed to Darryl and Ethan. "Your three, long lost brothers showed up on your door step at the same time! All because we found out you were dying...can't you see, Kendrick? Are you so blinded by your own self pity that you can't see what God is trying to show you?"

Ethan and Darryl walked over and stood behind Moses.

Moses looked at Kendrick with tears in his eyes. "I'm sorry, Kendrick. Sorry I didn't try to get in touch with you all these years. I'll admit it; I had given up on you spiritually."

Moses looked hopelessly at the floor. "I know what you're all thinking *he's a preacher, there's no excuse for that.* But I'm human, guys."

Moses looked at Kendrick. "I was afraid to face your homosexuality. Kept wondering how it was gonna affect me, you know? What would folks think if they knew? What would my church think? My kids? I made a mistake. I'm still your brother, Kendrick. I'm sorry."

Kendrick stared at all of them.

"But God..." said Moses pointing upward, "God loves you, Kendrick. And every moment that you breathe is proof of His love. Every day is another opportunity to experience the miracle of life from Him."

"Moses is right," said Ethan to everyone's surprise. "All things, good or bad, begin with us, ya'll. Mom and Pops are off the scene now."

"Yeah," said Darryl, "nobody thumpin' us up side the head tellin' us right from wrong."

"So whatever we want for our family," continued Ethan, "is gonna have to start right here and right now. And it's okay, man, that our family has some imperfections."

"The power to make things better is within us," interjected Moses. "It's our decision as to what this family will be known for, what we'll leave behind and what we'll start afresh." Moses looked at Kendrick, "just like last night; it was the hardest thing I've ever done, leavin' you in the hands of the Lord to make up your own mind. But it was your decision, Kendrick. And you came out triumphantly."

"...I did, didn't?" Kendrick placed the statue on the table and wiped his tears. "You wanna know what I want, Moses?"

"Yes, Kendrick," sighed Moses happy to have made a little leeway with Kendrick, "I wanna know. We all want to know."

Kendrick closed his eyes as if dreaming. "I'd like to be invited to sit in the stands at a Kings game and cheer my brother on to the NBA Championship."

Ethan said reluctantly, "...you got it, Kendrick."

"But I don't know if I have that long to wait," he replied wiping some of his tears.

The Walker brothers smiled.

Kendrick turned to Darryl. "Maybe spend some time chick watchin' with my big brother Mr. Chicago four years runnin'."

Darryl pointed at Kendrick, with his eyes red from his own tears. "You might even teach me a thing or two about respecting women, lil' bro."

"But the one thing I want most of all?" Kendrick fell onto the couch wearily. "...The thing I've hated not having in my life. The reason I believe Roman killed himself. It's the thing you'll probably say no to, Moses, but here it goes." Kendrick took a deep breath and confessed, "I want to be a part of my family again. I want to meet my nephews, Moses. I want to see life in their faces, hope in their eyes. I know you and Stella have done a good job raisin' them. That's the best legacy anybody could ever want."

"Kendrick," said Moses giving access to his tears, "if God can look on us mere mortals with all our faults and still commit to love us and make us better than we were, then so can I."

Tears of joy poured from Kendrick's eyes.

"Stella and I have raised our boys to believe that the homosexual lifestyle is wrong," said Moses through cracks in his voice. "But we have also taught them to love people with a Godly love despite their choices."

Moses pulled a plane ticket from the pocket of his suit coat and placed it in Kendrick's hands.

"...Call it an unction. But when I booked my flight

yesterday, the ticket agent asked me how many would be returning. I said two." Moses looked at the ticket in Kendrick's trembling hands. "I thought I was goin' crazy or somethin' up until this very moment, Kendrick."

Kendrick doubled over and cried out loud.

Moses' voice quivered as he was overtaken with emotion. "This is what God had in mind all along. This time I listened. I guess there was no other way to convince you and me that *you* are loved and wanted, Kendrick. Unconditionally."

Kendrick looked toward heaven and said only two words: "Thank You."

Moses walked toward Kendrick crunching the shards of glass and broken clay under his shoes. "No more fear, Kendrick. No more distance. No more misunderstandings." Moses lifted Kendrick from the couch and wrapped his arms around him.

Darryl followed suit saying "no more assumptions. No more disrespect." He wrapped his strong arms around Kendrick and Moses.

Ethan stepped forward with "...no more indifference," and completed the fabric of brotherhood with his embrace.

Hand Me Downs

The Marriage Bed

Chapter One
The Bed Undefiled

To every story there are two sides.

This time, my side is told the way I tell it. It's not the wine and roses side like the fairer sex likes to tell it. But it is the sincerely in love side of one man's heart.

For some couples, a favorite corner of the couch or den is the most welcoming spot in their home. Others might say it's their garden or breakfast table that's best.

But for me and Camille, the favorite spot is our bed.

It's the only place where we're just Steve and Camille. Not Mr. and Mrs. Steven Torrance and not Mommy and Daddy. Not Brother and Sister Torrance. And not the couple next door.

In our bed we're two young lovers again growing old gracefully, planning a future together under crisp linens. There we were happy to have a private sanctuary to be ourselves. We make the rules. We play the games. Our bed is undefiled.

My wife Camille?

I'll bet you're wondering who this exceptional female is who merits this kind of adoration, huh? And how does she rank with such famed damsels as Romeo's Juliet and Jacob's Rebecca that an ordinary man would go to great lengths just to have her in his life?

Well, it's hard to describe someone who is my most treacherous opponent and my biggest fan. Even when I don't believe in myself, she sees something in me that justifies her love. The more I try to win her respect, the more she showers me with her love. It's a delicate give and take in which the getting is always good.

There are so many sides to this woman. Well, to be honest, she scares me!

She's wit tempered with wisdom. She's safety in one number. Her.

She's confident with drive that never runs low on gas. She's sweet tarts and cold punch on a hot summer day. Yet, I'm home whereever she is in life's cold winter.

She's the loveliest half of the whole.

Camille is the brown sugar, cream in my coffee, hitting below the belt, soft as a baby's bottom woman I'd marry again and again if I had more than one lifetime to live.

She's the opposite of rough and tough. But she can be.

To make it plain, Camille is the reason why men love women so much. Yeah, that's my Camille.

Now our bed is no different than anybody else's. We flip our mattress when we think about it. We sleep with just sheets in the summer and an extra blanket or two in the winter. It's no different except for one major adjustment that occurred early in our married life.

Matter of fact, I believe this one simple thing changed the course of our marriage forever.

It has kept us together.

It has driven us apart.

So, here's the long and short of it.

***

We had just met a couple named Drew and Antoinette Galton. Drew was a minister at the Haven Community Church where we'd recently joined.

Joining was Camille's idea.

I was never a big church-goer. I'd had enough of being forced to go to church when I was a kid. But it seemed to fit; newlyweds establishing themselves in the community and all that stuff.

The sermons were pretty good, too. Pastor Lukus was young, spirit-filled and the services were filled with contemporary music. There were a lot of messages about committing to God and living right.

We clicked with Drew and Antoinette from the jump. They were just plain old people like me and Camille. Not bible-thumpers using our time to get their preach on.

Haven Community Church was small and unpretentious. All the pomp and circumstance I'd grown up with didn't exist there. The restrictions that Cammy wanted

The Marriage Bed

more than anything to get away from didn't exist there either.

The Galton's, only ten years older than us, displayed a sort of freedom-slash-reliance on God that blew our minds!

They included God in everything. I mean everything. They talked about God like He was sitting within earshot. And it was natural, you know? Really natural.

They weren't loud and fanatical. Just cool and self assured that their lives included Him fully.

So, a few days after joining Haven Community, the Galtons dropped by. They said they had just deposited their kids at Drew's parents and were in the neighborhood.

Yeah right.

I'm sure they knew I was a hard nut to crack. When I was old enough to say no to my Mom and Dad without getting' my butt whipped, I stopped going to church. And it showed. I was no longer the neatly trimmed choir boy my parents paraded around each Sunday.

Well, we got to talking and then the conversation fell into all the important things to keep a marriage alive.

We talked about sharing household chores, making time for one another and stuff like that.

Needless to say, Cammy and I figured we had it down pretty well. I mean, we never once turned on the television the whole time we were on our honeymoon, if you know what I mean.

So they went on saying that communication was of the uppermost importance in a successful marriage along with mutual respect, fun and other things.

Then they asked if they could pray for us.

"Sure," we said.

"We want to pray for you in the most important room in your home," said Drew.

Cammy and I just looked at one another. At this point I took a good, long look at this guy and his wife. They seemed to be on the up-and-up.

So, pretty soon we'd made a circle, holding each other's hands at the foot of our bed.

I kept my eyes on Drew.

I gotta tell you, plenty of weird stuff went through my mind; like maybe this was some crazy cult Cammy and I got ourselves into.

"Lord," Drew prayed with authority, "we gather in this place because more than any other room, the test of love is given here."

I relaxed a little. I couldn't help but take a peek at the bed that had only served one real purpose, (well, two purposes) since before our marriage and it didn't look any different to me.

"Thank You, dear Father," he prayed while the women swayed, "for this place of comfort, this lounging place for dreams, this neutral zone after arguments."

"As You bless this couple, Steven and Camille, fill this family bed with children."

"Yes, Lord!" exclaimed Camille.

"Give it daily as a prayer alter," continued Drew, "a place for long talks with You well into the wee hours of the morning."

"Let conflicts end here and let the reward of love and happiness reign supreme here."

"Yes, Lord," I found myself saying.

"Let secrets cease to whisper guile here," prayed Drew fervently. "And let darkness cease to deceive."

"And may the quality of their love be measured in this place for many, many years to come."

That sealed it for me and for Cammy.

I mean I'd had people pray for my wallet, my heart, my headaches even. But this prayer that God would do something special for me and my wife surrounding our bed; it blew my mind!

There was a warm assurance that filled me after the prayer; almost like God was standing there with us.

In one swift swoop, God was even more real, more significant to me than I'd ever given Him credit for in my rebellious youth.

Camille and I became much closer the season following the prayer. Aside from the obvious, we ate breakfast and dinner, played board games, watched television and had long, long talks in our bed.

It became the hot spot in our lives. Our inside joke affording us winks and stares only we knew how to decode.

Sure, we went to church and work, dinner parties and stuff like that but the true meeting place, the end-your-day-on-a-good-note place was our bed.

Over due bills, angry bosses and rainy morning traffic had no affect on that time and that place. We thumbed through travel and food magazines as if we had all the time and money in the world to plan and spend and enjoy.

I guess it was then that I discovered how far reaching God's purpose for marriage extends and all the perks that come with it.

The Marriage Bed

I fell in love again night after night, day after day as Camille handled the role of working woman and newlywed homemaker with finesse and grace.

She kept the house spotless.

She prepared scrumptious meals for two that beckoned me from the game, the computer, and even the shower.

We'd spend entire evenings by candlelight or just laying around on pillows thrown in front of the stereo other nights. But it really didn't matter what we were eating or even where. She was the loveliest dinner companion in the world to me.

Candle light danced in her eyes and the golden glow from the flames illuminated her beauty.

I loved the way she insisted on feeding me the *first perfect bite* she'd call it; a fork stacked with a taste of exotic salad, the most tender meat and a swirl of pasta dripping with sauce.

I'd respond with moaning, groaning and chewing with a look of incredible deliciousness. I'd roll my eyes back, shake and shiver.

It would make her smile. That's all that mattered to me.

Being newly wed was a lot of fun. I grew up with three older sisters. But none of their stuff was half as interesting as Camille's was.

I discovered so much about myself as a man, a lover, a husband and a friend.

Like the time Cammy had taken this massage therapy class at the community college. She said it would keep our marriage alive and passionate.

Wouldn't you know it, I was her practice dummy.

Really. For a whole six weeks I let the woman I love hammer, poke and twist my back and neck muscles into mush.

I never let on but she had no idea what she was doing.

Her touch thrilled me.

Her attention lulled me further into love with her.

I can remember newlywed nights when we'd dance real slow to jazz content with just holding one another.

It was our way of shielding each other from the world, from time. For our own brand of fun we'd chase each other through the apartment behind a sock or an earring. But you know it; we'd end up in the same place every night discovering the blessing of pleasure God grants to a man and his woman bound in holy matrimony.

Those days could have dragged on into eternity without a mumbling word from me.

Chapter Two
Sleeping on a Time Bomb

I was at work standing at the receptionist's desk jaw-jackin' with some of my co-workers about the long 4th of July weekend.

"Geomax Software Consultants, how may I direct–well yes," said Sharon lowering her voice. We all stopped talking hoping the urgency in her eyes wouldn't soon meet one of ours.

"He's standing right here," said Sharon.

It was Camille. She was all shaken up and crying I could barely make out what she was saying.

I dropped everything and went directly to her job.

A cop stopped me while I was trying to push my way through the crowd in front of Camille's building.

"I'm Camille Torrance's husband!" I told the dude.

"Sorry, sir," he said looking right passed me. "No one is allowed beyond this point."

Sirens blared. Lights flashed. Emergency vehicles of every sort screeched to a halt at the scene. Paramedics were running around with blood on their clothes.

"But my wife!" I shouted right in his face. "Man, c'mon! What happened in there?"

"Three people were shot," he said remarkably calm considering all the commotion. "We don't have any other details–"

"But my wife called me and I need to get in there and

see about her!"

"Sir, if she *called* you, she must be okay!" he said trying to control the crowd.

A carefully wrapped body under a white sheet became the focus of the crowd as a deafening hush fell over us. The paramedics treated the body with delicate respect and discretion as they loaded it into the back of the ambulance.

One woman screamed in horror as another was rolled out.

The cop looked kind of guilty. "It's routine to hold witnesses for questioning sir," he said to me.

He called another cop over and said, "escort this gentleman to the holding area. His wife is in there. She'll want to see him when all this is over."

Pure adrenaline; that's what I was operating on. Camille was a *witness* meant she was alive. But how did the prayer hold so much magic when my ears first heard it? Why was I so willing to believe in the power of a god that only existed on pages in a book? And where was His power now? As far as I could see, this was something I had to deal with on my own.

Camille was brought into the corridor surrounded by five or six cops.

"STEEEVE!" she shouted.

She ran to me covered with blood. She grabbed me and jumped into my arms until we both fell over in the corridor.

"Steve, I can't believe what he did to those people!" She held my neck like a drowning person. "He shot 'em, Steve!" she cried hysterically. "Why did he shoot 'em?" She melted into helpless tears and anguish right in my arms.

"Mrs. Torrance," a white man said reaching for her arm.

"Hey, who are you?" I said pushing his hand away.

"I'm sorry, Mr. Torrance. I'm Dr. Hoag, the medical attendant here at KBI Hospital. Your wife may be suffering from shock. She *did* witness the shooting. I've called an ambulance to take her to the hospital for observation and a little rest."

"I won't go without you, Steve!" screamed Camille clutching handfuls of my shirt. "I won't!"

"Okay, Dr. Hoag," I said getting my first good look at the terror in her eyes. "Take her to the hospital. I think that's a good idea."

In the hospital, Camille slept and so did I.

"Mr. Torrance," said somebody nudging me in my sleep. "Mr. Torrance."

I woke up with a crick in my neck to find a nurse

whispering my name and shaking my arm.

"Visiting hours are over, Mr. Torrance," she whispered.

"I can't leave her here," I told the nurse. "We've never been apart even one night."

"I'm sorry, Mr. Torrance," she said. "But it's against hospital policy for you to stay the night. You can come back bright and early tomorrow morning. She'll be going home then."

"But you don't understand, I–"

"Tomorrow morning, Mr. Torrance," she said practically lifting me from the chair by my arm. "She'll sleep through the night and you'll need your rest, too."

The door shut softly behind me as I found myself in the hospital hallway surrounded by sterile white and haunting sickness behind each door. Then I noticed a cop standing outside Camille's door. He nodded

"What is this?" I asked him. "What are you doin' here?"

"Mr. Torrance?" asked the thickly mustached man wearing an overcoat and golf spikes. He pulled me by the arm. "Mr. Steve Torrance, is it?"

"Yeah."

"I'm Detective Gregorio," he told me with a firm handshake. "Will you step over here into the waiting area?"

I followed him and took a seat.

"Your wife, she's well, yeah?"

"She's sleepin' right now," I told him. "She'll be okay."

"Good," he said wringing his hands. "I must tell you this for her safety and yours."

"Tell me what?"

"The gunman, Roth O'Leary....well, we didn't apprehend him."

My heart started to pound out of control.

"Why'd he kill those people, man?" I asked him.

"It seems Mr. O'Leary, a convicted rapist and killer, spent the last 12 years in prison on DNA evidence used against him. Evidence tested by the KBI staff.

"He vowed he'd get those responsible back for his incarceration, Mr. Torrance. Today he made good on his promise."

I stopped breathing.

"Your wife's body was discovered next to the victims unharmed," he told me. "We don't know why he didn't hurt her, too. We can't rely on our hopes that he showed mercy toward her since she was only 12 years old 12 years ago."

The Marriage Bed

"We're afraid he may retaliate against Mrs. Torrance," said Detective Gregorio. "He is aware that she can identify him."

"But you know who he is, right?" I asked the guy. "Why should it matter that Camille can identify him?"

He took a deep breath. "We simply want to cover all the bases, Mr. Torrance. Surely you can understand that."

"Yeah, I understand."

"We'll put two men on your apartment until we can nail this guy," promised the detective like it was his wife this Roth O'Leary was after.

But it wasn't *his* wife. It was *my* wife. I didn't trust anybody. Was this some put-on?

I looked back at the cop at Camille's door. He looked like he could've been a family man; in good shape, pretty confident even. But I made up my mind right then and there, I couldn't be certain he would risk his life to save the other half of my life laying in a hospital bed behind that door.

"You do what you have to, Detective Gregorio," I told him. "I'll do what I have to do."

My head was fuzzy. Ugly images of what that scum intended to do to Camille stuck in my head and made me a little crazy.

I took a cab back to the apartment.

A cold emptiness breezed past me when I opened the door.

There were no smells of marinated chicken grilling.

No soft music played.

Nothing to remind me of the evidence of Camille in my life.

Nothing except the hollow hole in my heart that in some sick, primitive way ached with blame for not protecting her.

I went into the bedroom and leaning against the door frame I just stared at our bed.

It hadn't been made and I could still make out the shape in the sheets where Camille's body had lain. If I closed my eyes, I could feel her warm softness in my arms. Her scent filled my nostrils.

The marriage bed was just an empty relic of memories once sweet without Camille.

I grabbed my coat and headed out into the night in search of a gun.

When I brought Camille home from the hospital the next

day she was quieter than usual.

She headed straight for the bathroom and then for the bed.

Luckily, I had changed the sheets and cleaned up the house. She slept restlessly for hours tossing and turning at the slightest sound.

Over a steaming cup of tea, she explained, "I was in the back of the lab mixing some compounds. And then I heard a pop. I thought it was a mild explosion or something. You know, maybe one of the burners had malfunctioned. It happens all the time." "But then I heard screaming," she told me. "I looked out the window of the mixing room and there was Dr. Ephraim laying on the floor with his head just gushing blood.

"I could see Fiona and Loraine crying, begging that man not to shoot them too."

She closed her eyes.

"Fiona kept saying 'no, por favor! No! Mi bambinos!' But he just turned, pointed the gun at Fiona like she was nothing and shot her in the face. Then he turned to Loraine. She was on her knees begging. He shot her. Maybe I moved or something and he looked right at me. His eyes were cold and empty. I blacked out; all I remember was hitting the floor. Then the police were there."

"Do you know how you got blood on you?" I asked cautiously.

"I guess he pulled me into the lab area to shoot me too. But the police got there before he could do anything." She covered her face and cried. "I don't know, Steve. It was so terrible I know God must've been watching out for me."

"More than you know, Cammy. More than you know."

"Why me?" she kept saying. "Why did God spare me?"

I just grabbed her and held her in my arms. In my mind, God better had spared her life. I knew it was arrogant and selfish but losing *her* wasn't an option for me.

I pulled the gun from under the bed and showed it to her.

She backed away slowly. "Steven Jarrod Torrance, have you lost your mind? Why would you bring a gun into this house?"

"Ssshh! For protection, Camille, what else?!" I took a quick look out the window. "I'm not gonna let nobody come up in here!"

"But Steve," she said, "there are police right outside watching the place!"

The Marriage Bed

"You think one of them is gonna lay down his life to protect you?"

I touched her face.

She snatched away. "This isn't right!"

"Don't be silly, Camille! I'm a man! And a man's got to protect his family!"

"But Steve, Christians don't live in fear and we don't respond to confrontation with violence."

"That's the peace-loving female talkin' through you right now!" I pressed bullets into the gun. "But it'd be a whole different story if somebody was tryin' to hurt your kid or somethin'. Don't tell me you'd be all calm and ready to talk it through. You'd be on that joker's back tryin' to beat the mess outta him!"

We didn't talk much about the gun after that.

We just spent some of the most restless and sleepless nights of our new lives together.

I revolved Roth O'Leary's name through my mind day and night. I played Russian-roulette with his face in my *mind*. It kept me awake and kept me distracted at work.

One morning I kissed Camille goodbye and headed for the door. She was barely awake and she hadn't slept well the night before.

I came back into the apartment remembering some papers I left on the nightstand. I walked into the bedroom. Camille looked a little troubled in her sleep so I leaned over to kiss her gently on the forehead.

Her eyes popped open. She screamed.

She rolled over and began scrambling across the bed. She was screaming "No! No!" and reaching for the gun.

I grabbed her leg and shouted "No, Camille! It's me Steve! It's me, Cam! It's me."

She looked back at me with tears in her eyes. She came to her senses and started to shake.

"I thought I saw him hovering over me, Steve. I would never hurt you...."

We both sat on the bed dazed. Suddenly we reached for each other and cried.

"The weapons of our warfare are not carnal," she whispered in my ear, "but mighty through God to the pulling down of strongholds."

"I don't want to lose you, Camille. I don't want–"

"For we are not given a spirit of fear," she told me holding on for dear life, "but of power, love and a sound mind."

I picked up the gun and headed out the door.

"Where are you going with it, Steve?"

I looked at Camille and for the first time I saw the damaging effect of what violence had done to her. "I'm gonna get rid of it. It doesn't belong in our lives."

I tore through the mean streets of Seattle listening to my mind's recollection of the marriage bed prayer.

Too much was at stake for me. Just too much to lose. I blocked out the words and headed downtown to pawn the gun in case I needed it later.

Chapter Three
Mama's Baby, Daddy's Maybe

Camille had gone through a lot since the killing at KBI.

There were too many sleepless nights. Newspapers and talk shows wanted interviews. Months later, Camille was still sorry for what happened. But she wanted more than anything to put the past behind her and get on with life.

Sitting at home, dodging phone calls and all the media attention made Camille a nervous wreck.

Eventually she changed jobs and started working for another laboratory testing FDA proposed preservatives for microwaveable, prepackaged foods.

Our lives started to return to normal.

The soft music played when I got home. The smell of grilled meats and veggies met me at the door.

I was home.

We'd spend long Saturday mornings naked under the sheets doing nothing at all or anything that came to mind.

We were back to bliss trying to outdo one another with tokens of our affection.

Camille had never been more beautiful; her skin was almost always perfumed, her nails were polished, her hair was long, thick and shiny. She had a wonderful glow about her overall and I was falling in love with her all over again.

One morning during our 3rd Saturday morning trinket-giving contest, she handed me a gift-wrapped box. I opened it to find a small rattle inside.

When I looked up, Camille was smiling with tears in her eyes nodding yes.

"A baby?!" I asked quickly putting two and two together. "My baby's havin' my baby! Thank you, Jesus!"

I jumped all over the bed and finally fell off and knocked the wind out of myself.

By her fifth month, it was evident that it was time to move to a larger nest. Baby accessories had taken over whole corners in the living room, bedroom and closets.

I watched my buddy Drew and his brother Tyrone haul our precious bed out to the moving van. Camille followed them and gave supervisory directions to the fellas. They were nice to her but did it their way instead.

No one could know how much that one piece of furniture meant to me; how it became the centerpiece of my life. Sometimes, I was even a little embarrassed of the high place it had in my life. I didn't worship it or anything like that, but for me, it was the place I associated God with marriage.

I mean, what did Drew and Tyrone care about that 400-pound mattress made of coils, wood and fiber?

Sure, it was just an object. But God had blessed us just like Drew prayed that He would.

I hadn't noticed as much before as I watched Camille carrying a clipboard and giving out soon-to-be-forgotten instructions, but I missed the hourglass figure that shaped my wife. She was stretching into motherhood physically and my mind started wandering.

She'd say things like "I'm fat."

I'd say "you're not fat, you're pregnant." But what I really meant *was you're not going to look like this forever.* At least, I hoped not.

Trying to curb my true opinions, I did some stretching of my own; the truth. I complimented her skin, her hair, her overall loveliness. In all actuality, her nose had spread across her face and her feet and hands were puffy like croissants. I had to cut her wedding ring off to keep her finger from turning blue.

Hey, I almost broke myself financially and physically taking her to dinner, long walks, massaging her feet and painting the baby's nursery. She changed her mind about the color of the nursery three times, but I never let on that I could have strangled her. You'd have thought I was competing for Husband of the Year or something.

Finally, on January 12th, Nichelle Lynn Torrance was

born. I remember because that was the day my resident lover-boy status changed to resident bottle-washer, poop-diaper-changer and all around house slave.

And as much as I loved that baby girl of mine, it was difficult to accept the reality that now Camille's passionate being no longer belonged solely to me. Every time I turned around, she was whipping her breast out to feed the kid, or laying in our bed trying to put the baby to sleep. And as she got older, the kid insisted on sleeping in our bed! If I protested, I was labeled as the big bad wolf!

"Daddy means well," she'd whisper to Nichelle as they slipped away into living room to sleep on the couch. "He's just not a Mommy."

Camille was right. And she knew way more about being a Mommy than I did.

But what she didn't know was that I wanted the warmth of her hips pressed against me while I slept. I wanted to reach over and stroke her beautiful hair. I just wanted her near me.

Seldom did I ever get what *I* wanted.

I can recall many nights waking up with little Nichelle's feet in my chest or her head shoved into the small of my back. Or my all time favorite, waking up to notice that I had less than an inch to move before I'd fall out of the bed all together!

Camille decided to decrease her hours at work in order to stay at home with Nichelle.

She was so good at being a mother, it frightened me. I wondered where I fit in. I mean, Camille was so self sufficient, so complete.

But she would complain about everything. Things like I didn't appreciate her any more, the gifts had ceased and that I didn't look at her the same way. Her nails were going undone, her hair was going undone; not enough money for this and for that.

Well, she'd gained about 20 pounds since Nichelle's birth (which for a woman means a whole new wardrobe). I started doing some consulting on the side to make ends meet.

It was a difficult time. I was missing things, too.

But because what I was missing had nothing to do with being an *80's Super Mom*, my things went unnoticed until I stopped noticing them myself.

Drew and I talked man to man at the church clean-up day.

I told him all about the changes in our lives; the baby, the jobs, the new place, everything.

He offered me three words. He said "pray, my brother."

And pray, I did. I asked God to restore what had been lost under all the new responsibilities. I asked Him to curb our complaints and to help us find the greatness of our union all over again.

Camille dropped twenty pounds (which meant a whole new wardrobe) and was better than she ever was before.

The romance engine got a tune-up and we drove as often as we could.

And wouldn't you know it, one 3rd Saturday morning I got another rattle as a token of her affection.

For this pregnancy, we were better prepared. Well, we were up until Matthew was born. I remember it was like the calm before the storm.

There I was; dead tired and trying not to move around too much so not to disturb Cammy when all of a sudden she groaned like some hurt animal.

I jumped up not even really knowing where I was for a few seconds. And then I looked over to find my near-delivery wife in a pool of fluid.

I snatched the sheets back and there was his head crowning.

"I didn't know," said Camille reading the horrified look on my face. "I just didn't know."

"It'll be alright, Cam, just hold on."

Talk about adrenaline; I hopped around that room and down the hall to call 911 as if I'd slept all day.

"How many minutes apart are her contractions?" asked Georgie, the 911 operator.

"How many, Cam?"

"Four minutes!" she shouted.

"Four minutes!" I shouted into the phone.

"Calm down, dad," said Georgie. "Prop her head and back up with as many pillows as possible, Steve. Looks like you're gonna deliver this one yourself, dad."

"I'm scared, Steve!" screamed Camille between contractions. "Do something!"

It was all up to me, I kept thinking. *All up to me...*

Maybe it was the screaming. Or all those long instructions. Maybe it was the blood but I started gettin' a little scared, too.

"Wait!" I told Georgie.

"Steve. Steven!" hollered Camille. "Steve, where are you going?!

Don't leave me!"

I stepped into the hall and raised my hands high. "God, help."

I went back into the screaming, the instructions and all the blood. But this time, God became my hands.

He replaced fumbling with finesse.

He became my mind. I tell you, I didn't recognize my own voice as I soothed Camille with simple words and instructions.

He dismantled my fear and gave me instant knowledge.

Camille, the Lord and I delivered an 8 pound 5 ounce boy named Matthew right there in our bed.

"The prayer," I whispered in awe of my wiggly little son crying in my arms.

"What?" asked Camille still out of breath and looking at the two of us adoringly.

"The prayer," I told her. "Remember? Fill this family bed with children."

Camille shook her head, reached for her son and cried tears of joy.

Chapter Four
Whispers in Bitter Gray

Camille's mother died suddenly.

A tidal wave of woe swept through our home like nothing we ever imagined.

Camille was the oldest of three siblings. She carried the weight of everyone's burdens. She has always been the shoulder to lean on when life hits you hardest.

A kind word, a pot of soup, an unexpected card, a phone call out of the blue–yeah, she's quite the encourager.

This time there was no one to encourage Camille. Her dad was just out of it. And her younger sister and two brothers were too busy feeling guilty for treating their mother so badly that they were useless to Camille.

I remember her making every phone call from the quiet privacy of our bedroom.

Our bed was lined with used tissues from where she'd have to stop and just let it all out. Then she'd pull herself together and make another phone call. I felt sorry for her. Nobody should have to relive gut-wrenching sorrow like that.

"Anything *I* can do, Camille?" I asked her after the second outburst.

She just waved me out of the room gently.

Camille called her Aunts Raynell and Edenia. She called her mom's closest friend Geraldine Porter. She called out-of-town cousins, nieces and nephews until she covered the entire family.

Even with all the funeral arrangements and fighting off

the family vultures, Camille insisted on caring for 2 year old Nichelle and 6 month old Matthew as she always had. She never missed a bed time story or day at the park.

When it came to the kids she lit up like pure sunshine. To look at her with them, you'd have never thought she'd just lost her own mother.

During this trying time, it seems I gained a new significance, too.

I became the keeper of family secrets. Curled up in my arms where it was safe to speak her mind, Camille would tell me how her uncle got on her nerves, or how her cousins and nieces who never spoke kindly of her mother now spoke so lovingly of her. And I'd never look at her hypocritically when Camille had to smile at them or embrace them.

"Uh, Stuart," said Camille's nosy first cousin Luella as I was coming out of the bathroom.

"It's Steve, cousin Luella," I told her. "My name is Steve."

"Well, whatever," she said getting annoyingly close to me. "Camille's mother had a diamond cocktail ring that I loaned her back in 1956 and I..."

"Cousin Luella, Camille and the rest of the kids haven't been to the house yet to go through her mother's things," I said to her looking across the room and noticing that a mob of second cousins converging on her. "Maybe you should–"

"That ring is mine, Stuart!"

Death and money bring out the worst in people. That was my conclusion as I witnessed a kindly old woman's metamorphosis into a greedy grave-robber.

I went to Camille's side.

Yeah, the big shoulders and strong chest took on greater significance as Camille poured herself into my arms when she felt low.

One night she tried to explain to me what it's like for a woman to lose her mother when her mother is her best friend.

They would talk for hours on Saturday mornings sometimes beginning at 6:30 a.m.! It was their way of confirming a sister-like, supportive bridge across their age difference. And when Mother would visit, they'd sit on the bed chattering and giggling like two little schoolgirls. Camille said that moments like that cemented the need for mother and daughter relationships.

"I feel like a part of me has died, Steve," she told me laying in my arms in the dark. "In a weird way, I feel like I have to step into her shoes."

"Everything about me," she confessed, "every choice I've ever made somehow affected my Mom. She's the one that taught me to be a lady.

"The older I get, the more I look like her...."

"When I told her you wanted to marry me, I needed her approval of you to some degree...."

I have to admit, I didn't fully understand their woman-to-woman bond. All I knew was that Camille felt disconnected and lonely. That's all that mattered to me. I was determined to do whatever I could to make the sad shadows go away.

All during the funeral proceedings, which Camille arranged by herself, Camille's brothers and sister buried their grief and guilt in her lap. And Camille soothed them through their guilt despite her true feelings. They were using up all the tear time.

When did Camille mourn, I wondered.

After working well into the night, that question was answered for me.

Camille cried into her pillow without end. Every angry protest, every shred of hostility was forced into that piece of cotton stuffed with feathers. She even moaned through her sleep.

I guess it was only right to use our bed as a sort of weeping altar. What other place was there for her? I hoped the sadness would be removed quickly so Camille could get back living; even without her mother.

I came to a philosophical conclusion holding my hysterical wife in my arms; we employ a bed as a place of comfort. We pay it with the stillness of our tired bodies.

Among all the valuable pieces of equipment in our homes, it is almost never stolen. It lasts longer than most TV's. At best, it's a practical object.

The words of the prayer floated through my mind once again. I felt safe.

Death. Unanswered questions. Sleeplessness and theories plagued me into the blackness of morning.

It had been 5 years since the Roth O'Leary incident. He had been killed as the police tried to apprehend him but not before he took the lives of his girlfriend and her daughter.

So, the threat of a psycho-murderer stalking us and killing us was slim.

Still, the work hours had been long for me. The pay, a little short at times.

I kept having this reoccurring nightmare of crossing the

street with my sister and falling under the wheels of a car.

It kept me up. I paced the house investigating any noise, any shadow. It was weird.

I tried to fall asleep watching television. Sometimes I was successful. Most times I'd find myself trying to wake up from frightening whispers in my bitter gray nightmares.

The words of the prayer came back to me. But I blew it off. I mean, it's silly to rely on words spoken over eight years ago. At some point, doesn't life mature and take on it's own dimensions as far as protection and provision are concerned?

The prayer was fading out and phasing out quickly. I did nothing to stop it.

"Honey," whispered Camille at 1:30 a.m. as I laid on the couch. "Why not come to bed?"

"Okay, I'm comin'..."

But somehow I'd find my way back to the nightmare that had scared me since I was a kid.

The next morning Camille said "why didn't you come to bed last night?"

"I tried, honey," I told her faking sincerity. "I really did."

"I *tried* to stay awake, too." She slipped her arms around my waist and kissed my neck. "I thought we could enjoy ourselves...maybe I could've given you a massage, huh?"

I felt like a dope. But there was nothing I could do about it. I peeled her arms from around me. "Gotta get to work."

I prayed constantly.

I asked God to again restore what had been lost. But this time I asked almost embarrassed by the request. I mean, my wife was certainly attractive. Our marriage was pretty solid. But why was I being haunted by something that my mind had put together from stories my mother and older sister *told* me happened? And why was it robbing me of sleep and life?

When Camille thought I was sleeping, she'd reach over and lay her hand across my head. I could feel her praying for me. She'd never said a word, but I knew she was praying. I know she sensed the error in me.

Her prayers worked.

But then I started falling in the other direction. I was sleeping every chance I got; during outings, family night with the kids, parties. You name it, I was always kicked-back in some corner unconscious to what was happening around me.

I couldn't blame her for getting mad at me. After all, I was making life difficult for everybody. My internal clock was off, that's all. I wasn't avoiding life and God, like she said. Was I?

At least I was getting the job done. Consciously, that is. I was the bread-winner in the family. And the nights spent in front of the television stopped. I reinstated my "husbandly" duties and for the moment, Camille seemed to be happy.

But you know how women are; she had to find something to complain about.

One night after being too frustrated with life in general to explain anything to anybody, I told Camille that absolutely nothing was wrong with me.

"Cam, just pray for me, okay?!" I shouted at her. "You've been goin' to that church and to all those women's meetings! Is that what they teach you there; how to nag your husband to death?"

I know she wanted to get me straight after that but she didn't. Matter-of-fact, she didn't say a word.

Our marriage bed was colder that night than it had ever been.

She wanted to see results and who could blame her.

I had no time for this. I was busy providing, protecting, juggling bills and being the ultimate father. Just trying to keep my head above water.

She had no idea that romance, vulnerability, attentiveness were all back-burner issues that had to wait.

Something occurred to me.

The reoccurring nightmare that bit at my heels for almost a month was announcing to me that I was afraid.

"Afraid of what?" I asked God in a half-hearted attempt at prayer.

"Afraid of being consumed," I heard His voice say. "Afraid of being hurt, separated from those you love."

I had tried to avoid the fear, deny it even. But even in our marriage bed there loomed an enemy who attacked in dreams and turned me into a defiant monster.

Maybe Camille didn't know how to deal with the sudden changes in me. But I knew.

I had become aware of the deep seated plague fear has on a married couple's place they call their own.

Fear intends to separate, to interfere and to confuse.

So why would it happen again and again?

Chapter Five
Sleeping In the Bed You Made

If there was ever a time when my feelings for Camille, the love of my life, were in question, was the time when money, enthusiasm about life and the desire for intimacy were at an all-time low.

How do you explain it? A healthy man. A healthy woman. Attractive. Both old enough to know how but somehow not smart enough to know better.

We were looking at 8 years into this thing, you know.

Two kids.

Living paycheck to paycheck.

Able to compete in the job market.

And ready to argue when the question arose of who would stay home with the kids if they got sick.

How broke were we? Let me count the ways; the cars needed new brakes, the credit cards were maxed-out, we were $718 behind in childcare expenses, little Matthew needed his front tooth looked at by a pediadontist , Camille needed her monthly beauty maintenance of nails and hair, the church asked for donations of cash so that some neighborhood kid's Christmas would be a joy and staring at the $13 dollar balance in my check book wasn't making the cash appear any faster.

On top of that, we were at each other's throats constantly, I don't know, maybe for some thrills–hurtful as they were. My daily routine was just as tedious.

In the morning I didn't hesitate to get out of bed with no

proposition worthy of swaying me back in.

At night I lingered in front of the flickering blue of the TV screen. I took distracted steps to the bed with no proposition worthy of hurrying me to it.

Camille constantly bugged me about church, about money, about spending time together.

"Steve," she nagged, "when are you going to join me and the kids at church?"

"I don't know," I growled staring at the game unaware of the score, fouls or anything else of significance.

"But I feel like some single mother on the prowl when I go without you," she explained. "The kids want their dad there, too. Would you consider coming to this special men's day service next..."

"Look, Camille, just get off my back about that, okay!"

"But, Steve," she said, "you're always talking about the prayer. And now you're actin' like you..."

"The prayer!" I shouted slamming my soda can on the table. "What's it doin' for me now, huh, Camille? Is it payin' my $200 phone bill? Or the $2,300 property tax bill, huh? Is it keepin' my job from downsizing, is it?"

"Don't talk like that, Steve," said Camille closing her eyes on her tears. "I know times are rough right now but God has blessed us!" she shouted in defense.

"You believe what you wanna believe, Camille." I told her. "I'm not goin' to that church to skin and grin like my life is just wonderful, okay!"

"It's not about that, Steve," said Camille waving the kids back into their rooms. "We're blessed by faith."

"Faith?" I laughed.

"Yes. Faith," she said. "Look around you, Steve. Look what we have!"

"Camille," I said, "we have a broken down sofa, a second-hand TV, a stove on its last leg and..."

"Two healthy children who get straight A's in school!" she shouted. "Our health. Two cars that run when other people's cars aren't! Food in the cabinets! A good marriage!"

I walked away from Camille and went for a drive.

There we were in our marriage bed unable to sleep. Endless possibilities of pleasure and exploration were before us. All we could do was lay there like two strips of raw bacon with no sizzle and no fire.

"Steve."

"What?" I groaned wishing she'd just leave me alone and let me sleep.

"I'm not happy," she said.

You're not happy? I thought to myself. *I'm the one who's not happy!*

Her voice cracked with sorrow. "I've done just about everything I can think of to make you happy with me but you complain constantly."

You oughta hear yourself sometimes, I thought.

"Steve," she asked, "are you listening to me?"

"I'm listening," I snapped. "What do you want me to say?"

"Something...," she said hopefully. "Nothing," she huffed and turned over.

To know that Camille felt the same way I did scared me. But I was nursing my own anger and dissatisfaction. How could I give a second thought to her complaints?

Besides, I knew where she was going with this. By the end of the night she would end up in tears. And I'd be the bad guy. Like always.

A brother just can't win, I thought.

But the argument ensued.

We pointed out each other's part in the kid's problems, our money problems and marital problems.

She called me names like jerk, idiot and caveman.

I called her names back like mouthy, know-it-all and childish.

"Well let me tell you something, Steven Jarrod Torrance," she began. "I may be your wife but I'm not your property. Don't you dare think that I don't still turn a few heads when I walk down the street! Don't you fool yourself into believing that if you don't want me, nobody else does!"

"Oh, yeah, Camille?" I asked. "Well, ditto for me."

We went at it in the dark with whispered daggers like two punks in a knife fight to the death.

Then finally, Camille said, "Steve, lately I've developed a layer. A layer that says I don't want to take any stuff from anybody, you know? I can take it or leave it. And mostly I want to leave it."

"Me too." Silence dropped on us like a tarp in our precious marriage bed.

Neither of us moved.

I don't remember breathing, either.

"Then that's it," said Camille in a brave whisper. "It must

be the devil at work."

"How you figure?"

"If one of us loses patience, okay, 'cause there's always the other one to help and encourage," she explained. "But if we've both lost simple tolerance of one another...well you know where that's headed; a one way ticket to divorce court."

She was right and I told her so.

That night we made love.

Not passionately like in times passed. It was awkward and we probably hugged or kissed too long making it seem like pity friendship more than anything else. But it was a reminder that God had brought us together for reasons other than surface glee or money.

We were and always will be a part of each other that is private unto us. Our union.

Up until then, I hadn't realized how hard it was to sleep in the bed I'd made.

After all, shouldn't a man be concerned about overdue bills, bounced checks, ballet and Taekwondo lessons?

If not, a man is labeled sorry, right?

I tell you, there's a thin line between being a loving provider and a totalitarian dictator. Really. And the one thing a guy measures his status by is the look in his wife's eyes. She can slice him up with those eyes. Or she can make him feel like the icing on a cake with one look.

It's a tight rope to walk!

***

My day at work was going well. I spent a long time just looking at Camille's picture on my desk. I went over all the things I loved about her. All the things I hated, too.

"You've got mail," chimed the programmed voice on my computer. I opened the e-mail. It was from Camille.

"This money thing is killing us, babe. That's all life seems to be about. But I want the best marriage has to offer. I want to laugh again. I want to enjoy myself with our friends. I want to be a couple. I want to go places with someone who really loves me. I want little gifts for no other reason that I am who I am to someone who thinks the world of me. I want love demonstrated, not assumed. Is that someone you?"

The man of the hour. The hardworking black man trying to hold all that is right and good together had been spoken against! I had been found guilty of neglect and indifference.

I didn't say much to Camille about the e-mail. She knew

I'd read it. And yes, I took it to heart. So much so, that I offered a half-hearted prayer to God that He would enable me to be that someone Camille needed. That same someone I used to be.

It cost me, though. I shorted the electric and telephone bill a couple of months to treat her to a weekend getaway. I fumbled through the lingerie section of the department store and bought a nightie.

For a tough, macho guy like me, this wasn't easy. But I got through it by remembering how beautiful she really is. How statuesque, how creamy brown her skin is. How great she looks in red, green, purple, gold. It wasn't so hard after that.

I just found whatever it was that fit my mind's image of her.

And it wasn't all about buying for her. Sometimes, honestly, I just wanted to hear her laugh, to see her smile, to sense exactly what that look in her eyes meant.

It was worth it.

Treating her like my girlfriend/queen became fun and I found myself much more satisfied and relaxed.

The bills?

They continued. But the quality of life improved. I learned how to relax and take one day at a time. From then on, the bed I'd made was made just right.

Thank God.

Chapter Six
Never Say Never

Inez Vera Cruz smelled of expensive perfume and was always so well put together. She was the newest consultant at Geomax and the only female of our all boy executive club.

She had an engaging, *in-yo-face* personality. A great laugh. She wasn't intimidated at being the only woman in our weekly staff meetings. She was gracious and hardworking. She made a good impression on both the administrative and the executive staff.

The workload was distributed more evenly because she came on board. We all loved that.

Now, I must say here that Inez wasn't runway-model gorgeous. But she had all the right things working for her that made her noticeable. You know, that polished look.

Her and I had a lot in common. We both drank decaf coffee. We both preferred the medical sciences branch of consulting.

She was married with two children.

So was I.

She was notably unhappy at home.

So was I.

I asked myself time and time again why I longed to see her in the mornings? Why did I look forward to bumping into her at the copy machine, the fax machine, the coffee machine?

Further than friendly scared me half to death. Now I've never been one of those guys who tells himself he can handle a little romp on the side. And unfortunately, the few times I've been in love, I fell really hard. So, I know my limits.

Nevertheless, I was drawn to Inez Vera Cruz like a magnet.

She reciprocated in subtle ways like brushing against me when I held the door open for her. And sitting directly across from me in meetings so that she could make eye contact with me.

I found myself hovering around her office for no reason at all. I'd strike up conversations with employees I hadn't said two words to in five years just to be where she was!

It was weird. I still loved Camille. But Inez was a tantalizing distraction. My thoughts embarrassed me. Still, I enjoyed them while they played in the secrecy of my mind.

Instantly Camille noticed something different about me.

"So, you got a little honey on the side, do ya?" she asked jokingly one night after I didn't respond to her attempt to kiss and cuddle.

"...What me? No."

"If I didn't know better–"

"Aw now, woman," I said snapping back into reality, "you know you're the only one in the world for me."

"Yeah...." she answered looking into my eyes. "Well, you're lookin' good for a 32 year old man," she said stroking my cheek with an open, perfumed palm. "You're starting to look a little more distinguished. A little more debonair. Women like that, you know."

I didn't say anything.

"And this body!" She smiled and tickled my sides. "Who could ignore this big, wide chest and all these muscles?"

We laughed together.

She pressed her head to my chest. "Steve, you don't know how much I want to be left alone."

"Left alone?" I asked.

"Yeah, honey. Left alone to love you," she said. "An uncomplicated, unaffected life without bills, debt...like Adam and Eve before that apple thing."

We kissed and cuddled until we found ourselves enthralled in passion and on our way to our marriage bed.

I lay awake that night staring at the ceiling.

I tried and tried to get Inez's face out of my mind.

Camille is my wife, I kept telling myself. *I could never hurt her. Could I?*

Comparing the two women to each other was useless. Camille had years of my love invested in her. Hell, she was the mother of my children!

Inez was an insignificant fantasy that would go away with time.

I hoped to God I was right.

It was the following day's events that brought me face-to-face with what men and women are capable of.

I was having coffee with a few fellas from the office. Inez walked into the coffee house, waved at us and sat down at the counter.

The conversation naturally turned to her.

"She's hot!" said Paulie nudging me. "She's hot."

I purposely stayed out of it. I didn't want the guys to pick-up on my attraction for her. But the guys mentioned all the same things I'd been thinking about her; beautifully perfumed, department store fashionable, likable, good looking.

Then Wesley Keniston slid into the conversation that he and Inez were messin' around.

We all got quiet.

"But, Wes," I said, "you've got a good thing with your wife. Why risk it?"

"Are you kiddin', Steve?" He smiled at me. "It was free, man. Fantasy, you know. No strings attached. No commitment."

"Man, you–"

"I'm surprised you didn't get to her first, Torrance," he said devilishly and punching me in the shoulder.

"She's pretty hot," said Paulie groping her with his eyes over his coffee cup. "Wish it was me getting' *that* instead of you."

"Yeah," said Big Dan starting to sweat, "she's certainly sending all the right signals."

"What do ya' mean?" I asked knowing full well.

"She told me she had her eye on you, Torrance, from day one," said Wes. "But I guess just like with the Octagon account in '92, I beat you to the punch, man."

"Naw, man," I said reaching for my briefcase suddenly disgusted with my own fantasies. "I don't mess around."

"Oh, don't deny it," challenged Wes, "you've thought about it."

I didn't say a word.

"C'mon, Torrance," said Wes, "every married man messes around. Even if it's in his mind."

"Sometimes," said Paulie nudging me again, "that's the best way to do it."

Wes laughed. "Stop trying to be the innocent one!"

"How long have you and Camille been together?" asked Paulie.

"Nine years," I said still surprised at the their confessions and accuracy.

"You mean, you've never had another woman in nine years?" asked Big Dan.

"No," I said feeling like the virgin who confessed his purity to his college buddies. "For some men, one woman is enough."

They laughed and cracked jokes about me.

On my way out of the coffee shop, I passed by Inez sitting alone reading a newspaper. We shared only a look.

Her eyes were dark and deep. She pulled my attention in with the creamy-plum of her mouth that curled devilishly at the corners. She inhaled and then exhaled. My eyes followed the rise and fall of her ample cleavage.

I walked by her without saying a word.

I had never touched Inez; never went any further except to shake her hand. But I felt like I knew her the way Wes knew her. Maybe it was because I didn't realize how well I knew myself.

I mean, I had to ask myself *was I capable of such infidelity? Could I turn to the bed of another woman? A woman who offered nothing less than the pleasure of her body; could I be so desperate or so stupid?*

Camille and I golfed with Wes and his wife. His kid came to Matt's birthday parties. He was a husband and father just like me.

What made him do it?

What kept me from doing it?

I realized that it was the marriage bed prayer. The far reaching words spoken directly to the Lord for protection and guidance and honor. Somehow that prayer had fused me with power to do the right thing when the wrong thing would bring me pleasure. And be so easy.

I sat there taking their quips on the chin. Years of Sunday school lessons and scriptures came rolling to mind; *can a man take fire into his bosom and not be burned? Resist the enemy and he (or she) will flee from you. What God has put together, let no man put asunder....*

I felt bad for Wes.

I felt really bad for Inez.

They were both fired for improper conduct. And I heard

their marriages fell apart shortly thereafter.

Paulie and Big Dan never teased about infidelity again.

Now, there are some things even a happily married, innocent man doesn't discuss with his wife. This was one of those things.

Camille was the only woman in the world for me. Deep down in my heart, I knew that.

One day when the house was quiet, I just laid down in the bed.

No TV. No music. Just quiet.

I was amazed at how something I'd invested life, love and body in for so many years could be over and done with by signing my name to a piece of paper. Too easy. Could it be so simple as to condition myself to taking a new route home? Maybe to my own apartment? Or seeing the kids only on the weekend? Or worse yet, changing the dynamic of the marriage bed to, let's say, the pleasure bed or the freak-daddy bed? Okay, so Inez wasn't the only woman my mind had gone to be with over the years.

That wasn't good enough. I needed something with more adhesive than Steven J. Torrance's brand of wisdom and escapes. I started on a mental list of reasons to either stay married or not. Every married person entertains the idea of how they'd make it on their own, right? We try on the single parent hat and the dating hat just to see if it fits. Well, so did I.

The process that began begrudgingly ended up being a pleasant stroll down memory lane.

So many good times, significant times competed for my immediate attention. I was surprised. Under all my reasons for being angry, displaced and bitter were these forgotten pleasantries with my wife Camille

I laughed out loud. I reminisced.

Somebody up there was tenderizing my heart. I could feel it.

Two hours later, my list was complete. I decided to stay married; to unplug the issue of divorce and its get-glad-quick philosophy. I can honestly say it wasn't because of splitting up the kids or selling the house or having to pay alimony. It was because of commitment. The commitment I made to Camille on our wedding day.

Maybe that sounds corny. But that's not the half of it.

When I decided to stay, a whole new door opened up to me. Like in that two hour period, I grew up. And some new challenge was waiting to be experienced and conquered.

The Marriage Bed

It's hard to explain but a brand new level of sacrificial love was calling to me. Over the mountain of unresolved arguments and nights Camille and I fell asleep without speaking to each other, I found my heart rushing to partner with this new love. Love I had not anticipated nor believed I needed. But I came face-to-face with it and suddenly my life needed it like the body needs blood. A warrior-like voice whispered inside my head, "you're ready."

Chapter Seven
The Bed of Affliction

One Sunday, I was out in the backyard digging the same hole with a shovel for the greater part of an hour.

Why? No reason at all.

I heard the doorbell ring. "I'll get it!" said Nichelle.

Before long, I heard Nichelle say "Mommy! Mommy! Uncle Drew and Aunt Toni are here!"

I kept digging.

"Where've you been?" asked Camille.

"We had to go to Louisiana to settle my mom's estate," said Drew.

"Oh, I see," said Camille.

"We just came by 'cause the Torrances haven't been at church," said Drew. "Ya'll not disenchanted with the Lord, are you?"

Camille hesitated. "No," she said. "Nothing like that."

I stabbed at the moist earth purposely killing worms.

"Is Steve home?" asked Drew.

"Yeah," said Camille. "He's out back."

The patio door slid open and Drew stepped down near my project.

I didn't turn around.

"We're gonna take the kids around to the park, fellas," shouted Antoinette.

"Steve, man," Drew asked still wearing his clergy collar from church, "what's wrong with you? You're not yourself today."

"I've got a lot of things on my mind, Drew," I said, raking up some leaves.

"You wanna talk about it?"

"Not really," I said reaching for my shovel.

"...Okay," he said smiling, "well, did you see the Clippers game last-"

"Camille told me last night that they found cancer in her breast," I told him stabbing at the same hole with the shovel.

Drew was silent. The smile drained from his face into a frown.

"She doesn't know the extent of it yet," I said pulverizing a family of worms as sweat poured from my face. "Her doctor, Dr. Prescott, is suggesting surgery to know how far the cancer has gone."

Drew was stunned but managed to say, "the Lord moves in mysterious ways, my brother. Sometimes our actions get His attention and bring about negative consequences."

"Drew, I don't believe you, man!" I looked at him like I could've killed him. I mean, was he referring to my secret thoughts about Inez? The very ones I hadn't even told anybody? Or was he suggesting that I hadn't been a good enough husband to Camille?

"You've got a cut and dried answer for everything, Drew! Sometimes I don't even think you're real. You live by this code of *I'm the Man! Nothing can hurt me!* Well, I'm real. And this cancer *thing* hurts me!"

"Look, Steve man. I didn't mean to...I'm sorry."

"Yeah right," I said throwing the shovel to the ground. "Are you saying that somehow *I* brought this on Camille? My wife has cancer, man!" I hollered at him. "I didn't put it in her alright!"

"God only wants to make-"

"Don't mention God to me!" I shouted loud enough for every neighbor to hear. "Look, how do you know what God wants, huh? Who are you, his lawyer or somethin'! God don't love me or Camille! I don't even know if *I* believe in Him anymore!"

"Steve, what are-"

"I don't wanna hear His name or that butcher doctor's name either!" I started for the door. "Radiation therapy? Exploratory surgery? They wanna kill my wife! And from the looks of it, God's gonna let 'em do it!"

"Steve, Antoinette was brutally raped and beaten five

years ago and she never really got over it!" he shouted.

I just stared at Drew who up until this moment seemed flawless. I saw my friend, the minister, whither into a helpless, nervous mortal right before my eyes.

He started to sweat suddenly and sat on the porch under the weight of the confession.

"When?" I asked. "Where?"

"She was workin' late at the school one night 'bout a year ago," he told me. "I was preachin' that night out of town."

"Drew," I said seeing that same look in his eyes that I had to justify purchasing a gun, "did they ever catch the guy?"

"Nope." He turned away. "Whoa," he said wiping his forehead, "I never thought I'd ever say that again out loud and here I am tellin' you."

"Drew, man..." I didn't know what to say. "You never told us."

"It hurt too much to say some things, man. Folks always look at church people funny when really bad stuff happens to 'em...Antoinette is a shadow of herself, Steve," he said staring into space. "A shadow. Remember how she would sing and sing and sing in church? Not any more, man. Nothin' moves her."

He started to cry. "I still see the fear in her eyes. I can tell when she's forcing a smile. I know when she's drifting back. When it happened I said how could God allow this to happen to a woman who never hurt anybody?" He dropped his head in sorrow. "I even asked Him why He just didn't let her die.

"I'm ashamed now," he confessed, "but I wondered what my life would be like if she had died. If I knew she wasn't gonna suffer from it, you know?"

I couldn't respond.

"But He let her live," he said with difficulty. "And just as Antoinette relives it day after day, *I* have to remind us both that God never leaves us not even for a moment.

Her tugged at his clergy collar. "Imagine how *I* feel when I'm not sure I believe *that* myself?"

He looked away like he was gonna really bawl. "...I've got to believe," he said clenching his fists. "I'm a minister of the gospel. I have no choice."

He turned to me, stood up and asked, "you wanna know why I stay at that church? Why I preach so hard? 'Cause I've got to believe that God doesn't punish people like that. He loves us. Even when bad things happen and tear up lives. He loves us. There has to be hope for all people, Steve. Camille, Antoinette, you and me."

Then he said, "I've been where you are, Steve; scared, helpless. Even feeling like part of it is somehow your fault; if you had loved her more, understood her better. Life's not equipped with absolutes and logical solutions. Or even justice, man."

He stood up, grabbed my shoulder and said, "I *am* real, man. Real as you. I'm sorry I came at you like that." He walked away.

"Couple nights ago," I said so Drew would stop walking.

He did. And breathed and smiled knowing our friendship was intact.

"I asked God to teach me how to love my wife, man," I admitted on the verge of tears. "'Cause I was mad at her...not feeling like I used to about her."

He put his hand on my shoulder. I knew I could trust him with this vulnerable, tender area of my life.

"Is this cancer thing a test or something?" I asked him. "Does God wanna know how much I really love her?"

"He's not cruel like that, man." He said putting his arms around me to let me cry. "He loves you. He loves Camille. You just love Camille like He loves her and through it, His love is demonstrated in you."

"In me?" I asked him.

"In you," he confirmed with a pointed finger at my chest.

In me, Camille wanted for nothing.

I held her during the night when she cried. I encouraged her when she felt low. I kept her secret from the church members and pretended that nothing was wrong when they asked about her.

I kept the kids busy when she needed rest. I washed clothes, cooked, well, burned dinner. But I would have done anything to show her that my love for her ranked somewhere near God's love for her.

My divine love lasted exactly two weeks.

You see, the cancer snuck-up on us like a whispering bullet. And then outta nowhere, POW!

Our lives changed. She changed.

I wasn't God. I couldn't stand in His shoes. I was Camille's husband. Sure, I had rank but nothing like God's. He could see all and maneuver the alignment of the stars and planets to benefit Camille.

I could only see the woman I love wounded and afraid.

Even in my denial of things, I tried to seem as normal as possible.

I mean, she didn't really look sick. And I desired her more than ever.

When I started seein' her get more and more depressed, more and more withdrawn from me and the kids, I wanted to give her the part of me that always made her feel good.

I did everything. I lured her into bed. I touched her. Nothing unlocked the passion she'd tucked away safely from view.

The house had settled. The kids were tightly tucked into their beds. Camille and I laid in our bed watching the last of Bob Hope's Road to Rio.

I put my arm around her. I kissed her hair and rubbed her hips under her gown.

"When I'm gone, Steve, I want–"

"If you start another sentence with 'when I'm gone, Steve', I'm gonna kill you myself." I said trying to sound playfully serious as I kissed a path around her shoulders to her back.

"...I know it's hard to understand, honey," she replied pulling her nightgown straps back over her shoulders, "but I just don't want to anymore."

"If you give into this cancer, Cam–"

"It's not that I've given in, Steve!" She snatched the blankets over her head. "It's a reality I can't ignore."

"But what about me?" I had the audacity to ask.

She threw the blankets off and screamed "what about you?"

The fear of losing her engulfed my mind like a tidal wave. I grabbed her and just held her while she screamed into my arms until she cried herself to sleep.

The darkest of night surrounded us finding Camille sleeping with her fears and me unable to sleep with mine.

I called on the Lord as best as I knew how. Not eloquently like Drew, but with one word; *help*.

We stayed there huddled in our marriage bed awaiting daybreak.

Nichelle came in from school the next day. She leaned against the door-frame of our bedroom.

"Where's mom?" she asked looking as if the day had gotten the best of her.

The Marriage Bed

"Doctor's appointment," I said patting the bed.

She dragged in letting her backpack hit the floor with a thud.

She hung her arms around my neck and just sighed.

I know she didn't want to lose her mama and neither did I. But the cancer wasn't just taking over Camille's body, it was taking over our lives. It showed on our faces. It dominated our thoughts.

We were quiet when maybe we should have been making the normal noises of life around Camille. We were solemn, understanding, and a little lethargic when we could have been our usual spontaneous selves.

I don't know why, but we maintained this mortuary like existence ignorantly trying to make life easier, I guess.

"Daddy," said Nichelle wiping her tears, "I know you guys don't tell us everything but I wanna know. *Everything*, daddy."

"*Everything* is complicated, Nichelle," I explained. "You've gotta understand, Nichelle. It's not that we're trying to keep things from you and your brother."

"But I've been hearin' kids at school talk about cancer and stuff," she said still crying. "They say things like cancer patients go bald and die real soon. And that sometimes they get so sick just before they die that they can't talk anymore. And have to be hooked-up to machines. And live in the hospital and–"

"Okay," I said. "Okay, Nichelle."

"I wanna know if Mommy's gonna die, Daddy."

"Pumpkin, I don't have all the answers right now," I told her. "We'll just have to pray for–"

"I have been *prayin'* for her. Every night! Why doesn't God answer, Daddy? Why does He take so long just to answer?"

I didn't know how to answer her. She was seven years old, full of questions and full of worry.

Yeah, she was busy worrying about having to grow up without a Mom and I was busy wondering how I was gonna love my wife with one breast.

Don't get me wrong, Camille is and always has been an exciting woman and I had to keep telling myself that certain parts of her didn't matter.

But in all honesty, they did.

As a matter of fact, I found out how dirty Satan fights, too. I can't tell you how many times I've heard this little voice in my head say *why don't you call Inez? And you fool, you should've went for that when you had the chance! At least you could be getting some right about now.*

Lord, I begged, *help me.*

"Nichelle, Mommy's goin' through a lot right now," I told my daughter holding her in my arms. "She hasn't been herself lately, you know? But she's still Camille." I said just to convince myself.

"There's no reason to feel differently about her just because she's sick," I explained to Nichelle's hopeful face. "She'll get back around to doing all the things that make you love her so much like youth club parties and skating, shopping and things like that."

"But what about you, daddy?" asked the kid sensing something awry in me. "Will you feel differently about Mommy?"

"What do you mean?"

"I mean if she has to have the operation," she explained playing with the button on my shirt, "will you feel differently about Mommy?"

I closed my eyes.

This was the moment of truth. "...No pumpkin," I answered with sudden assurance. "I've decided to love her even more if she has to have the operation."

Nichelle flung her arms around me and just squeezed my neck.

That sealed it for me.

Chapter Eight
A Private Thing

Nichelle, Matt and I tried to give Camille as much space as we thought she needed after her mastectomy.

We didn't make the same mistake of keeping the house as quiet as a tomb like we did before.

Dr. Prescott's advice to Camille was solid: *have the surgery and later he could replace the breast with an implant. There's no sense in relying on remission to save your life.*

We took his suggestion in stride.

But Camille got on the internet and researched the whole procedure and all the options. Saline implants were best, she concluded.

If it was okay with Camille, then it was okay with me.

During the time that lead to the surgery, Camille developed this sort of gutsiness that I never knew she had.

She may have had her moments, but she never missed a dance rehearsal or a taekwondo sparring match. She cheered, she clapped, she even debated at the PTA meetings. There was nothing she was incapable of doing. And depression couldn't stay in the same room with her. I admired her for that. I fed on her moxy.

One day, in an effort of black humor, I told her that her cancer would have to kill her on her feet.

She gave me this strange look as if I stumbled upon something she was trying to hide and said "...I wouldn't have it any other way, Steve."

With that door to her unspoken thoughts thrown open

to me, I was afraid to go near her. Would I find out even more about my wife that would scare the crap out of me?

Camille was extraordinary! Just the fact that she refused to take this lying down made me proud that she was the mother of my children and the wife of my love.

After the surgery, Camille decided she wanted to remove the bandages in the privacy of her own home.

"Enough people have poked and prodded me, Steve!" she shouted in the car on the way home from the hospital. "This is still my body, you know!"

Dr. Prescott protested when his nurse called to schedule Camille's follow-up appointment and she told the nurse she wouldn't be there.

My Cammy wouldn't even listen to the guy. She said she didn't want Dr. Prescott, his nurses or even that clinical psychologist he had waiting to counsel her anywhere around.

It was a private thing with Camille.

So there she was; holed up in our bedroom for about three hours alone and in the dark.

Nichelle was at a slumber party. And Matt was with the Galtons on a ski trip.

You know me; I had stretched out on the couch to watch the Clippers game. I don't even like the Clippers. But I had to do something to get my mind off Camille.

Nothing worked.

I was watchin' the game, but all I could think about was her.

Like this voice kept sayin' *what are you gonna do without her, huh? Who will you find to love you like Camille? Can you afford to start over again? What kind of god is God to give you a wife like her and then take her away?*

Was this *my* thinking? Did *I* doubt God that much? I wondered.

Then suddenly from the bedroom, "Steeeeve!"

I hopped up off that couch so fast I knocked over my glass of punch.

"What, Camille!" I said busting in to the room. "What is it!"

She was sitting at her vanity table with her back to me still wrapped in the bandages that held her from the whole truth. There was a chilling cold in the room.

"...Don't touch that light, Steven."

"Okay, honey." My mouth went dry.

"I'm afraid," she said as she started to cry. "Hold my hand, Steve...."

The Marriage Bed

I walked over to her stiff as a board. I was afraid to touch her. Can you believe it? Afraid to touch my own wife?

With one hand she tugged gently at the bandages in the absence of light.

"Honey," I said, "I'll turn on the light for–"

"No." She whispered. Then she took a deep breath and peeled the last bandage away from her wound.

She cried out into the darkness. The flicker of her wedding ring caught my eye as trembling fingers touched the area that used to be her breast.

Her pain filled the room.

I cried, too.

"C'mon, Camille," I said trying to get her to look at me. "You and me. We're in this together."

"...The light, Steven," she said closing her eyes. "I want to see myself in the light now...."

I gulped hard. "You sure?"

"Yes..."

I got up enough courage to do as she asked.

There it was in the mirror; a scar, red and raw, where there used to be a healthy mound of flesh.

Her mouth stretched into a frown. Tears welled up in Cam's eyes again.

I went to her and dropped to my knees. I kissed the scar. I cried and held her tight knowing her shock would grow into a scream.

"Cam, you are still the most exciting woman in the world to me!" I said while she slammed her fists against my back.

She pulled away from me and strained to get another horrifying look in the mirror.

"You are everything God created you to be!" I shouted over her screams. "What God created is right, Camille!"

"How am I gonna live like this, Steve?" She rambled on. "I'm not a whole woman...not whole..."

"I'll never stop loving you!" I shouted at her. "You are more to me than a breast!"

She stopped finally. Then she looked at me and the scar in the mirror a long, long time.

"...I'm still a woman," she declared in a hardy whisper.

"*My* woman," I said stroking her hair.

"You'll never stop loving me, Steve?"

I looked into her eyes. "Never."

Three months later, Dr. Prescott found cancer in Camille's other breast. Camille swore me to secrecy.

Dang it!

We were just starting to get back to normal when all of a sudden it looked like we were going to have to go through that surgery thing all over again.

Sometimes I thought if Camille would just die-then it would all be over.

I finally realized what Drew meant when he confessed to me about wishing the same for Antoinette. Needless to say, I couldn't think about that very long.

My little prize-fighter who could take it on the chin was reduced to this shadow of a woman I didn't recognize half the time.

She would prop herself up in the bed surrounded by photo albums touching Nichelle and Matt's faces and crying. "I want Nichelle and Matt to have a good mother...somebody who'll really love them. Somebody like me, Steve."

There were some nights Camille didn't come to bed at all. And when she did, I could bank on conversations in the dark that consisted of *"I want you to remarry, Steve* and *find someone who will love you as much as I do, Steve."*

"That did it!" I shouted at her. "Enough with this mess, Camille! You'll get through it, okay?"

"I don't know about that this time, Steve," she said completely drained of hope. "I'd rather die than to live as half a woman with no breast and no hair!"

"Cam, there's only you! Do you hear me?"

Initially, she wouldn't even look at me. And when she did, she looked right through me.

Before long I was shouting at her and shaking her. "Only you! I can't think about anybody except you. I mean, what do you want from me, huh? I can't plan to marry anybody else while I'm lookin' at the woman I love!"

Her eyes looked back at me lacking the brilliance, fire and life I was used to.

I grabbed her and shook her again. "Cam! Camille, do you hear me?"

Her mouth quivered. "Hollerin' at me won't keep me alive, Steve," she whispered.

I could tell she was missing me already. I refused to long for what I could see and feel.

I pulled her into my arms. "Fight this, Cam! Fight it! Please, babe. I need you, Camille."

She went limp and slid from my arms-the big, strong

arms that comforted her when her mother died. She rolled onto her pillow, "I don't have the tears left to cry any more, Steve. God has let me go. Now you do the same."

My mind rushed up to Heaven's door. I banged on it.

You can't take her, God! I shouted inside my head. *You can't! Remember the prayer? This isn't a deathbed. It's a marriage bed. A place for dreams. A place for us. You can't take Camille. Without her, Lord, I'm just a man. Just like Adam before Eve; not a husband, not a lover. Without her, Lord, this is just a bed. Please.*

The next day, I broke my silence.

It was windy, wet and cold when I caught up with Drew on his milk delivery route. I explained Cam's condition.

I told him everything; how she wouldn't get out of bed, clean the house or go to work. I told him about the secret; the privacy she insisted on.

He must have stayed with me well over an hour intent on listening.

I ranted. I raved. As a matter of fact, I think he would've let me take a few swings at him if I needed to. He understood anger and helplessness. Drew is a friend like no other.

Before I went back to work, I asked him to pray for Camille. If anybody could get a prayer though, Drew could.

On my way home from work that night, I was numb to the news on the car radio. Somebody got killed. Somebody stole something. Some politician was trying to take over the world!"

All I could think about was Camille.

I tell you, as sure as I'm writing this, I heard a voice say *I have her now.*

I woke-up, if you know what I mean. I drove that car like a bat outta hell questioning God and begging Him not to take Camille's life.

When I finally got home, there were cars everywhere. My heart pounded into my throat as I ran to the front door.

It was dark inside. I could here a strange but familiar voice singing upstairs. It wasn't Camille's voice and that scared me even more.

All over the living room and dining room were people from Haven Community Church. They were stretched out before the Lord praying and crying.

"Spare Camille's life, Lord!" some cried.

"Remember her children, Father!" others groaned.

"Work a miracle in this place, Jesus!" prayed the pastor's wife.

On the stairs, I stepped over even more of them who were wailing and lifting up the name of the Lord unconcerned about me.

"*We are standing...*" sang the voice, "*...on holy ground...*"

Down the hall were still more of the members young and old.

"*...And I know that there are angels all around....*"

I reached the bedroom door not sure of what I'd see.

"*...Let us praise Jesus now....*"

I opened the door to find that it was Antoinette standing over Camille singing with even more people covering our bedroom floor.

"*We are standing in His presence on holy ground...*"

Camille sat in the middle of the bed; her cheeks washed with tears.

Her color had come back and she was smiling.

"Steve," she whispered reaching for me to join her. "Oh, Steve...They all just showed up at once this afternoon and started praying."

I basked in the rays of her smile.

"More of them came," she said looking around the room, "and more of them." She touched her breast and closed her eyes. "I felt something pull away from the inside."

She started to cry as she told me. "I can't explain it but the cancer, it's gone, Steve! It's gone..." She laughed and cried at the same time. "Oh, God, I know it's gone! God didn't let go of me, Steve," she said grabbing my hands. "*He* has me now."

God had her. The misunderstood words on the freeway. God was letting me know that sincere, faith-filled prayer got His attention. Not my anger. Not my desperation, goodness, near-misses or threats.

The whole scene played before me like a dream–a dream come true–with unanticipated joy for dessert.

Breaking my silence had life-changing consequences. Drew and Antoinette were at the center of it all. That didn't surprise me.

Up until that day, I could only make aimless guestimations at how a miracle comes together.

Now I know that it's a faith thing. What God really wants to know is how much we really believe. How much do we actually trust Him? And if we are willing to believe Him instead of the difficult things that are so obvious in our lives.

Oh, and by the way, the following week Dr. Prescott didn't find a trace of cancer anywhere in Camille's body.

Chapter Nine
I do. Ditto.

Okay, so it's safe to say it was my idea. After all, I had to show my woman that she meant the world to me.

What? A guy like me can't plan a wedding and a second honeymoon?

Oh, but I did.

I reserved the church, invited the guests, and ordered the cake and flowers. I even rented a limousine to take us to and fro in style. There would be nothing but the best for the woman I love.

Simple, right?

All my lovely bride had to do was show up in a dress of her choice.

Wouldn't you know it, she held up the entire ceremony. I kept sending Nichelle to the dressing room to find out what was going on in there. She would come back with the same answer each time. "Mommy's eyes are a little puffy and she doesn't want to be seen like that."

Three times!

The same answer!

Finally, just to kill some time I went to the front of the church, grabbed the mike and thanked everybody for coming.

I was a little nervous and Drew picked-up on it. He got a kick out of it.

"Why are we here, Steve?!" shouted Drew egging me on knowing I couldn't resist the urge to pledge myself openly about the woman I love.

"As many of you know, my wife had been ill for some time," I said. "This day is special for all of us. But especially for me.

"You see, I've gotten a hold of some real wisdom lately," I said recalling the good years and the challenging moments that made up my life with Camille.

"And I want my wife Camille to know just how wonderful she is to me, to our family. That's why you're all here. I gotta tell you, this woman is an excellent mother and friend to her children.

"She is my best, best friend," I said remembering her laugh and her smile. "And today, in light of so many blessings, I wanted more than anything to claim my love for her in the presence of God and you, our family and our friends."

Camille's aunts held hands and cried.

"Twelve years ago I stood in a church next to the woman God blessed me with and I said I do. And believe me, since then, I've done!"

Everyone laughed.

"Today," I said feeling nervous, "I stand in this church waiting for that very same woman who has stuck by me, held onto me, ignored me and loved me beyond what I could imagine.

"Without Camille in my life," I said looking at Drew, "I can't guarantee that I'd be the same man I am today.

"So I'm waiting," I said looking at my watch, "to look into her eyes once more and pledge my love with the words I do."
"Ditto!" shouted Camille from the back of the church looking absolutely stunning.

I tell you, everybody in that place turned around and found themselves treated to the most beautiful sight in the world! They cheered their heads off.

Her lines were long and tailored. She stood gracefully and proud. No sign of illness or weakness. She was the bride of my youth. My heart thanked God as it jumped around in my chest.

It's a memory I could relive over and over again and never tire of.

That night, our marriage bed took on a totally new and different meaning. We were a newlywed couple for the second time. But what we brought to that special place in our lives was a greater sense of the marriage vows laid down by Our Heavenly Father.

The Marriage Bed

In sickness and in health.

Those words used to scare me. But I've decided that I like them. They mean more to me than just some rushed-through preliminary one repeats in front of a minister. Or words we'd care not to think about.

In sickness and in health....

God knows how we're gonna react to sickness, threat...scarcity. And He has so graciously allowed a place to deal with it. In our case, a bed.

He has given us a place where we can close our eyes on the world, a place to wake up next to the one you love. A place to retreat unto. A place from which to awaken feeling renewed. I sound a little like Drew, don't I? But it's real, I tell you. Really real.

And in that place that we yield our busy, worn minds to rest, He is probably closest. Watching us; sewing together the ripped parts of our lives while we are quiet and undisturbed. Camille and I took the concept of our marriage bed to beautiful Jamaica. There we frolicked, we drank tropical fruit drinks, we danced under the moonlight.

Everywhere we sat, walked or slept together, the beautiful blessing of our marriage bed prayer went with us in togetherness, familiarity, honesty, passion and triumph.

Even fourteen years into marriage, love is still a funny, funny thing. It has a life all it's own. It develops, it grows. It warms you up. It makes you aware of good things. It angers you.

You want to know what's best about love?

It renews itself.

Just last night, I was on my way home; fighting traffic, makin' my way through the rain.

I got to the front door, turned the key and I could smell flowers. I even heard jazz playing softly.

I got excited and opened the door. My senses were met by the most exotic scents, sights and sounds.

Tiny candles lined a path of rose petals that led to the staircase.

At the top of the stairs was Camille absolutely radiant, dressed in this sheer black nightie.

"Take your shoes off, lover boy," she cooed as her perfume filled my head.

I did.

Leaning over the banister, she whispered to me, "now walk along those petals."

I kicked my shoes off and snatched my socks off, too, and walked.

"How does that feel?"

I closed my eyes and smiled. "Almost like heaven," I said with rose petals smashed between my toes and under the bottom of my big, crusty feet. "It feels soft, cool. It feels great."

"Steven Jarrod Torrance," she said sweetly, "that's how you make me feel."

I started up the stairs peeling the office attire from my body. The petaled path lead to where else? Our bedroom.

I walked in to find tiny lit candles everywhere. And our bed was covered in rose petals, too.

Camille had thrown pillows on the floor in front of the stereo and my lovely dinner companion had prepared plates of delicious food. She insisted on feeding me the first perfect bite; a fork stacked with a taste of exotic salad, the most tender meat and a swirl of pasta. The best of our first years together came rolling forward with sweet, new and appreciated excitement.

After eating, we danced barefoot on the petals to the slow, soothing sounds of the music that filled our home and our hearts.

So this is my life as I lay here writing this love story from, where else, our marriage bed.

Camille is fast asleep as the first sign of morning has washed our room in pale gray.

Look, I could go on and on. I have a mountain of stuff that proves even more how great this is and how wonderful that is. But Camille just woke up and is now smiling at me.

She's looking around the bed that is covered with not only rose petals but papers.

"What've you been up to?" she asks reading a few lines from a page.

I just smile.

"...Camille is the reason why men love women so much," she reads aloud. Then she looks up with tears in her eyes. "...Is this how you feel about me?"

"Yeah," I tell her taking her in my arms.

She grabs a handful of petals and sprinkles them gently on my head.

I tell her "I must be the most blessed creature on this earth to have you as my wife."

"Why?" she asks.

"To have you as my wife," I tell her, "and the showers of your love, your smile and rose petals in our bed."

Gingerbread Men

Chapter One
Inquiring Minds

The familiar horns of *La Cocarocha* danced through the three-story office building. Like lab rats, employees spilled from its doors into the brisk morning breeze to secure breakfast from The Roach Coach.

Three Black women, Shallondra, Lisa and Terri, found themselves first in line. They ordered breakfast specials from the personable cashier and stepped to the side to await the morning's sustenance.

"I wish that elevator hadn't been so full," said the elder Terri nudging Lisa who was trying to warm herself by rubbing her hands together. "'Cause I was about to say make room for daddy! Mmmm," she groaned eyeing the handsome Black man that every female employee was raving about since his arrival two weeks prior.

"Yeah," said Lisa as her thin blouse whipped against her in the sudden wind. "He's a hunk."

"He ain't *all* that," concluded Shallondra tightening her leather coat around her full figure. "He's probably gay," she concluded rolling her eyes.

"Oh, him?" asked Lisa disappointed. "He can't be. It always seems like the good ones are gay."

"Naw, naw," said Terri checking him out from head to toe. "You can tell by the walk and by the way they stand."

"Girl," said Shallondra with a hearty laugh, "you trippin'."

"Listen here, young girls," said Terri lighting up a cigarette, "take a lesson from a more experienced woman. A woman old enough to be your–your older sister."

Lisa and Shallondra snickered.

"*That* man," exclaimed Terri pointing discreetly with her cigarette, "he don't have no sugar in his tank. He's 100% Grade A beef! Check out his walk, girl," said Terri as her friends leaned in. "He knows the ladies love him. And look at the way he stands, feet spread apart. Girl, that means he's not through 'til you're through, okay? He's ready for anything."

Lisa and Shallondra nodded their heads. They were impressed.

"Just look at how he carries himself, ya'll," said Terri directing their attention to the details of his every move. "He's a ladies man I tell you." Terri covered his entire muscular physique with her imagination. "...I'd leave my husband for that."

"Terri," said Shallondra stomping her foot and putting her hand on her hip, "you already left your husband for your boyfriend, remember?"

"Honey," said Terri still mesmerized as she took a drag on her cigarette, "I might have to leave my boyfriend next."

"I still say he ain't all that," declared Shallondra folding her arms across her hefty bosom. "Since he been here, he ain't tried to talk to one *sistah* yet," she said pointing with a long sculptured nail. "Not even Debra up in Accounting. You know, the one tryin' to break into movies who thinks she has to sleep with everybody who starts workin' here?"

"Oh, come on," said Lisa laughing and thinking warm thoughts. "You don't know that that's true, Shallondra."

"Well, Debra's gorgeous," said Shallondra, "by some folks' standards and he ain't tried to mess wit' her yet. I guess she's too Black for *him*."

Terri peered over her glasses. "What you sayin'?"

"I'm sayin' it's obvious Garrett Hunter ain't interested in the *sistahs* 'round here," declared Shallondra. "He's probably white-washed!"

"What does that mean?" asked Lisa now jumping to keep warm.

"A sell-out brother, Lisa, who says *sistahs* got too much attitude so he goes and gets some white chick and treats *her* like a queen! They a trip. Humph! They came outta a Black woman, but now suddenly Black ain't good enough!"

Gingerbread Men

"Lisa!" shouted the cashier from inside the catering truck. "One breakfast special, two hot cakes, eggs scrambled and two pieces of turkey bacon!"

Lisa walked away from her co-workers to settle her bill.

"Sensitive ears, Shallondra," whispered Terri slapping her on the shoulder, "Lisa's mom is white and her father is Black. Watch what you sayin', girl."

"Humph," exclaimed Shallondra keeping a tight grip on her phony-pony tail as the wind whipped around her, "that's *her* problem."

"Breakfast special! Breakfast special!" shouted The Roach Coach chef again. "Cherrie and Shwallwondra!" he shouted massacring their names with his Vietnamese accent. "Two hot cakes, scrambled eggs and regular bacon! A dollar ninety-nine each, ladies!"

The two women joined Lisa as she finished paying for her food. "Wait up, Lisa," said Terri blowing smoke, "we'll walk back with you."

"Well," she said grimacing. "That's okay. I've got to stop by the reception area to get some coffee. I'm freezin'." She waved to them with cold fingers. "See you upstairs."

Shallondra looked at Terri and rolled her eyes. "What? Don't you say a word to me about little miss half and half."

"Hey, Shallondra, look," said Terri pointing to a woman standing patiently in line reading a small pamphlet. "There's Aileen the church lady who works in Personnel. She knows everybody. We'll ask her about Mr. Garrett Hunter."

The two women hurried to the end of the line to talk with Aileen.

"Hey, Aileen." Terri greeted her as if they were the old friends. "Tell me, honey, what's the scoop on the new brother up there?"

Aileen adjusted her glasses. "Who? Garrett Hunter?"

"Yeah," said Terri enjoying her view of him from behind. "The fine one."

Aileen smiled. "What's there to tell?" she asked returning to her inspirational reading. "He's a nice young man with a Masters in Computer Science, 28 years old with a great wardrobe and a two year-old Porche. He's a consultant with Daylor Computer Software Systems here at Wide World Information Technologies to supervise the programming of our new financial system. He's well-traveled and works out religiously."

"Yeah," said Shallondra opening the lid of her container

and biting a piece of bacon, "but is he gay?"

"Oh, Lord, no," said Aileen grabbing her heart. "Nothing like that."

"He married?" asked Shallondra biting her bacon again.

"No," said Aileen. "I don't think so."

"Kids?" inquired Terri pressing in closer.

Aileen looked up as if annoyed. "No."

"Livin' with anybody?" demanded Terri in a whisper.

"Really, now," said Aileen recoiling. "I wouldn't know."

"I'll bet he is," accused Shallondra consuming the bacon and then pointing at Aileen. "And she probably white!"

"Come on, girl," said Terri pulling Shallondra's arm.

The two women came upon a Middle-Eastern-style scarved Black woman walking into the building from being dropped off at the curb.

"Karmena Muhammed," said Shallondra.

"Asalama Lakum, my sisters," she replied full of peace and order.

"Hey, Karmena," said Shallondra snapping her finger as she remembered something, "you work in the same department with that new dude Garrett Hunter, right."

"The new *brother*?" Karmena smiled pleasantly and nodded. "Yes, I do."

"Personally, I don't think he's all that," said Shallondra glancing at Terri, "but we were wonderin'," she probed, "is he livin' with anybody that *you* know of? Is he gay?"

"My sisters," said Karmena softening into broad smile, "this wouldn't be one of those female attempts to berate the Black brother, now would it?"

Terri shook her head. "Oh no. We just–"

"Because too often," interrupted Karmena planting her feet firmly to deliver her message, "the Black male is reduced to unidentifiable mush in the mouth of his female counterpart as she grinds him with her words. She must respect him and honor him. For the world he seeks respect and honor from does not recognize him as a valuable addition, but a treat. A threat economically, socially and yes, spiritually."

"Society and the media," continued Karmena gaining momentum and animation as she spoke, "have inducted the Black female in its strategy to cripple the Black man. The Black female rips at his image due to her mistrust. She bites at his armor due to her ignorance of his power and his glory. Remember, the Black man is a descendent of royalty. Of kings and of warriors who–"

Gingerbread Men

"Karmena," interrupted Shallondra taking her second piece of bacon out her breakfast container, "we think he's livin' with a white woman."

Karmena's gaze tightened. "He's dog spit," she exclaimed and pushed the glass double doors open to begin her day.

***

By 4 p.m., Garrett's pager had logged the same message sixteen times.

He quietly excused himself from his meeting and ducked into the washroom to think. He took a lingering look at himself in the mirror and wondered what cruel deed he had committed, in this life or some past one, that warranted such punishment.

The pager vibrated on his hip once again. He snatched it from his belt and looked at the LCD screen. The words *CAT CALL* appeared logging in at an astounding seventeen times.

Garrett put the pager on the sink and sighed. He straightened his tie and flattened his pirate-style mustache and beard with his hand. He smoothed his tight hair cut down and made up his mind to leave work early. Garrett reached for the pager and then had a change of heart. He left the pager behind.

Outside, fallen winter leaves blew in circles around Garrett's feet. He pulled the collar of his taupe cashmere coat up and around his neck against the biting cold.

A red knit hat tumbled toward his feet. He picked it up with his gray, leather-gloved hand and noticed a fellow employee running toward him to retrieve it.

"I guess this is what you need," he said handing the hat to the attractive Black woman.

"Thanks," she said balancing a brief case and a stack of loose papers. "The wind was blowing so hard, I barely noticed my hat flew off."

"Glad I could be of service to you," said Garrett making his way to his car.

"Uh, aren't you the new guy?" asked the woman causing him to turn around.

"I'm Debra Dane. I work in Accounting, third floor. But this is just temporary," she said nodding at the bundle in her arms. "I'm pursuing an acting career."

Garrett reached to shake her hand. "Garrett Hunter. I'm consulting with D.C.S.S., third floor. Pursuing, uh, getting your financial program hooked up."

"Yes, yes," said the young beauty, "I've seen you around."

Garrett noticed a familiar sports car as it screeched into the parking lot. Then the driver haphazardly swung into a handicapped space.

"Will you excuse me, Debra?" said Garrett walking away before she could answer.

Garrett moved his 6 ft. 3 in. frame swiftly toward the car hoping against hope that he was wrong.

His hopes were dashed when a tall white woman unfolded herself and stood next to the sleek white sports car. Her red tresses blew fiercely in the wind licking and snapping at the cloudy sky. From his distance, her hair looked like fire.

"What are you doing here, Cat?" he asked putting his briefcase on the hood of her car.

"I've been paging you all day, Garrett," she said sharply putting her hand on her hip. "And don't give me that line about you were busy. You just don't care about me."

"Cat, this is a major account for D.C.S.S.," he returned getting a strange feeling that he was being watched. He controlled his body language trying to appear calm. "I've been in meetings most of the day. I gotta tell ya', it's annoying to look down every half hour and see *CAT CALL* on my pager!"

"Well," she snapped pointing to Debra, "I see you were able to make time for little miss tall brown sugar over there. Humph!" spat Cat. "Men."

"Oh, now you sound like that listed twisted, fruity roommate of yours Trevor."

"You leave him out of this!" returned Cat.

"I just met her, okay," explained Garrett unconsciously punching his gloved hand. "You women just don't understand."

"Women?" asked Cat. "Who else have you needed to explain this to?"

"I'm not makin' any promises or playin' with anybody's mind, alright?" Garrett rhetorically inflected "Been there, done that. I've made a lot of mistakes. I'm focused on God and my career right now. And, to tell you the truth, I'm really lookin' for the Man upstairs to guide me. A real life. A real relationship that's blessed, you know?"

Cat shook the fiery red strands from her face and continued to glare at Garrett unconvinced. "God, huh?" Cat snarled. "Since when did you get so holy?"

"Look," he said snatching his briefcase from the car, "we're not together. I don't have to explain anything to you."

Gingerbread Men

Garrett walked away.

"Wait, Garrett," said Cat while the clicking of her heels came fast behind him. "Ride with me, huh?" she asked tugging at his coat sleeve.

"My car is right over there," he told her pointing across the parking lot. "I've had a bad day. I'd just like to go home, Cat. I don't want to argue or create a scene, alright?"

"I promise, Garrett," she said sweetly touching his shoulder. "I'll be on my best behavior. I just wanna talk. That's all."

"Cat," sighed Garrett, rubbing his forehead, "maybe we can have lunch tomorrow or–"

"No!" Cat shrilled. "I mean, Garrett, it's urgent or I wouldn't have paged you so many times today. You can understand that, can't you?"

Garrett thought for a minute. "Okay," he said holding his hand out for the keys, "but let me drive."

"No," said Cat quickly turning from him. "I'll drive and then I'll bring you right back to your car."

"Cat," Garrett looking her pretty well over this time, "are you feelin' alright? You haven't been drinkin' or anything? Have you."

Cat laughed nervously. She pointed at herself. "Me? No."

"Is everything okay downtown?" inquired Garrett. "Last time we talked, you were under a lot of stress. Weren't you lobbying for that–"

"I don't wanna talk about work," she interrupted. "Just ride with me, Garrett," plead Cat simply. "I just need to talk to a friend."

Garrett reluctantly got into the car with the willowy, red-headed Cat.

From the third floor window, four women peered down at the scene.

Shallondra began, as she bit into a chocolate bar, "See, I told you he was white washed. Watch, next time we see her, she'll have a crown on."

"Honey," said Terri fluffing her short crop of bleached blond waves, "don't you fool yourself. Queen or peasant, I could teach a young buck like that a few new tricks."

"Maybe he's in love with her," said Lisa happily gazing at the couple. "Love *is* color blind, you know."

Karmena glared at them as they drove away. "Dog spit."

The following morning's wind whipped rain sent Wide

World Information Technologies employees sending them scurrying into the building for warmth and comfort.

"Excuse me, but are you Theresa English?" asked a black trench coated bald man with sparkling blue eyes.

"I am," said Terri shaking the rain drops from her coat and securing her purse in her desk. "But, if I called you yesterday about your claim, you'll need to make an appointment with the–"

"I'm Detective Larry Desmond with Baltimore Police Department," he said holding up his badge.

Terri studied it and then studied him. "What's this all about?"

"Your supervisor mentioned that you and some other office workers knew Mr. Garrett Hunter," he said whipping out a pad and a short pencil. "Is that true."

"Wait. What do you mean *knew* him?" asked Terri now concerned. "Is he alright?"

"Mr. Hunter was in a near-fatal car accident, Ms. English," said the detective. "He's in a coma. The woman that was driving the car died unfortunately."

Terri held her heart and plopped down into her chair.

Just then, Shallondra's voice was heard as she rounded her friend's cubicle. "Terri, girl, you wanna go down stairs and get a breakfast–who's he?"

"Shallondra," said Terri grabbing her arm. "This is Detective Desmond of Baltimore P.D. He said Garrett was in an accident."

"Shallondra," said the detective flipping through his notebook. "Shallondra MacNabney?"

"Yeah," she said suspiciously.

"Ms. MacNabney, did you see Mr. Hunter with Catherine Fuller?"

"I saw Garrett with a white woman last night around four o'clock outside in the parkin' lot," offered Shallondra. "He was treatin' her like a queen. But I didn't know her name."

Detective Desmond wrote quickly. "A queen?"

Shallondra waved her hand. "Inside joke."

"Did you also see him, Ms. English?" continued the detective.

"I did," Terri said still stunned.

"Did they appear to be arguing or having a quarrel of sorts?" probed the detective.

"No," replied Terri. "They just talked for a few minutes and then got in the car together."

"Was there anyone else who saw the couple together before they left?" he asked continuing to scribble on the note pad.

"No," lied Shallondra crossing her arms.

"Yes," said Terri. "Two other employees. But we all saw the same thing."

"I'd like to talk to them." The portly detective closed his notebook. "Are they here?"

Shallondra looked around and then looked at Terri. "Yeah," she sighed, "over here." She lead Detective Desmond to Lisa scantly clad in yet another clinging, little blouse and a mini-skirt.

"Lisa, this is Detective Desmond," said Shallondra making her disdain apparent. "Garrett was in a car accident and he–"

"I'll take it from here, Ms. MacNabney," the detective injected, "but thank you."

Shallondra rolled her eyes.

"Lisa, what is your last name?" he asked.

"Tinsley. Lisa Tinsley," she told him.

"Ms. Tinsley," began the detective, "did you see Mr. Hunter and his female companion last night along with your co-workers Ms. English and Ms. MacNabney?"

"Yes," she answered cooperatively. "We were standing near that window over there that faces the parking lot," she explained. "Just talking around four o'clock like always. Garrett, I mean Mr. Hunter just stopped to talk to another lady in the building and then made his way over to a little white sports car."

"Then what happened?" asked the detective. "Did they appear angry at one another or anything like that?"

Lisa laughed a little. "Even from this distance, I could tell they really cared about one another."

Shallondra laughed.

"Uh, Ms. MacNabney," said the detective, "could you excuse us?"

Shallondra rolled her eyes and headed for Terri's desk.

"Go on, Ms. Tinsley," said the detective continuing to write.

"Well, like I said," Lisa gulped, "it was obvious they cared for one another. But the red-headed lady seemed like she was agitated or something. It's hard to describe because we couldn't hear what they were saying. Is Garrett, I mean Mr. Hunter alright?"

The detective closed his pad and slid it into his pocket.

"Mr. Hunter is in a coma. The red-headed lady died at the scene of the accident. We're gathering information to make some sense out of what happened. Tell me, Ms. Tinsley, did anyone else see them?"

"Yes," she said, "one other employee was talking with us at the window."

"Can you take me to him or her?" he asked.

Karmena turned around from the copy machine as Lisa and the white stranger approached her.

"Karmena Muhammed," said Lisa for the benefit of the detective. "This is Detective Desmond."

"Good morning, Ms. Muhammed," he said pleasantly.

"Mmm-hm," she returned without cracking a smile.

"Ms. Tinsley was telling me that you saw Mr. Hunter from the window last evening around 4 o'clock."

"Mmm-hm," she said again raising one brow.

Just then, a younger detective came over and whispered to Detective Desmond. "The guy's pager was found in the men's room last night," he began. "A message from *CAT CALL* was logged seventeen times."

"Okay, okay," said Detective Desmond returning to Karmena. "Did you notice who drove the car away, Ms. Muhammed?"

"Mmm-hm," she said crossing her arms across her purple gauze outfit.

The detective ran his head across his balding dome and spoke discreetly to his obstinate witness. "Ms. Muhammed, I understand that many people have a mistrust of the police. But Mr. Hunter has been badly injured in a car accident. His companion, possibly the woman you saw him with, is dead this morning. Now Mr. Hunter is lying in a coma. Any information you can share might help him."

Karmena smiled. "An accident in which a Black man survived and his white female companion has died?" Karmena bit her lip and tapped her temple mimicking deep thought. "Oh, I don't know," she ridiculed. "By the look in your eyes, Detective Desmond, it's got O.J. written all over it." Karmena turned away and closed her office door.

Chapter Two
Rude Awakening

Garrett blinked twice and looked unfamiliarly around the sterile hospital room. His eyes fell on flashing monitors and his ears recorded bleeping sounds. Although his memory was fuzzy and he felt hungry and weak, the absence of flowers, balloons and get well cards reminded him of his lack of concerned friends and family.

A Hispanic male nurse walked into the hospital room. "Oh, you *are* awake, Mr. Hunter. Now don't get excited," he said patting Garrett's shoulder. "You're at Mercy Hospital."

Garrett opened his mouth to speak. "How long have I been here?" he asked in a painfully scratchy voice.

"You've been in a coma, Mr. Hunter," said the nurse checking the monitors. "You were in a car accident, three weeks ago to the day."

The news settled painfully in Garrett's head.

"Cat!" he shouted in an impotent whisper.

The nurse rushed to him and held his shoulders against the bed. "Now, Mr. Hunter. The doctor will be in to see you. Please calm down."

Garrett's mind slowly fed him the details of the accident. A single tear rolled down his face and into his ear. He slammed his fist on the bed and covered his eyes.

There was a knock at the door. A salt-and-pepper-haired little Jewish woman poked her head in. "Garrett?"

"Ingrid," he said recognizing her. "Aw now this is

pathetic," he said grabbing his throat. "A brother knows he's all alone in the world when his lawyer is the only one who comes to visit."

Ingrid smiled at Garrett and cupped his cheek with an expensively perfumed hand. "How you doin', kid?"

"I've been better," admitted Garrett sniffling a bit.

Ingrid whipped out a business card and handed it to the nurse. "The police are on their way here to see Mr. Hunter. Will you tell them that Ingrid Thaxton, Esquire, is advising her client and wishes not to be interrupted? And tell that nice nurse Kim Patrini thanks for calling me as soon as his monitor showed signs of consciousness."

"Sure," said the male nurse taking the card and walking out of the room.

"Police?" asked Garrett. "What's goin' on here, Ingrid?"

"Garrett," she said putting a heavy hip up on his bed. "I need you to tell me what happened. The car accident; do you remember?"

"Of course, I remember," snapped Garrett as his voice got stronger. "But what do the police have to do with it?"

"They just have questions, Garrett. There's nothing to worry about," assured Ingrid pushing up her red-rimmed glasses on her nose. "I've already spoken with the District Attorney and no charges will be pressed against you. They're lacking evidence for a conviction."

"Conviction!"

"Ssshh!" Ingrid waved her hands. "Now Garrett, just tell me what happened, okay? Trust me," urged Ingrid with a smile.

Garrett closed his eyes and took a deep breath."...Cat came to my job at Wide World Information Technology. She wasn't herself. I knew that. She had been cryin' and I thought probably drinkin'. But me like a fool, got in the car anyway. Possessive. Neurotic. A little crazy," said Garrett of Cat as he shook his head pitying her. "We started arguing over that stupid apartment key."

"What apartment key?" persisted Ingrid.

"Cat was always demanding stuff from me, Ingrid," explained Garrett. " Like my time mostly. She wanted to know my every move, who I was seeing, when I'd be back." He shook his desolately. "Okay, so at one point when we were seein' one another, I gave her a key. I let her talk me into it. That was dumb."

"She wanted to talk to me," explained Garrett. She said she'd been to my place and found a letter from an old girlfriend and ladies' uh...underthings. I told her to give me my key back and stay out of my life!"

"Ingrid, do you know she even insisted on making my plane reservations for me?" he asked having difficulty focusing.

"She was pretty needy, huh?"

"That's not the half of it," said Garrett now angered. "Let's just say Cat could be vicious and vindictive. I know she wanted to make sure that I was traveling alone. For a while I thought it was cute. Until I started feeling trapped. So, I broke things off with her. That was seven or uh, eight months ago. I'd heard from her every now and then. But yesterday–I mean last week, I mean...three weeks ago she paged me seventeen times. Can you believe it? It's all kinda fuzzy, Ingrid."

"Okay," she paced the floor to think. "You argued with this woman over your apartment key...Garrett," asked Ingrid repeated solemnly and returned to the bed, "what happened in the car just before the rig hit it?"

Garrett swallowed hard and began to sweat. "She took her gun out from under the seat," he remembered. "She started wavin' it around. Pointing it at me. Pointing it at herself. She said, if I can't have you no one can. I knew then she was gonna do somethin' stupid, Ingrid. I managed to get the gun away from her by distracting her for a quick second 'cause she was easing into the rig's path. I said look out, Cat! She straightened up the car. It must've scared her. And then," he said staring at the playback in his head, "like she wanted to die, she turned the car into the guy's tire. All I saw was headlights. Out of the corner of my eye she just disappeared." Garrett turned away. "That's all."

Ingrid leaned in. "Are you saying, Garrett, that Cat deliberately killed herself?"

Garrett turned to Ingrid's inquisitive face. "As much as I hate to admit it, yeah. Cat committed suicide."

"That car was badly damaged. And not a scratch on you." Ingrid figured the angle of her case. "Okay," she said patting his hand. "The police will want to ask you some questions, Garrett. Just tell them what you told me."

"You sound like you don't believe me, Ingrid."

Ingrid got right in his face. "I believe what you believe."

Garrett grimaced and sighed realizing that Ingrid's integrity was on retainer. But half of something was better than all of nothing.

"Now let's get you in a position of authority and wellness," said Ingrid busying herself with fluffing his pillows and helping him sit up in the bed.

"Okay," said Garrett, "at least I know *you know* how this looks then, right, Ingrid? A Black man? A white woman?"

Ingrid stopped suddenly and looked at Garrett. She removed her glasses and smiled at him. "Do you remember how we met, Garrett?" asked Ingrid returning her heavy hips to his bed.

"I dislocated that dude's shoulder and almost put his eye out for callin' me Black-sambo," said Garrett.

"That dude was a councilman's son, remember?" asked Ingrid.

"You got him to drop the charges 'cause he was violating parole bein' in that bar. You were a pro, Ingrid." Garrett looked out the window. "Fight was all in me back in those days. When your mom abandons you, you gotta fight to survive."

Ingrid nodded. "I know how this looks. But you're going to be just fine. There was no criminal act involved. Except maybe on Ms. Fuller's part. But in all my years of practicing law, I've never seen a deceased person convicted of first degree manslaughter." She patted Garrett's hand reassuringly. "You just answer the detective's questions. He's doing his job, that's all."

Ingrid exited the hospital room and returned a few moments later with Detective Desmond.

"My client will take your questions now, detective," said Ingrid taking a bold stand at Garrett's side.

"Mr. Hunter," said the detective. "I'm glad to see you're getting better."

"Thanks," said Garrett.

He whipped out his note pad. "I'm not going to pull any punches with you, Mr. Hunter. We found a gun at the scene. Your finger prints were all over it."

"I gave her the gun," said Garrett in full voice. "For protection. Cat was a paranoid person who always felt the bad guy was out to get her, you know? She'd been mugged before. It spooked her. The gun gave her a sense of power, I guess."

Detective Desmond raised a brow. "Was the gun a part of this particular road trip, Mr. Hunter?"

"If you mean, did I threaten her with the gun," stated Garrett. "No. She threatened *me* with it. I managed to get it away from her before she could use it."

"You understand, Mr. Hunter," spoke Detective Desmond gravely, "there's no way to corroborate that statement for us.

Gingerbread Men

We're just trying to get to the bottom of—"

"I understand, Detective Desmond," said Garrett intellectually. "It's my word against what *you* think."

Detective Desmond ignored Garrett's sarcasm.

"A witness said the decedent's car appeared that it would go safely past that rig and then at the last minute turned right under the driver's front tire. Almost like someone else turned the wheel suddenly."

Garrett didn't answer.

Detective Desmond showed him the picture of Cat's little convertible in an unidentifiable ball.

All the color washed from Garrett's face.

"The two of you should be dead by the look of it," said Desmond, "wouldn't you say, Hunter?"

"Detective Desmond," Ingrid interrupted.

Garrett's heart raced.

"They tell me that they had to use the jaws of life to get you out of there," he continued on his psychological attack, "and a spatula for Catherine Fuller!"

"Enough, detective!" Ingrid shouted.

"Now," he said getting close to Garrett who was resisting any emotional display, "either God loves you a whole hell of a lot, Mr. Hunter, or you're guilty as sin."

"That will be all, detective." Ingrid pointed to the door. "My client has nothing further to say."

Detective Desmond slapped his notebook closed and left the hospital room without another word.

Garrett slammed his fist onto the bed in anger. "I'm not guilty of anything!" he shouted.

"I know, I know," said Ingrid soothingly.

"Did you hear that, Ingrid?" asked Garrett laughing hysterically. "Did you hear the racial undertones? That joker tried to punk me! White man spook the Black man. Watch him squirm. Did you see that? I hate it!" He punched his hand. "They use the same exploited list of physiology and stigmas we cannot change; skin color and the majority's decision that Black men will never be worthy to keep company with white women!"

"Calm down, Garrett," said Ingrid. "I told you—"

"I make more in three months than this clown makes in a year!" continued Garrett at the top of his lungs. "And here he is breathin' his funky breath in my face remindin' me that he had power over me 'cause I'm layin' in this bed! Every word was like he was shovin' it down my throat!"

"You did fine, Garrett," assured Ingrid picking up her briefcase. "You handled yourself well. So what Desmond has his prejudices. Everybody does. But you can't convict a client of *mine* based on personal prejudices."

Garrett sighed. "You're right, Ingrid. But you're wrong, too." He shook his head doubtfully. "I didn't do so well."

"What's that *I'm right, I'm wrong*?" asked Ingrid taking off her glasses. "What do you mean, Garrett?"

"While he was talkin' to me," Garrett closed his eyes, "I went inside myself for strength. It wasn't there. Just an empty box."

"Not because of Detective Desmond," continued Garrett against the sounds of bleeping monitors, "and not because of Cat Fuller. But because God wasn't there. It's been so long since I felt His presence," whispered Garrett, "that I can hardly remember His leaving."

Garrett reached for a pad and paper. He scribbled out an address. "Something tells me this isn't gonna go away over night, Ingrid. When I get outta here," he handed her the paper, "you can reach me at this address."

Ingrid slid her glasses back on her nose and looked at the note. "New York?"

"Yeah," he said. "It's where I grew up. It's the last place I knew anything about God. And I'm goin' back there to find Him."

Ingrid stepped outside Garrett's hospital room checking her watch. She bumped into Detective Desmond waiting for the elevator.

"Counselor," he said sarcastically.

"Detective," she returned, "the way you spoke to my client was completely uncalled for. I'll thank you to direct any further inquiries directly to me."

Detective Desmond shrugged his shoulders. "...Guys like him," he said as he shook his head and grinned mischievously. "You didn't really believe that line about Catherine Fuller threatening *him* with the gun, do you?"

"My client deserves the benefit of the doubt, Detective, until proven guilty in a court of law." stated Ingrid.

Detective Desmond smiled. "Just like I thought. You know those kind are never what they seem."

"That's not what I–"

"But you won't say whether you believe him or not, will you?"

Ingrid tightened her gaze on the police detective who

was beginning to reveal dark layers to his thinking.

"What have you got against his kind, Detective?"

Detective Desmond's face went blank. "My wife ran off with one of them back in '93," he said. "Took my little girl with 'em. He was a big, dark one like Garrett Hunter. Fatal car crash in the rain, just like this one. He survived. They didn't. The, the mystery remains one-sided forever. The survivor's word against...no one's."

The detective's bald head glistened with perspiration.

"He was guilty. I know he was. Just like Garrett Hunter. I can smell it in him." The detective turned to Ingrid with a piercing blue-eyed stare. His mouth and eyes twitched. "I hate the black that covers 'em."

Ingrid's courtroom training prepared her to stay unemotionally detached from the detective's prejudices. "What ever happened to the man, Detective?"

Detective Desmond shoved his hands in his pants pockets and smiled. "I guess the pressure got to him."

The elevator bell rang and the doors slid open. Desmond stepped in and turned to Ingrid who couldn't move.

"He killed himself, Counselor." Desmond put his finger to his temple and whispered, "poof."

The doors slid closed. Ingrid feared for Garrett.

***

It wasn't until Garrett saw the familiar sights of Townsend, New York, that he felt the leech-like pressures of his ordeal finally fall away.

Aunt Lena, dressed in pearls with opaque stockings and terry-cloth house slippers, stepped from the simple two-story home that fostered Garrett's youth wiping her hands on her apron and smiling. Time had stolen her swiftness and gray topped her head, but the same warmth and sincerity sparkled in her eyes. Garrett wasted no time hopping from his sports car and rushing to her arms.

"Thank you, Jesus," she whispered in his ear as she embraced him smelling of her signature scent of delicate lilacs. "...Thank you, Lord."

Uncle Tyrone moseyed up wearing his employer's t-shirt and his church slacks. He slapped Garrett on his back and reeled him in for a vigorous hug.

"It's good to have you home, Son."

Garrett fell into the old gentleman's arms.

"It's good to be seen, man." He smiled at the two of them. "Uncle T., man, you still workin' out, huh?" asked Garrett playfully punching his uncle's pecs.

"Yeah," said the aging but debonair man, "gotta stay in shape, man. Old ain't out!"

Garrett shared a laugh with them. "And look at you, Aunt Lena." Garrett gently kissed her cheek, "still glamorous even in an apron."

Aunt Lena smiled and pressed her beautifully manicured hands against her shapely frame.

"Oh, go on! You always had a way with the ladies, Garrett."

"Gingerbread man! Gingerbread man!" shouted a familiar voice from the stairway.

"Oh, Lord..." breathed Uncle Tyrone shaking his head miserably.

"Catch him if you can!" returned Garrett pointing at Blake, his well put together cousin who always had a certain panache even in jeans and a t-shirt.

The two men slapped hands and pulled each other in for a macho hug.

"Looks like I made it just in time for dinner," said Garrett taking a long whiff of the baking meat spiced with garlic that tickled his brain reminding his stomach it was empty. "Aunt Lena," said Garrett removing his coat, "My favorite garlic-roasted chicken, huh? I couldn't wait to have some of your cookin', girl!"

"You'll have to get some of my cookin' tomorrow, Garrett," she said making her way into the kitchen untying her apron.

"What?" Garrett was flabbergasted as he got little support from his cousin and uncle.

"This food is for the church service this evening," said Aunt Lena from the kitchen.

Uncle Tyrone frowned. "We're havin' cold cut sandwiches, boys."

"Naw, naw..." moaned Garrett rubbing his empty and disappointed stomach.

"So, come on upstairs, man," said Blake throwing a supportive arm around his shoulders. "We'll eat, man, I promise ya'."

Garrett drug himself up the stairs.

The second floor of Garrett's childhood home hadn't changed much. Proudly displayed were pictures of him and Blake donning Afros, posing for wrestling team photos and impersonating the funk group Cameo in a high school talent show with Blake out front dressed as the notorious Larry Blackman.

Everything about the wood-paneled hallway in which he and his cousin had sneaked many-a-girl, suggested that the passing years had little influence. All the high-tech gadgets in which Garrett took for granted in his condo paled in significance to the rush of simplicity and memories that crowded his gaze.

Blake opened his bedroom door. "Come on in, man."

Garrett was surprised to find Blake's room exactly as it was when Garrett left for college over twelve years ago.

"You still stay here, Blake?" asked Garrett waxing nostalgic at the faded posters of the Gap Band, Tower of Power and the Isley Brothers.

"I been back and forth, you know," explained Blake admiring his own chiseled features in the mirror above his dresser. "Had a place of my own for a while. Things didn't work out." Blake bolstered his sadness and embarrassment. "But not like you, man! You been livin' here and there, getting' the ladies, huh? Really livin', huh, man?"

"Yeah, well..." Garrett found nothing about the recent events of his life amusing. "So what's this I hear, Blake, you and Vivi not together anymore?"

"Naw, man," said Blake methodically trimming the hairs of his mustache. "I'm hookin' up with Sister Slaid's daughter, Yvette. Remember her?"

"Yeah," said Garrett sweetly reminiscing, "who could forget *her*?"

"But, what happened with Vivi?" asked Garrett eyeing the numerous prom photos on Blake's dresser and tucked under the wood surrounding the mirror. "You two were supposed to be getting married, weren't you?"

"You kiddin', right?" he asked staring at his cousin.

"No, Blake, man," said Garrett seriously. "What happened?"

"What happened *is* Lena Hunter talks too much!" clowned Blake attacking some wild hairs that marred his otherwise perfect eyebrows.

"Listen man, we're the gingerbread men, remember?" he asked punching his cousin in the arm. "You and me, Garrett. We're not supposed to get that serious about anybody."

Garrett let Blake laugh by himself. "So, goin' to church," began Garrett, "and bein' a Christian, it don't mean nothin' to you, man? Man, I thought you were still holdin' up the

155

bloodstained banner, B. I came back here hopin' you all would be the anchor that *I* need right now."

"Lay off, Garrett!" Blake turned from his primping. "Now c'mon, this is the way it's always been. Why you actin' so surprised all of a sudden? We been goin' to church all our lives. We know these girls inside and out. Get a little kiss in the bathroom. Take 'em to the prom when they turn seventeen. Now it's just on a grown-up scale. Nothing's changed. Everybody gets what they want and everybody's happy."

"And Vivi," asked Garrett securing himself on the corner of his cousin's bed, "is she happy?"

"Now you're in *my* business, man," said Blake gravely pointing his mustache brush at his cousin.

"I got a wedding invitation, man," said Garrett.

"Come on, G.," Blake said tossing his tool to the dresser. "You tryin' to tell me, you've never asked a woman to marry you just to get a little somethin', somethin'?"

"No," answered Garrett. "Marriage is a serious thing. You can get sex without it, Blake. Everybody knows that. I can't believe you've taken it *that* far. I couldn't do that."

Blake laughed. "Then you've never gotten very far at all, huh, player? You know, it's better to marry than to burn. Look, I don't care what you think, man, sisters like Vivi are on fire. And if you mention marriage, they'll give you the world!"

"I'm just tired of this game, that's all," said Garrett rubbing his neck. "You know how we used to do it; hoppin' from this church to that. Checkin' out this one and runnin' from that one. This city is only so big."

"And then there's the next city," encouraged Blake growing in hysterics as he continued, "and the next. Man, all these church women want is somebody to practice all this lovey-dovey stuff on they've been learnin' about in these women's meetings. They're freaky! They're all hyped up about it. That's where we come in." Blake grabbed his cousin's shoulder. "Just think of yourself as a practice dummy."

"I don't know anymore," groaned Garrett flopping back on the bed and noticing a poster of a g-strung brunette sucking a red cherry. "Somethin' about all this just isn't right. You've got a kid now, man. Maybe you should just–"

"Look," said Blake pointing at his cousin, "don't start pullin' that holier-than-thou crap on me, G!"

Garrett hopped to his feet and threw up his hands. "Alright."

"Hey, man," said Blake changing his tune, "we ain't seen

each other in close to eight years, man. Get your gear outta the car. We'll stop by Mom's and Pop's church."

"Alright," said Garrett excited at Blake's suggestion. "It's been a long time since a brother's heard the Word!"

"Yeah, you know my motto," Blake glanced at himself in the mirror with arrogant satisfaction, "follow the food."

Garrett trailed his cousin out of the bedroom. "Some things never change," he said under his breath as he took one last look at Blake's room and closed the door.

Chapter Three
Snails, Shells & Puppydog Tails

With their stomach's full of Aunt Lena's prime rib, mashed potatoes and fresh collard greens, Garrett and Blake arrived at a small church on the other side of town to find piously skirted women gathering outside.

Amidst a sea of sequined hats, one young woman stood still as others shook her hand and spoke pleasantly with her.

"Didn't I tell you, man," said Blake discreetly to his cousin. "This place is spread thick with butter, huh?"

"Whoa, whoa," breathed Garrett playfully noticing the young woman now standing alone. "Butterfly at 2 o'clock, man. But don't turn around. She's lookin' this way."

"See, I knew you were still true to the Gingerbread Man code, cuz!" Blake laughed. "Okay," he said bracing himself. "Give it to me quick. Skirt?"

"Long and snug, my brother," Garrett told him thinking little would come of their return to adolescent folly.

"Ahh," said Blake with a wink, "she's churchy but sexy. Make-up?"

"Modest."

"Lips?" inquired Blake.

Garrett smiled. "Red."

"Uh-huh. Churchy but rebellious." Blake rubbed his hands together and licked his lips. "Hair?"

"Flowing," said Garrett. "As a matter of fact, it's

cascading down her back."

"Yeah," said Blake now intrigued. "The dreamy, feminine type. Bible?"

"None."

"*That* means she's open to anything," he said obviously excited. "Okay G, your call. You wanna holler at her or should I?"

Garrett laughed. "Naw. You take it this time, Blake."

"Cool," said Blake making sure her first impression of him would be memorable as he straightened his Neru collar and squared the shoulders of his black wool suit. "Uh, fake intro like we used to, alright?"

Garrett nodded surprised that his cousin was so into this thing. They approached the young woman. "Girl you look good!" said Garrett giving the stranger a hug. "Angela, it's good to see you again. This is my cousin Blake and–"

"Excuse you," said the young woman shoving him away. "My name's not Angela."

"Oh, wow, I'm sorry," said Garrett faking embarrassment quite convincingly. "You look just like Angela Malcolm a friend of mine. I can't get over the resemblance. You look like her twin. I'm sorry Sister uh..."

"Naomi Pierce," she answered pleasantly.

"Sister Pierce," said Garrett holding his heart, "accept my apology. I'm brother Garrett Hunter. This is my cousin Blake."

Naomi shook their hands.

"You know," said Garrett getting a signal from Blake to disappear, "I think I see, Brother Smith. Would you two excuse me."

"So, Sister Naomi," said Blake with excellent timing, "how long you been comin' to Prayer Temple?"

"This is my second week," she said warming up to Blake's engaging demeanor. "I really like it. I've noticed you before but not your cousin."

"Oh him?" Blake shrugged his shoulders. "He just pops in from Baltimore every now and then," he lied. "So it's only natural that he gets the pretty faces mixed up sometimes."

Naomi blushed.

"Sorry," said Blake perpetuating the crafty illusion. "He doesn't mean any harm. And I keep tellin' him to wear his glasses. He's blind in one eye. But his glasses are pretty thick and he doesn't think he looks good in 'em." Blake laughed. "He's right. He doesn't. He wasn't tryin' to grope you or anything like that."

"It's okay," said the young woman. "Really."

"Can I walk you to your car?" asked Blake offering his arm.

She slid her hand around his arm. "Sure. I'd like that."

***

Garrett laid on his cousin's bed with his eyes closed to the sensual poster that loomed over him. His thoughts were introspective lingering on the recent events that were changing the dynamic of his life.

Cat's desperate face flashed before him.

He remembered staring down the barrel of her gun.

Detective Desmond's questions rang in his ears.

The smell of Ingrid's expensive perfume stung the memory center of his brain.

The rig's horn blew in his mind. And then Garrett remembered waking up in the hospital.

He sat up on the bed and put his head in his hands.

Uncle Tyrone knocked and then poked his head in. "You wanna hit the weights, man? Let's see if you can out-lift a 50 year-old like me, huh?"

Garrett hopped from the bed. "You're on," he said needing no further encouragement to escape the grim memories that were trying to cage him.

Outside, Uncle Tyrone pulled the heavy wooden door open. Garrett noticed that the same ripped and rusted weight bench was still in his uncle's employ. And that the same dusty, oil-stained piece of beige carpet covered the cracked concrete floor. The familiar dampness of the space reached his nostrils and brought back the sounds and images of his youth. Garrett smiled.

"What you laughin' about, boy?" asked Uncle Tyrone carefully selecting the weights he would need.

"Not laughin', Uncle T.," explained Garrett, "just smilin'."

"Oh, yeah?"

"So, you're still haulin' for that dairy, huh, Uncle T.?" asked Garrett taking a 30 lb. weight from his uncle and sliding it on the weight bar.

"Yep," he replied. "Just about five years from early retirement, too. Me and your Aunt Lena, we gonna fish and travel, travel and fish."

"Sounds like a good life, man," said Garrett.

"I think so—say, uh, Garrett?" Uncle Tyrone pointed to a near-by chair. "Move that milk hook and have a seat. I'll pump first," he said strapping on a pair of gloves. "Give you somethin' to shoot for," he teased.

Gingerbread Men

Garrett picked up the milk hook and laughed out loud. "Back in the day, you wouldn't let me or Blake even touch this milk hook. You said you always wanted us to do better than you. You said *don't get used to holdin' things that won't do you any good.*"

Uncle Tyrone huffed and puffed through his reps.

"...Yeah, the milk-hook was never good enough for us," said Garrett as he stared at the thick metal rod. "But you just don't know, Uncle T. You always made it seem like your life was so much less than everybody else's. Man, I'd give anything to have this kind of simplicity–the nicest house on the block, two cars that are paid for, a family. It's everything."

The weights clanged against the metal rest and Uncle Tyrone came up sweating. "I didn't really ask you out here to pump iron with me, man." He grabbed a towel and wiped his face. "Now your aunt told me bits and pieces about what happened. I wanna know from you, are you guilty of anything?"

Garrett took a long look at his father-figure; the man with whom he had entrusted many secrets in his youth. "Yeah, Uncle T.," he said quietly, "I'm guilty. I'm guilty of hoarding my money and trying to make as much of it as I can. I'm guilty of knowing that I can't just be *good* at something, but the best because of my skin color. I have to be the best if I wanna get ahead! I'm guilty of indulging myself. And I'm guilty of dating a white woman!" Garrett flung the milk hook to the ground. "Everything that people are jealous of or don't understand or can't accept, I'm guilty, man!"

Uncle Tyrone reached for a 45 lb. hand weight and began his curls with his left arm. "Used to know this fellow in Vietnam back in '63. Tall dude with a big neck and broad shoulders, little teeny waist and man, you should've seen his shoes! Size fourteen!"

Garrett continued to fume about his own disappointments.

"The Army didn't have nothin' to fit this dude," continued Uncle Tyrone feeling the burn and enjoying it. "Had to have his uniforms custom made! On top of that, the brother didn't eat pork or beef. Rations, most of the time, were pork or beef and this dude just wouldn't eat. He'd say if it didn't fit what he wanted for himself, he didn't want it." Uncle Tyrone smiled and switched hands. "That's how you are, Garrett. Only certain things are gonna fit you, you know what I mean?"

Garrett nodded breathing in this wisdom.

"Now the problem is most people condition themselves to accept whatever comes their way," explained Garrett's uncle sweating and grunting to finish the exercise.

"Sort of like, just grin and bear it, right?" he asked.

"That's right, Garrett," answered Uncle Tyrone. "Believe it or not, not everybody is willing to make sacrifices even for themselves. But this dude was decisive," he said pointing to hand. "He knew what suited him. So, what suits you these days, Garrett?"

"God," he replied enjoying the question as much as the answer. "God suits me, Uncle Tyrone. When I look over my life and try to determine my purpose, all the arrows point to Him. He's the only one who hasn't judged me or made me second guess my decisions."

Uncle Tyrone smiled and laid back on the bench. He gripped the bar balanced with a whopping 250 pounds And began to pump it into the air.

"Since God is your choice, man, you'll never have to be worried about bein' let down." Uncle Tyrone grimaced and then thrusted the cold iron into the air with ease. "He'll stick by you," he said, "and make His presence and approval known when you need it most."

The weights clanged onto the bar rest. Garrett's uncle hopped from the bench and wiped the sweat from his brow. "Your turn, man," he said pointing to the opportunity for strength and stamina. "Now what you gonna do with it?"

Garrett looked at his smiling uncle and then at the weight bench. Without a word, he secured himself under the poundage and began hoisting the burden above his head.

Meanwhile, across town, a striking, honey-colored woman walked into the Black & White Museum Gallery & Café in Greenwich Village dabbing at her eyes with a tissue. She rushed past the diners and museum guests who stood captivated by the talents of African-American artisans.

She dashed into a door marked *Employees Only* to the seclusion of her office.

"So, I suppose this means you forgot, Nadine?" asked a familiar voice hidden behind the high back of the executive chair.

"Forgot?" asked Nadine hanging her coat on a rack inspired by metal coat hangers. "What are you talkin' about, Dixie?"

The voluptuous, blond cropped Caucasian woman

spun around in the chair and displayed a wealth of diamonds that decorated her daintily polished nails. "It's first Thursday, Nadine. Hello? Remember, we lunch at some fancy little bistro and turn the town upside down with gossip? How could you forget our monthly treat to ourselves?"

Nadine folded her arms and leaned against the wall. "...It's November 19th, Dixie. I went to the cemetery to put flowers on Evander's grave."

"Oohhhh," cried Dixie standing up to wrap her arms around Nadine. "I'm sorry. I totally dismissed the date. Why didn't you call me? I would've gone with you."

Nadine patted her friend's arm reassuringly and broke gently away from her. "I know, Dix. But I already feel stupid about it. Evander's been gone three years now and it's still so, so, so fresh." Nadine broke into tears again.

Dixie lead her to the office chair and sat her in it. She exited Nadine's spacious seclusion and returned moments later with a steaming cup of tea. "It'll be okay, Nadine," she encouraged.

"I know," said Nadine refusing the tea. "I've just got to get myself together," she said bravely wiping her face. "Evander was the love of my life. But now, he's gone. I've got to face life without him."

"Nadine," said Dixie, "when are you going to start dating again, huh? You know, put yourself back in the market?"

"Dixie," said Nadine shaking her head, "I'm not like you. I can't just pick up and pretend Evander never existed."

"Like I pretend my Charlie didn't exist after 14 years of marriage?" Dixie put her hands on her full hips. "Believe you me, I've got the credit card receipts from plenty of motels to prove he existed!"

"And you married again exactly 15 days after he died!"

"That's because when his plane went down," sassed Dixie, "we were in the middle of a messy divorce. That low life, two timin' son-of-a–"

"Watch it, Dixie," said Nadine putting a corrective finger up.

"You know," she said whipping out a compact to powder her nose, "I really need to stop talking like a sailor. It's terribly unlady-like."

"You're right."

"But let me just say if marrying Arny turned old Charles over in his grave, well, serves him right!" She snapped the compact closed. "But enough about me. Now I met this fellow

163

named Reynaldo Buenaventura at my country club and he'd be perfect for–"

"Dixie," said Nadine engaged in reading a contract, "no more match-making."

"Oh, come on, Naddy," begged Dixie knocking on the glass topped desk. "What about that blind date I set you up with, huh?"

"How could I forget, Dix? He was actually blind!"

"Yeah, but did you notice the body on him?" Dixie fanned herself and let her eyes roll around in her head. "A world champion body-builder with spontaneous blindness disorder." She wrinkled her nose. "A small hurdle, to say the least!"

"I need more than that," said Nadine putting some files in a cabinet.

"Honey, you could go blind, cross-eyed and crazy with a body like his when it really matters."

"Get your mind out of the gutter, Dixie!" Nadine slammed the file cabinet shut.

"Oh, you just want somebody to needlepoint with and roam around this drafty old gallery!" Dixie crossed her arms and pouted. "You need some excitement, Naddy," said Dixie shaking her full bosom. "Something that makes you smile whenever you think about it. Just like that fling I had last summer with–"

"Needle point." Nadine stopped and smiled. "Maybe that *is* what I want," she said sarcastically.

"You know," said Dixie peering out of the one-way glass that showed the entire gallery floor, "I admire what you've done with this place." Dixie looked around at the museum's bold prints and up to the air-duct exposed ceiling. "But the Black & White Museum Gallery & Café needs some color, don't you think?"

Nadine shook her head. "You don't get it, do you, Dixie?"

"Get what?"

"The Black & White Museum Gallery displays black and white photos, Dixie, taken by African-American photographers. I've explained that to you so many times, Dix."

"I still say you need some color, Nadine," said Dixie returning to her view of the gallery. "Sort of like your life, dear. It needs some spice. And that's why you should let me introduce you to–"

"Dixie," interrupted Nadine strategically, "I've been meaning to ask you, does your church still have that ministry rally around this time of year?"

"Yeah." Dixie frowned. "But what do you wanna go there for? That's no place to find a man."

"I'm not looking for a man," explained Nadine. "I'm looking for purpose. Something outside of the gallery. Something where I can roll up my sleeves and get involved."

"And all you can think of is church?"

"Yeah." Nadine smiled. "And you can go with me, okay?"

"Oh," said Dixie thinking of a way to get out of it. "I don't know."

"You can pray about that cursin' thing. And I can find something meaningful to lift me up out of this rut. I mean, how long can I chase Evander's ghost? He's not comin' back."

Nadine sighed and rubbed her shoulders. "All I have is the gallery to remind me of his passion for photography. But what about my passions? I need to do something that says this is Nadine's *thing*."

Dixie looked Nadine in the eye. "You really wanna do this?"

Nadine nodded. "I really do."

Dixie pouted and hesitated. "Oh, well, alright. It just so happens that I got an announcement about the ministry rally in the mail. It'll be Tuesday night at 5 p.m."

"Great!" shouted Nadine. "And look, I'll make it up to you. How about dinner and a movie tonight?"

"Sounds good," said Dixie.

***

Upstairs, Garrett snatched off his sweaty shirt and opened the door of his cousin's bedroom just in time to see Blake hiding something behind his back.

"Oh," breathed Blake and sighing in relief, "I thought you were Lena. You want a beer, Garrett?" he asked opening the small refrigerator in his bedroom.

"Naw, I don't drink anymore," said Garrett. "Not since I dislocated a dude's shoulder in a bar fight back in college."

Blake laughed. "You always did have a mean streak, man."

"And since when do Uncle T. and Aunt Lena let you bring alcohol in their house, B.?"

"Since they don't know about it." Blake tipped the can on his lip and poured some into his mouth. "Besides this is not drinkin'. This is beer."

"So, you still play hoops?" asked Garrett enjoying his relaxed feeling after his workout.

"Naw," said Blake with a loud belch as he flopped onto

his bed to channel surf.

"What happened with Naomi, man?" asked Garrett. "You two just disappeared."

"...She wasn't what I thought she was," said Blake focusing his attention on the TV

"Translation," began Garrett, "she wasn't givin' nothin' up, huh?"

"Somethin' like that," said Blake not giving it another thought.

"Have you read that new book written by Marcel Francis *In The Footsteps of a Black Man*? It's really–"

"Naw," said Blake gulping his beer and belching. "Don't read much."

"What do you do, man?"

"Work," he said belching again. "Go to church. Hit the night clubs every now and then–whoa!"

"Blake," said Garrett following his cousin's gaze to an adult scene on the TV, "don't tell me you're into this porn stuff on cable, man."

"Get it, girl!" shouted Blake standing to his feet and slapping his backside repeatedly.

Garrett grabbed the remote and turned the TV off.

"What you do that for?"

"C'mon, man." Garrett threw the remote on the floor. "We're cousins. More like brothers. We haven't seen each other in years. Let's catch up, alright?"

"Alright," said Blake taking a seat. "So who are you seein' these days?"

"Nobody special," said Garrett.

"That means you got a bowl full of strawberries!" Blake rubbed his hands together. "Tell me about 'em."

"Man, I'd rather talk about deeper stuff," said Garrett. "I've had enough of females for a while. Is Bible study still on Tuesday night at your parent's church?"

"You've had enough of females?" Blake stood to his feet and backed away from Garrett. "Don't tell me, man, that you went to Baltimore and got some sugar in your tank and think you gonna come up in here actin'"–

"Naw, man!" Garrett laughed. "Nothin' like that. I'm just really into seekin' the Lord right now, you know what I mean?"

Blake scoffed. "You sound like Naomi Pierce." He looked Garrett up and down. "You supposed to be a Gingerbread Man, remember? Dark, sweet, irresistible? And hard to catch! Now you up in here talkin' like John the Baptist or somethin'. Seek ye the Lord!"

"C'mon, Blake. Don't try to clown me."

"Naw, G., what's with you, huh?" Blake pounded his chest with his fist. "The Gingerbread Man! You ain't true to it no more?"

Garrett laughed. "B., we used to go to the youth rallies and church services to score with the church chicks. Get a little kiss in a dark corner. Get a little feel in the bathroom. But we're grown men now. There are more sophisticated ways to approach women."

"And I suppose *you know* all about these sophisticated ways?" Blake laughed. "Listen, man, you had me goin' for a minute there. Now I'm willin' to take this as far as you want to. But save that holy crap for the honies. *They* like it." Blake reclined on his bed, grabbed the remote and surfed the channels.

Garrett headed for the door.

"Maybe you should ask Lena when she's gonna get that stuff out of the guest room for you," said Blake as his cousin left the room.

Chapter Four
Cupid's Bent Arrow

"Now," said evangelist Cissy Whitaker, "I want everybody in here to close their eyes."

Nadine looked around at all the mid-twenties participants and leaned over to her friend. "I told you we were too old to be in this class. Look, these are mostly kids. We should've waited."

"Stop complaining, Nadine," spat Dixie. "It'll be good for us."

"Now," said the evangelist, "I'm gonna ask some questions and raise your hand only if it applies to you. Who in here is looking for a husband?"

There was snickering and no one raised their hand.

"C'mon now," prompted the evangelist. "Don't be shy. That's why we all have our eyes closed. Not even your best friend will know how you answered."

Almost every hand went up.

"A wife?"

Some of the men raised their hands but Garrett and Blake didn't.

"Alright. Who in here has never been married?"

Almost every hand went up including Garrett's.

"Divorced or separated?"

An alarming number flew up.

"Widowed?"

Nadine and Dixie sheepishly raised their hands.

"Okay, now everybody open your eyes." Evangelist Whitaker turned to her dry erase board and wrote as she talked. "First I want to say that single is not a synonym for incomplete! You're a whole person by yourself. Marriage doesn't make you whole. It adds to and enhances what is already there."

"Coming to the church means that you're looking for God," she admonished. "You should want to have a closer walk with Him."

"Let's face it, the modern church has turned into a meat-market of sorts," she said. "The church, the holy house of God has taken the place of the nightclub for many of us. Let's be careful."

"Dix," whispered Nadine, "I'm going to the ladies' room."

"But there'll be sign-ups for a single's ski trip after she—"

"I've gotta go, Dix," said Nadine.

"Oh, I'm sorry," said Nadine accidentally hitting Garrett with the door that led to the lobby.

Garrett laid eyes on the seasoned beauty and was rendered speechless.

"Are you alright, young man?" she asked.

"Yeah," said Garrett remembering that he could speak English. "No problem. Nothing's broken."

"Good," said Nadine finding herself strangely attracted to him. "Why are you standing out here? The seminar seems to be pretty informative."

"I uh, it's not really for me," he confessed. "I'm uncomfortable in there. They're just goin' over what I already know. I'm not here lookin' for a wife. I need God. And I know that."

"I see." Nadine laughed and shook her head. "I told my girlfriend, I'm just too old to be in there. I'm widowed. Three years now. My romance days are behind me."

"How old are you?" asked Garrett

Nadine raised her brow.

"I mean," recovered Garrett, "if you don't mind me sayin' so, you look so young."

Nadine smiled at the handsomely dressed young man. "I'm forty-four," she said proudly.

"That's not old!"

"How old are you?" She asked.

"I'll be twenty-nine," said Garrett feeling like a scruffy third-grader in her gaze, "...next year."

Nadine laughed. "Well, it was nice bumping into you."

Nadine turned to walk away.

"Wait," said Garrett willing to do anything to detain her. "I don't even know your name."

Nadine raised a brow at him again.

"It's just that if I see you around," explained Garrett as gentlemanly as possible, "I'd like to call you by name, that's all."

She reached her soft, slender hand out to him. "My name is Nadine Manhassette."

"Nice to meet you, Sister Manhassette," he said relishing in the moment to shake her supple hand. "I'm Garrett Hunter."

Nadine looked at him suspiciously. "You wouldn't be related to Blake Hunter, would you?"

"Uh, yeah," said Garrett uneasily. "He's my cousin. But how do you know–"

"He dated my niece for a hot second," explained Nadine. "Really broke her heart."

"He and I are nothing alike," said Garrett quickly and shaking his head defiantly.

"Oh, I see." Nadine's eyes fell appreciatively on Garrett whose choice of gray linen suit accented with a black turtleneck fit him dashingly. "Well, no matter," she said collecting her thoughts. "My niece won't be coming to New York for a long time."

"Sister Manhassette, you uh...wanna grab a cup of coffee?" Garrett thought quickly. "There's a coffee shop just down the–"

"No," she said quietly. "Thank you, Brother Hunter. I came with my friend."

"Not like a date or anything, just–"

"That's really kind of you," she said touching his arm. "Such a rare breed of a young man...mannerable, kind, well spoken." Nadine chuckled. "Where were you when I was nineteen?" she asked rhetorically.

"Startin' second grade," spoke Garrett so captivated by her beauty that he didn't even realize the words were coming from his mouth.

Nadine stood erect at his answer.

Garrett shook himself into reality.

Suddenly, the playful flirtation wasn't funny anymore. A wall of years and time stood between them and they both hurried away from each other.

Garrett returned to his seat next to Blake.

"We'd like to thank Evangelist Cissy Whitaker of The Single's Advantage," said the perky mistress of ceremonies.

"And those of you who would like to participate in the events she has planned for single Christians, please feel free to sign up with her after our meeting."

The audience applauded.

"Last on our list, we'd like to welcome old friends of ours," she announced. "They are the Freidmans from the Trinity Care Feeding Program!"

The audience burst into applause again.

A plainly dressed young woman who put one in mind of a librarian escorted a hunch backed, white haired man to the podium. "Saints, my Father and I are so glad to be back in New York for your annual ministry rally. We have gotten such tremendous support from this congregation over the past few years. Thank you. Some of you who own businesses have sponsored our feeding program and others have volunteered their time."

"We're asking that you join us again this weekend," requested the young woman. "We'll be going to the Bronx to distribute school supplies to children there. We will also supply groceries as well as a hot meal. We're looking for volunteers. Right outside these doors, you can.."

The old man tapped the young woman on the arm.

"I'm sorry," she said sweetly, "Trinity Feeding Care founder, Tugwell Freidman would like to have words."

The old man took the microphone in his shaking hand. "We started T.F.C. back in 1972," said the feeble old man. "It began in our kitchens and from our pocket books. Now we are a nationally recognized program of helps that not only feeds but also counsels and encourages youngsters and their families! To date, we have fed an estimated 4 million people with the gospel and by faith!"

The church exploded with praise.

"The Lord said to me this morning," continued the old man, "that some of you are looking for purpose."

Garrett leaned in.

"You won't find a greater opportunity to fill a void or get closer to Our Lord and Savior than by extending yourself to the needs of others." The old man pointed randomly throughout the audience. "You know who you are. God's talking to you. Go right outside that door and sign up for this weekend. God bless you."

The congregation clapped their hands.

Garrett got up from his seat.

Blake grabbed his arm.

"Where you goin', man?" he whispered.

"To sign up," he said.

"Cissy Whitaker's single thing is after the meeting," whispered Blake. "Just wait, man."

"It's Trinity Feeding Care for me, B." Garrett made his way out into the lobby with many others.

Blake sunk down in his seat. "When's that brother gonna learn that that ain't no way to meet the ladies?"

***

A fine gray mist covered the slumberous streets of lower New York. The rickety, old school bus pulled to a squeaky halt. Garrett opened his eyes. He checked his watch; 5:30 a.m.

Reverend Freidman fastened his clergy collar and moved diligently from the driver's seat. "Up and at'em, children," he said to his groggy volunteers. "The lambs have gathered."

Garrett peered out the window to find the promised sum of over 5,000 people lined up around the circumference of the Hadley Perone Community Center. Mothers with whiney babies. Old men leaning on canes. Whole groups of school children. Some appeared as if they had spent the entire night in line.

Garrett trailed the other volunteers off the bus. Across the scores of people, he noticed Nadine's familiar beauty as her arms were hastily filled with stock pots before she was rushed into the back door of the Center.

"Hunter!" said a wormy-looking man carrying a clip board receiving instructions from the old Reverend. "We'll need your brawn this morning, Bro. Hunter."

"Yeah," said Garrett, "anything I can do."

"Good man," he said patting him on the shoulder, "the boxes of school uniforms will need to be unloaded from a semi parked around the side. We'll need you to distribute uniforms, too."

"I'm on it," said Garrett without reservation.

"And Bro. Hunter," asked the coordinator, "the sign-up sheet mentioned that you are a computer programmer."

"That's true, I am."

"Encourage these kids, Brother Hunter. Don't be shy. Let the Lord use you."

Garrett smiled and made his way around the Center. He hoped to get a confirmed look at Nadine. But continued on without seeing her.

Gingerbread Men

Before the noon hour, the sun had smiled generously on the crowd of volunteers and needy ones. Garrett had met his stride and routinely asked the young people what they wanted to be when they grew up before distributing the school uniforms.

Careers like doctor, lawyer, teacher, cop and nurse spilled from the lips of the children with eagerness.

"Stay in school," he'd say to them, "the Lord loves you."

There was a ruckus in the line between two women.

"How you just gonna cut in front of me!" shouted the African-American woman.

"I've been in this spot for hours!" fired the Hispanic one.

Garrett hopped from the lift-gate of the semi and did his best to separate the two women while getting his shirt ripped and his face slapped in the process.

The crowd, however, moved safely aside and continued to wait patiently for their child's free school uniform. They all knew that other lines for groceries and a hot meal had to be tackled, as well.

With the two women safely pulled apart and scolded, Garrett looked up just in time to see a lone teen-ager grab an arm full of uniforms and tear across the busy street.

Garrett took off after the kid with incredible speed.

Between cars, they ran, across parking lots and down some basement stairs.

"Wait!" the youngster cried out as he raced down an alley. "Wait just a minute, man!" He stopped, pulled out a .32 and pointed it directly at Garrett.

"Whoa, man," said Garrett as calmly as possible. "Just put the gun down, alright?"

"You just shut-up, man!" Some of the uniforms fell around his feet as he needed room for his chest to expand due to exhaustion. "What you chasin' me for, huh? They're just school uniforms. Material things. What they mean to you, huh?"

"They're a gift," said Garrett resting his hands on his knees, "from some real dedicated people, man." Garrett tried to rationalize his chasing the youth as he caught his breath. "They belong to whoever needs 'em."

"Well, I'm a *whoever*," stated the teen. "What's so important about all this stuff anyway?"

Garrett stood up and raised his hands slowly to surrender. "People need this stuff. That's why we came here. Put the gun down, kid."

"Naw," said the youngster. "I ain't puttin' nothin' down!

This is how I get mine!"

"Let me ask you somethin'," said Garrett, "if they don't mean much and they're just material things, like you said, why'd you steal 'em?"

The teen shrugged his shoulders. "I don't know....shoot, 'cause they were there, man, what you think?"

"Look, if something's free, man, you don't have to steal it, right? You just wait your turn and you get it. Just like God's love, man. It's free."

The youth revived in strength and pointed the gun squarely at Garrett's head.

"Look, instead of taking more than you can wear," braved Garrett, "and I see you accidentally picked up some girl uniforms, why don't you come on back and help us pass them out to those kids."

"Naw, man, you ain't gonna punk me like dat!" The youngster held the uniforms clumsily. "I get back over there all cool wit' you and you turn around and call the police!"

Garrett remembered his own rude awakening complete with a racist detective and a manslaughter conviction. "I give you my word, kid, no police. You put that gun down and I can handle you myself."

The youngster didn't move.

"Alright, I tell you what," said Garrett, "you keep the uniforms and we'll just forget all about it." Garrett began to back up slowly.

"Wait," said the youth, "I uh, I would come with you, man. But..."

"Well, come on then, man." Garrett smiled feeling he was no longer in danger. "Do some good for your neighborhood."

"What about my piece?" he asked nodding toward the gun. "I can't go with this, can I?"

Garrett scratched his head. "I don't know if this is in the Bible but I've heard it said often enough; the Lord'll accept you as you are, man. Let the Lord talk to your heart."

The youngster walked over to Garrett and handed him the armful of the uniforms. "I just wanted to see what you'd say." He pointed the gun at Garrett's chest and pulled the trigger.

POP!

Garrett's heart skipped a critical beat.

The youngster laughed at Garrett's frightened face. "It ain't even real, man. It's a toy. Belongs to my little brother."

Garrett caught his breath and resisted the urge to slam the youngster to the ground.

"Welcome to the Bronx," said the teenager in tough, gangster gruff. "But I gotta give you your props, man; to chase a thief through the streets of New York over some school uniforms makes you either the biggest fool in the world or God loves you a whole hellava lot, man!"

"Yeah," said Garrett as his purpose came into focus however ironically.

"Okay," said the youngster tossing the toy in a near-by trash can, "now I'm ready to do some good in my neighborhood."

Garrett and the youngster returned to the charity site with the uniforms bundled in their arms. Garrett pointed to some boxes that needed to be moved. The young man went about his assignment with supernatural vigor.

Reverend Freidman patted Garrett on the back. "You're a good man, brother Hunter. There are seeds of a fine disciple in you yet, young man."

Garrett squinted. "I don't understand."

"That youngster steals two arms full of uniforms every year," explained the kindly old Reverend. "Nobody's ever chased him. And you, you not only chased him, but you brought him back.

"Yes, sir," said the old man walking away, "the Lord moves in mysterious ways."

***

The end of the long day of ministry was sweetened with numerous prayers and hugs, promises to keep in touch and random TV and newspaper interviews.

Garrett and his young helper, Zeke, made their way over to the Community Center cafeteria.

Garrett was pleased to lay eyes on Nadine wearing a food stained apron and busily serving families. Everywhere she moved, his eyes followed her.

"She your lady, man?" asked Zeke.

"...No," said Garrett. "She's just somebody I know, that's all."

"Well, c'mon," said Zeke slapping Garrett on the shoulder. "Let's get some grub!"

"Brother Hunter?" asked Nadine holding some empty food trays and barely recognizing him.

"Sister Manhassette," said Garrett with a smile as he reached for a small plate of cornbread. "You remembered my name." She smiled. "What happened to your shirt?" she asked pointing to the rip that showed his bulging chest muscles.

"I had to break up a fight," he explained stepping forward through line. "All in a day's work, I guess."

"*You* volunteered for Trinity Feeding Care today?" asked Nadine.

"Yeah." Garrett picked up a knife and fork. "It was a pretty good experience, too, despite the obvious," he said nodding toward his shirt.

Nadine beamed. "Well, I'm impressed."

There was an awkward silence between them. The noisy cafeteria further manifested their awkwardness while pressured by an extreme attraction to each other.

Nadine shifted the weight of the trays and looked toward the kitchen. She noticed some of the other volunteers in need of her help.

"I'll see you around, Bro. Hunter."

"Nadine," said Garrett stepping out of line with only a small piece of cornbread on his tray. "I mean, Sister Manhassette, could we grab that cup of coffee tomorrow?"

"Brother Hunter, I don't know if–"

"Not like a date or anything," he said quickly. "I just want to see you again. We could talk about our experiences today, huh? Believe me, I've got a story to tell."

"Garrett, I'm, I'm just not...it's too soon for–okay." Nadine sighed. "I'd like to have coffee with you tomorrow."

"You just name the place," said Garrett sincerely. "I'll be there."

"The Black & White Gallery Museum & Café in the village," said Nadine. "Say around 9:30?"

"I'll be there."

Chapter Five
Appearances

"Garrett," Blake said donning his blue Food Company blazer as he passed by the open door of the spare bedroom. "Where you been, man? Haven't seen you all weekend."

"I volunteered with Trinity Feeding Care yesterday," Garrett said slapping on some aftershave.

"You sure were up and out pretty early," said Blake. "Man, I had to be at work at 6 o'clock."

Garrett strung his belt through the loops.

"Well, where you goin' now?" asked Blake leaning against the door frame.

"Gotta date," he said brushing his hair into place.

"On a Thursday morning?" Blake laughed hysterically. "Now that's more like it! The Gingerbread Man is back!"

"It's not really a date, man," said Garrett purposely deflating Blake's balloon. "I'm just meeting a friend for coffee."

"Oh, I get it," said Blake with his nose in the air. "That's the sophisticated way to approach the ladies, huh?"

Garrett snickered. "You still bent out of shape about that, B.?"

"Naw." Blake shrugged. "I knew you was just tryin' to clown me, G. You're still a Gingerbread Man to the heart! Just like me. Dark, sweet, irresistible and impossible to catch!" Blake slid his coat on. "See you later, Gingerbread Man!"

Garrett glared at himself in the mirror. He closed his eyes and listened to the shallow whispers of bottomless promises he'd made to unsuspecting females to satisfy his own animal lusts.

Garrett feared the residue of his indiscretions still showed on him.

Garrett shook himself. He checked his watch and grabbed his coat and headed for his car.

Garrett opened the glass and gold trimmed door of the Black & White Museum Gallery and Café. The melodious sounds of saxophone, bass and drum filled the space. He noticed Nadine sitting in a far corner typing into a lap top computer.

He approached her slowly never taking his eyes off her morning-fresh, captivating beauty. "Nadine," he said.

She looked up and smiled.

"Garrett, I'm glad you could make it. Sit down, please."

Garrett took his seat and looked around.

"Nice choice."

"Do you like this place?" she asked closing the lid of the computer and tucking it under her chair.

"Yeah," he said admiring the artwork that surrounded him. "It's trendy, unique and I like the artwork."

Just then a waiter approached their table.

"Good morning, Ms. Manhassette. What can I get for you?"

"Good morning, Carl. I'll have a mocha latté," she told him. "And you, Garrett, what will you have?"

"Uh, the same as Ms. Manhassette."

Carl finished the order and stepped quietly away.

"They know you here, huh?" he asked. "You must come here a lot."

"Everyday except Sunday," Nadine teased. "I'm the owner."

"You own this place?" Garrett was pleasantly surprised.

"Yep." Nadine smiled proudly looking about the trendy spot. "We've been in operation almost sixteen years now. We get artists and tourists from all over the world! We try to–"

"I'm sorry, Nadine, but *we*?"

Nadine sighed. "My husband and I started this gallery because he loved photography so much. He's gone now." She hung her head in embarrassment. "I'm sorry. I'm just used to being a part of a team, I guess."

"Nadine..." Garrett touched her hand. "I'm the one who's sorry. This gallery is wonderful. And you," he charmed,

"Nadine, you're a piece of artwork, yourself, girl"

Nadine laughed.

Carl carefully presented their beverages.

"So, Garrett," said Nadine blowing the froth, "what got you interested in Trinity Feeding Care?"

"Well, you know that night we bumped into one another?"

Nadine chuckled. "I sure do. I hit you with the door."

"My cousin–"

"Blake?" she asked.

"Yeah," said Garrett, "Blake. He really wanted me to go to that single's seminar. But when Reverend Freidman started talkin' about helpin' the kids and giving back, I knew I wanted to do that. You know, God has blessed me so much, I just want to give back. And I saw that as sort of a bridge back to the Lord for me."

"That's great," said Nadine sincerely. "It's so nice to hear a young man say that."

"Hey," said Garrett with a smile, "we're not gonna get into that age thing again, are we?"

Nadine sipped her latté. "No, I suppose we won't. So, you're a native of New York, huh?"

"I've spent the last six years in Baltimore," answered Garrett. "I'm a computer programmer and systems analyst for D.C.S.S.; Digital Concepts Software Systems. I've been consulting with them since I got outta college."

"Well, Garrett," asked Nadine, "what brought you back New York?"

Garrett took a deep breath and exhaled his uneasiness. "I was in a car accident. A friend of mine was killed. I lost three weeks of my life from a severe concussion but not a scratch on me. When I came to, I knew exactly what I wanted. I wanted something different for myself, for my life. I guess you can say I had a moment of clarity."

Nadine nodded.

"I'd made a lot of money for a man my age," he continued now taken with her butter cream complexion and the cocoa brown ensemble she wore to compliment it. "I've seen the world. I wanted to make a difference. So, I packed up my stuff. Sold my condo. And headed back to my roots. And here I am."

"This friend who was killed," inquired Nadine casually, "was it male or female?"

"Female," said Garrett disallowing the horrors of the

accident to take form. "Catherine was her name. We, uh, dated a while back. She was having some problems, I don't know. It was tragic." He put his head down. "I'd just as soon put it behind me."

"I see," said Nadine putting the warm brew to her lips.

"And you, Nadine?" Garrett sipped the warm mixture. "How long have you been widowed?"

Nadine turned away and rubbed her neck.

"Did I say something wrong, Nadine?" asked Garrett putting his cup down..

"...No," she said quietly. "I'm sorry, Garrett, I just have a hard time talking about myself. My husband Evander has been gone three years now."

"Well, don't you have any family? Or children?"

"No," she said with obvious regret. "Evander had children from a previous marriage. And my family...disowned me a long time ago."

"Disowned you?"

"Evander was 26 years my senior," she said with a tight smile. Her mind wandered fondly across time. "We loved each other. I can't explain it, but we did. My whole life was Evander Manhassette. He was a still photographer for a production studio here in New York. He was also a cameraman. I was working as a production assistant when we met."

Garrett smiled. "A gopher, right?"

"Yes," said Nadine, "a glorified gopher. Well, Evander was near retirement. He'd been divorced for years. He always had this dream of opening a gallery full of black and white stills. Fifteen years ago, the Black & White Museum Gallery was born. The café came later," she explained. "It was my idea."

"You miss him," said Garrett.

Nadine sighed. "I do miss him. But life goes on despite the ones we miss."

"C'mon, Reynaldo," said Dixie spotting her friend across the crowded café filled with the smooth rhythms of jazz. "There's Nadine right there."

"But she is talking with that fellow," said the casually dressed Spaniard. "Perhaps we shouldn't interrupt them."

"Oh, him?" She waved at the insignificance of it all. "He's probably some artist trying to negotiate a fee with her. C'mon."

"Nadine, sugar!" Dixie kissed her on the cheek. "Sorry to interrupt, but Reynaldo and I were in the neighborhood and decided to stop by so he could see this wonderful gallery of yours."

Nadine was uncomfortable with Dixie's obvious intrusion and glared at her friend. Then she softened. "Hello, Reynaldo."

"It's a pleasure to meet you, Ms. Manhassette," said the gentleman with a chivalrous bow. "Dixie has told me so many wonderful things about you."

"Hi," said Dixie putting her diamond studded hand out to Garrett and obstructing his view of Nadine and Reynaldo with her hip. "I'm Dixie Price, Nadine's dearest friend. And you are?"

"Garrett Hunter," he replied shaking her hand.

"Well, tell me, Mr. Hunter," she said with a fluttering finger, "which photograph is yours?"

"I'm sorry, uh, photograph?"

Dixie lowered her brow. "You *are* an African American photographic artist, aren't you?"

Garrett shook his head. "No. I'm afraid I'm not."

"Well, Reynaldo," said Dixie pushing her blond tresses into place, "I suppose we're disturbing Ms. Manhassette's interview for a new juice and sandwich maker."

Nadine turned red.

Garrett laughed. "No, I'm not here to apply for that job, either."

"Dixie, Reynaldo," said Nadine tactfully, "Garrett Hunter is a computer programmer and systems analyst. He's a friend of mine. We both volunteered for the Trinity Feeding Care Program yesterday."

Dixie looked Garrett up and down sensing his interest in her friend. "....Oh."

"Reynaldo," said Nadine as polite as possible, "it was a pleasure meeting you. And you're welcomed to tour the gallery."

"Ms. Manhassette," he replied, "I'd like very much to–"

"Oh me. Oh, my," interceded Dixie looking at her watch, "look at the time. We'd better be getting back to the club. Our golf pro shop is going on line today at 3 o'clock with some wonderful golf tips. It's my pet project." Dixie gave Nadine the evil-eye.

Then Dixie turned to Garrett. "A pleasure, Mr. Hunter," she said with a nod.

Garrett shared his warmest smile. "Nice meeting you, too, Ms. Price."

Dixie slid her hand into the bend of Reynaldo's arm. "Toodles, Naddy."

Nadine reached for Garrett's hand. "Can you ever forgive my friend Dixie?"

"Hey, it's no problem," Garrett reassured her. "Listen, you mentioned tourists. Well, I feel like a tourists 'cause I've been away from the city so long. How about a tour of the gallery for starters?"

Nadine brightened. "Of course. Right this way, Mr. Hunter."

Nadine spoke proudly of each piece introducing Garrett to artistic renditions that were rich in history and purpose. Garrett's eyes roamed between the showcased pieces and the exquisite artwork that defined his hostess.

Nadine kicked herself mentally for not being able to take her eyes off the handsome Garrett who proved to be every bit of a gentleman.

At the end of the ambling three-hour art excursion, Nadine and Garrett found themselves competing with the lunch crowd for a table. It was obvious neither of them were ready to end their *date*. They made each other laugh at the slightest things. And they relished each other's company.

"You know," said Garrett being pushed and shoved as many clambered for sandwiches and coffee, "when I was in Baltimore, I'd see pictures of New York and Central Park. They'd always show two people taking a carriage ride. I've lived here most of my life and, you know, I've never taken a carriage ride."

"Me neither," said Nadine as a hot beverage and sandwich was passed to a patron right between them.

"Then let's take one," he suggested grabbing her hand.

"But it's freezin' outside," said Nadine glancing out the doors at the icy-gray city.

Garrett smiled. "I'm sure they've got blankets."

With that, Nadine gave Carl a few hurried instructions and headed to Central Park with Garrett.

***

"Can you believe our luck, Nadine?" Garrett said happily as they pulled up to Aunt Lena and Uncle Tyrone's house. "Two tickets to see *Hand Me Downs*?"

"I've been wanting to see this play for a month," said Nadine happily. "It's been sold out for weeks. And that guy just gave us the tickets." She looked out the window of Garrett's sports car and got nervous. "Garrett," she said turning to him, "you go on inside and change. I'll wait for you in the car."

"That's crazy, Nadine." Garrett put the brake on. "We're friends. And we're havin' a great time today."

"Garrett," began Nadine. "...Garrett, Garrett, Garrett," she shook her head. "I've had a wonderful time with you today. But I don't want to risk anyone seeing this."

"Seeing what?"

"Garrett," she said leaning back on the headrest, "don't tell me you haven't noticed how people have stared at us and pointed."

Garrett's silence confirmed Nadine's suspicions.

"I'm such a private person," said Nadine painfully. "I've shared more with you in one day than I've shared with anybody. I'd just die if your aunt and uncle got the wrong impression of us too soon."

Garrett looked over her shoulder out the window. "I don't even see anybody's car, Nadine. C'mon, it'll be ten minutes–tops. You and me–in and out, I promise."

Nadine hesitated and then reluctantly agreed.

Garrett opened the front door and found the house silent. "See," he said closing it quietly behind her, "I told you nobody was here."

Nadine breathed a sigh of relief.

Garrett closed the door and noticed a personal-size envelope clamped in the mail slot. He reached down to pick it up noticing his name typed across the front of the envelope.

His hand began to shake.

"What's wrong, Garrett?"

"Nothin'," he said trying to laugh off his unexplained and sudden fear. He tore the open the envelope and slid out an obituary clipped from a newspaper. The word GUILTY was stamped across it in red.

"Garrett," said Nadine, "is there anything wrong?"

"No," he said crumbling the tiny paper in his hand.

His face lit into a smile. "Now, you sit down, right there," he said, "and I'll get dressed."

Just as Garrett began up the stairs, the front door flung open.

"Garrett! Garrett!" shouted Aunt Lena. "Come here! I was hopin' you'd be home. There's someone I want you to see!"

Nadine bolted from her chair out of fear.

Aunt Lena's eyes fell on her. And then slowly across the room to Garrett who was turning a deep shade of purple.

"Aunt Lena," he gasped.

"Oh," she said smiling quizzically at Nadine, "hello."

"Hello," said Nadine.

"Aunt Lena," said Garrett noticing a familiarly attractive young woman trailing his aunt carrying a sack of canned goods, "this is Nadine Manhassette. Nadine this is my aunt Lena Hunter."

Nadine smiled. "My pleasure, Mrs. Hunter."

"Like wise," said Aunt Lena bringing the young beauty into the awkward party, "this is Regina Baxter all grown up now. You remember her from junior high. You two had the maddest crush on each other."

"Yeah," said Garrett embarrassed as he shook her hand, "I remember you."

"Regina's a school teacher," said Aunt Lena carrying on as if Nadine wasn't there, "and I just thought the two of should get together to discuss old times."

"I'd like that," said Garrett flashing Nadine a confused look. "But Nadine and I were just on our way to see *Hand Me Downs* that new play. I just swooped to the house to change."

Aunt Lena looked at Garrett. Then she blinked slowly and scrutinized Nadine. "Well," she said breaking the silence. "I guess that means you won't be staying for dinner."

"No, Aunt Lena," said Garrett. "We'd planned to go to–"

"Garrett," said Blake traipsing down the stairs noticing Nadine and figuring the whole thing out faster than his mother. "A lady called you, man."

Garrett glared at his cousin who was enjoying his sadistic assault on the scene.

"Her name was Ingrid," he continued. "She said it was real important," said Blake winking at his cousin, "G, she said call her at the office, hit her on the hip, or call her at home late tonight or–"

"Okay! Okay!," he shouted. "Thanks, cuz." Garrett attempted to bolster his humiliation by excusing himself politely.

Nadine sat down in the chair and held herself nervously.

Aunt Lena and Regina Baxter disappeared into the kitchen to begin dinner.

***

Garrett awoke gently to the early morning sounds of the Hunter household. He remembered Ingrid's call and began dialing long distance to Baltimore.

"Garrett," snapped Ingrid, "it's about time you called.

Where've you been?"

"...Just tryin' to live normally, Ingrid. Just tryin' to live normally."

"Well, sorry to interrupt, Garrett, but there's something wrong. Really wrong, you know what I mean?"

"Give it to me straight, Ingrid," said Garrett deciding to take the expected bad news sitting up. "Don't tell me they're still tryin' to build a case against me."

"Well, not exactly," she explained. "Have you ever had any dealings with Detective Desmond before?"

"Nope. Why?"

"I don't know," she said. "That day at the hospital, he was pretty creepy."

"You're tellin' me."

"He's not a stable man, Garrett," said Ingrid. "Have you noticed anything strange? I mean, is everything going okay there?"

Garrett remembered the guilty-stained obituary. "Naw. Everything's been cool here. And besides, I can take of myself, Ingrid. But, uh, listen, if Desmond was nosyin' around my old job or somethin', he wouldn't be able to come up with my aunt and uncle's address would he?"

"Well, that depends."

"On what?"

"Whether or not he was able to get information from your personnel records."

"He'd need a search warrant for that, right?"

"Legally, yes," answered Ingrid. "But often times employees who you ate lunch with aren't as time consuming as a search warrant. It's been done before."

Garrett sighed. "Okay."

"Why? Garrett, is everything–"

"No problem, Ingrid." Garrett sighed. "...Just tryin' to live normally."

"Well, just the same. I've got my feelers out regarding Detective Larry Desmond. You watch yourself, kid, huh?"

"Talk to you later, Ingrid."

"Garrett," said Aunt Lena carrying a bundle of folded laundry into his room. "Here," she said practically throwing it at him.

"Aunt Lena," he asked with a sock hanging from his head as he hung up the phone. "Are you mad at me or something?"

"You weren't very nice to Sis. Baxter's daughter Regina last night," she explained. "And all I went through to get her here. Your favorite garlic roasted chicken and peach cobbler."

"Aunt Lena," he said getting up from his bed, "you were tryin' to fix me up with her, weren't you?"

"Okay," she snapped putting her hands in the pockets of her apron. "So, I was. But it's better than that Nadine Manhassette person you're draggin' around with. A woman old enough to be your mother!"

"Aunt Lena, she's only 16 years older than me," Garrett told her.

Aunt Lena puckered her lips and lowered her brow. "And you don't see anything wrong with that, Garrett?"

"Not when two people just enjoy each other's company," he answered.

Aunt Lena grabbed her forehead. "What do you see in this Nadine Manhassette?"

Garrett smiled and made dove eyes at her. "She reminds me a lot of you, Aunt Lena. Beautiful, warm, intelligent, sophisticated and–"

"Stop right there, Mr. Charmer," said Aunt Lena with a finger up. "I wiped the poop from her smelly behind, boy. Remember that. And I know what you're full of, alright?"

Garrett chuckled. He refolded his laundry items and tucked them into a drawer.

"You could talk a soldier's wife out of her chastity belt!" She folded her arms across her chest. "You and Blake always had girls callin', girls comin' by." She put her hands on her hips. "If I had a nickel for every midnight hour I thought I heard some girl gigglin' in my hallway–"

"Aw c'mon now Aunt Lena," he said grabbing her hands. "Nadine is a wonderful woman. We just went to a play together, that's all. Lucky for me, she was big-hearted enough to even find a little humor in what happened here last night. I thought she'd be mad at me. You and Blake went out of your way to make me look like a player. Huh?"

"Well, Garrett," said Aunt Lena, "you just have to be my age to see what I see."

"Aunt Lena," said Garrett proceeding to make up his bed, "times have changed. Men and women can be friends."

"In all my days, Lord," began Aunt Lena talking toward Heaven, "I've never seen more young people so unappreciative of appearances!"

"Aunt Lena, Nadine and I are just friends," explained Garrett fluffing his pillow. "She's a nice lady. We both volunteered for the Trinity Feeding Care Program. We met for coffee and just got to know one another. What's wrong with it, huh?"

"What's *wrong* with it?" she asked putting her hands on her hips. "What's wrong with it? Garrett, it looks perverted! Seein' you two together like that, well, it makes folks wonder, that's all."

"About what?" Garrett tried to see things her way but to no avail. "A man and a woman enjoying each other's company? It's innocent. What's there to wonder about?"

Aunt Lena tightened her gaze. "You know about *what*, boy. A May-December romance always makes folks' minds wander to places they shouldn't."

She shook her finger at him. "Sad to say, but that's just how your mama was. Never worried 'bout how things looked! Runnin' off with that musician just after leavin' your real father back in Chicago. You were only four months old! Sure, sure, your uncle Tyrone and I took you in and raised you as our own. But she was gonna drag you along! She never thought about how things looked!"

Aunt Lena noticed her nephew's look turn sour as he flopped onto his bed.

She joined him at his side. "...I know you're a grown man, Garrett," she said in a kind whisper. "And I don't expect that you've been an angel out there in Baltimore but–"

"Aunt Lena, there's nothing like *that* goin' on between me and Nadine," confirmed Garrett. "I've done a lot of runnin' around with the ladies. They're a dime a dozen when a brother's got a little somethin', you know what I mean? But I've learned you can't mistake *that* for the real thing. I wasn't kiddin' when I told you I need the Lord in my life. That's why I came back here. I'm not gonna let anything get in my way."

Aunt Lena patted Garrett's leg reassuringly.

"And that Regina you were tryin' to fix me up with?" he continued. "Now *she's* a barracuda!"

"What's that supposed to mean?"

"Let's just say she wanted me to make her a woman the night of the junior prom!" Garrett stood up and laughed out loud. "We couldn't have been any older than 14!"

"No, Garrett," interrupted Aunt Lena holding her heart. "Not Missionary Baxter's daughter. Why, that girl was peaches and cream sweet when she was–"

"Aunt Lena," said Garrett, "what I'm tryin' to say is that Nadine is a special lady. I've never met anyone like her. And I'm glad she's my friend. All the women I've dated ended up hurt one way or another. Either I've hurt them or they hurt themselves. Not this time," he declared. "Not Nadine. As far as my intentions are concerned, it's the right way or no way, you know. Mutual respect," he said counting on his fingers, "trust, no secrets, no agendas."

Aunt Lena smiled at her nephew's sincerity and integrity. "No man is ever that convincing when a woman's just a *friend*, Garrett. You remind me a lot of your uncle when he was young," she said with the glow of sweet reminiscence on her face. "He knew what he wanted. And this, this sounds like love."

"Whoa! After one day?" Garrett tried to laugh off the possibility but couldn't. He kissed his aunt gently on her cheek "As soon as I'm sure, I'll let you know."

"Uh, Garrett," said Aunt Lena straightening his collar, "...I still don't approve of this friendship, as you call it." She shrugged. "I'm an old woman who still cares about how things look. But I approve of *you*. I couldn't love you more if you were my own flesh and blood, Garrett. You've turned out to be a wonderful young man and I approve of *you*. You understand?"

Garrett wrapped his arms around his aunt.

Chapter Six
Tumbling Down

"Garrett," said Blake knocking on the door of the spare bedroom at 6:30 a.m., "phone for you, man."

Garrett aroused just in time to catch the cordless phone as Blake tossed it across the room. He spoke sleepily talked into it. "Hello."

"Brother Hunter," said a feeble old voice. "This is Reverend Freidman from the Trinity Feeding Care Program."

"Yes, Reverend Freidman," said Garrett coming alive in wonder.

"I apologize for calling you so early but there's been a terrible tragedy this week. I thought you should know. I'm afraid young Zeke has been shot and killed."

"...No. Not Zeke," said Garrett now fully conscious. "What happened, man?"

"...There's so much I want to talk to you about, Bro. Hunter. Could you come to the church this morning?"

"I'll be there in an hour."

Garrett approached the huge edifice feeling anxious.

Reverend Freidman met him at the door and led him down a long corridor past empty Sunday School rooms and administrative offices to a modest lounge.

"Reverend Freidman," asked Garrett taking a seat in a chair, "what happened to Zeke?"

"Mistaken identity, Brother Garrett," said the old man shaking his grayed head. "Some hoodlums robbed a liquor store and ran," he explained. "The police gave chase. Young Zeke, who was hanging out with his friends, was confronted by a patrolling policeman because Zeke fit the description of one of the boys. Zeke must've been terribly scared. He pulled a .32 from his coat pocket. The policeman fired..."

Garrett tightly closed his eyes and tried to shake the ugliness from his mind.

"...He was a kid, Reverend Freidman," said Garrett remembering the youngster. "That .32, it wasn't real. He showed it to me."

"The police discovered that it wasn't real after the fact."

"Why!" shouted Garrett bolting from the chair. "Why?"

"Brother Hunter," said the old man, "I asked you here this morning because Zeke's untimely and unfortunate death alarmed me about you."

Garrett turned to him. "Me? What you worried about me for?"

"You made a difference in Zeke's life. A significant difference, Brother Hunter," said the old preacher as Garrett shook his head doubtfully. "But there are too many variables. Things that are keepin' an old man like me up nights."

Garrett was puzzled by the old preacher's spilling conscious.

"I don't know what you said or what you did that made young Zeke follow you back to the site and pitch in the way he did. But I'm not willing to take that same chance with you."

"Rev Freidman," said Garrett, "I don't understand what you're tryin' to tell me."

"Do you know the Lord, Garrett?"

"Of course, I do," said Garrett.

"I mean, do you know Him in the pardon of your sins, young man?"

Garrett couldn't say anything.

"Zeke pitched in and helped the Trinity Feeding Care Program," said the old man as Garrett's eyes followed him around the room as he paced the carpeted floor. "He put his all into it for reasons only he and God know. And you, Brother Garrett, you pitched in and helped the Trinity Feeding Care Program for reasons only you and God know. But it's not enough, Brother Garrett. You must *know* God. You must believe by faith, do you understand?"

"Reverend Freidman," said Garrett with a smug laugh that sealed his uneasiness, "I was raised in the church, man."

"So was I," said the old preacher with a wink. "Daddy

was preacher. Mama was a missionary. Grew up in the heart of Texas; what y'all call the Bible Belt. But that didn't keep me out of Alcatraz for racketeering and murder."

Garrett's mouth fell open. The changing dynamic sobered him.

"Pick your face up there, son," said Reverend Freidman. "Volunteering does not a Christian make, my boy. Your salvation is not your ability or desire to do good deeds, Brother Garrett. I've seen your type before," he said shaking a finger at Garrett. "You're running. Oh, boy! Something has *scared* you holy!"

Garrett looked at him puzzled by his accuracy of untold details.

"Oh, don't worry," said the reverend. "I haven't been talking to anyone who knows what's happening with your life right now. Nobody except the Lord Jesus Christ. He told me," said the old man pointing to Heaven. "He woke me from my bed this morning at 4 a.m. with your soul on my mind. Zeke, Garrett, Zeke, Garrett. Your names played in this old head like a broken record. What's your vice, son?"

Garrett's eyes darted nervously. "...My vice?"

"Every man's got 'em," explained the Reverend. "Money, women, the races, booze. What's yours?"

"Rev, I...."

"C'mon now, son, it's time to confess." The old man's body convulsed. "Thank you, Father!" Reverend Freidman's eyes popped open and he clapped his hands. "Mistaken identity, Brother Garrett," he said pointing at Garrett's stunned face. "Somebody believes you did something you didn't do. But you can't defend yourself," he said moving toward Garrett, "'cause you think they've got power over you!"

Garrett went pale and held a near-by chair for support.

"God's offering you a choice today, son," said the little preacher with his eyes closed and his hand on his ear as if receiving some transmission. "Either accept Him in your life or die a spiritual death many times over. God's promising *today* that He will be by your side when the storm comes but only if you enter a covenant with Him today!"

Garrett wiped a tear from his face.

"Do you believe, son?! Will you enter into covenant with Him today?!"

"What good am I to the Lord if I'm scared, man?"

Reverend Freidman smiled. "God said that that question answers itself because He's the only one who can turn fear to faith. So, ask it again. Go ahead. Ask the question again."

Garrett was confused. "What?"

"Ask the question again?"

"What good am I if I'm full of faith?"

Reverend Freidman smiled. "It changes everything, doesn't it?"

Garrett took deep breaths and exhaled the shudder of tears. "...Women," Garrett whispered falling slowly to his knees to talk to God. "Women are my vice, Lord. I've used them, taken advantage of them. I've never said this out loud but I feel responsible for what happened to Cat. I was so busy getting what I could out of the relationship that I ignored the fact there was something wrong with her...I'm sorry, Lord."

"Romans 10:9," said Reverend Freidman appearing at Garrett's side with a bible, "if thou shalt confess with thy mouth and believe in thy heart that Jesus is the son of God and rose from the dead, thou shalt be saved, my boy! Do you believe?!"

Garrett read the scripture himself with fresh, new eyes. "Yeah, Reverend Freidman, I do."

"Do you believe God has saved you from your sins?"

"Yes..."

"Do you repent of your sins?"

"I repent," said Garrett in a purifying mixture of sincerity and freedom.

"Then you're saved, Garrett," said the old preacher backing away slowly. He gave Garrett a pat on the shoulder as he rose wearily to his feet. "Whatever happens, good or bad, from this point on, you have an ally greater than any lawyer, any evil force, any self-important, confident ability you have and greater than any friend."

Garrett sighed and found pleasure in the flood of peace that filled his entire being. "Thank you, Jesus."

***

"Nadine! Nadine!" Garrett banged on her townhouse door. "Open up, girl! It's me Garrett!"

Nadine flung the door open wearing a silky, floral robe. "Garrett," she said looking around for her neighbors, "do you know what time it is?"

"Nadine," he said putting a quick kiss on her lips and shutting the door. "I've taken it a step further!"

"What are you talking about, Garrett?"

He grabbed her shoulders. "My purpose, Nadine. I met

the Lord this morning. The first time ever in my life! It was incredible!"

"I-I don't know what to say."

"Don't say anything," he whispered stretching a joyous smile across his face. "I know my purpose now. I know who I am! All these years I've been wondering. I've been trying to find satisfaction in the women I've dated. They are nothing compared to what I'm feelin' right now! Clean and new!"

Nadine was speechless. She turned away.

"C'mon now, Nadine," he said turning her around with his big, strong hands. "Now don't be a hater. You know I came to you with a past."

"A past?" asked Nadine with false savvy. "Why should your past affect me one way or the other?"

Slowly, he met her eyes with his own and spoke only inches from her mouth. "You sayin' you don't feel the same way about me I feel about you?"

Nadine lingered. She crossed her arms and moved away from him to think. "Garret, we barely know each other."

"Love knows love when it meets its soul-mate, Nadine."

"Love?" she asked with surprise. "Garrett, I-I-"

"I know. I know. We barely know each other. But you, Nadine Manhassette, you are a part of my purpose. When I gave my life to the Lord this morning, everything fell into place for me, Nadine."

"Garrett," she said rubbing her forehead, "this is all moving so fast, I-"

"Just say it, Nadine," he encouraged looking into her eyes. "Just say you feel the same way about me that I feel about you."

"Garrett, I'm so glad for you that you have come to know the Lord. I have to admit I'm a little jealous even. Evander never let me pursue church work like I wanted to. He kept me under spiritual lock and key in a way. And I'm glad we have volunteering in common. But as far as my feelings for you, I need time to think." She took a deep breath. "I need space to think..."

Garrett kissed her shoulder. "You take your time, Nadine." He rubbed his hand down the back of her head and bare neck. "Nothing's gonna change the discovery I made this morning about my ability to commit. Nothing's gonna change the way I feel about you."

Nadine heard the door open and close gently.

Amidst the refined chatter and the gentle clang of sterling silver against bone china and fine lead crystal, Nadine and Dixie sat strategically centered in New York city's Diamond Bistro.

"Oh, Nadine," said Dixie covertly covering her mouth with her napkin, "look there. Look there. It's the owner's wife Emelia nick named Trinket. Can you believe it? According to The *Rovert Report*, you know that gossip web page I'm shamefully addicted to? Well, word is Trinket over there is having an affair with the–"

"Evander loved hot coffee and ham sandwiches," mumbled Nadine staring desolately at her endive salad. "I used to get up every morning at 3 a.m. when he was on a local shoot and make him a ham sandwich for his lunch and a fresh pot of coffee for this thermos. He hated the catered food on the set."

"Nadine, sugar," Dixie reached for her friend's hand and whispered, "where've you been all afternoon? This is first Thursday, remember? Hello. Earth to Nadine."

"I don't even drink coffee," said Nadine closing her eyes filled with tears that wouldn't fall out. "Never have. But somehow it ends up in my basket at the market. And I get nervous. I feel like I'm just gonna burst out in tears if I put it back."

Dixie rubbed her hand.

"It's okay, Nadine. You just need to–"

"My eyes still pop open at three in the morning." She dabbed at her eyes with the pretty cloth napkin at the side of her plate. "I know he's gone...I know."

"Why won't you consider, Reynaldo?" offered Dixie in an attempt to lighten the mood. "He's more–oh I don't know–your age."

"It's not an age thing with me and Garrett!" said Nadine promptly noticing that her outburst got the unwanted attention of other diners. "It's deeper than that," she whispered.

"Deeper, huh?" asked Dixie winking and leaning forward. "So you've slept with him, is that it?"

"No, I haven't," said Nadine blushing. "He's surprisingly old fashioned about a lot of things. He's charming and gentle."

"He's come into your life with notches on his bed post, Nadine, no doubt," warned Dixie. "You couldn't possibly be his first."

"He received salvation this morning, Dixie," said Nadine plainly. "He was so excited. I think he wanted me to be the first to know. That says a lot about his values and his character."

"Tsk, tsk, tsk," said Dixie sitting back in her chair and shaking her head. "Poor, poor, Nadine. Don't you know it's physically impossible for a twenty-eight year old man to be old fashioned when it comes to sex? I ought to know," said Dixie proudly, "I've corrupted enough of 'em." Nadine rolled her eyes and pushed some salad into her mouth.

Dixie grabbed her wine glass and swirled the gold mixture around. "I can almost guarantee that your Garrett is either gay or he's gettin' supplied elsewhere." She took a sip.

"Stop it, Dixie!" whispered Nadine vehemently. "Just shut-up! Why does Garrett have to be only 30% of the ideal, huh? He's 100% okay! He loves me."

"Oh," said Dixie straightening up in her chair.

"As crazy at that sounds, Dix, he loves *me*," explained Nadine laying her hand on her chest. "With Evander I always felt like a little girl waiting to grow up." Nadine shook her head and laughed at the irony. "Evander loved me. But there were times I know he kept me a secret. Around his friends, he treated me more like a daughter more than a wife. And I was screaming inside to be taken seriously as a woman. Dix, there were just things he knew, I couldn't even pretend to know. So I kept myself sheltered from the world. Few friends." Nadine took a deep, cleansing breath. "I loved Evander with all my heart but with Garrett I feel like a woman. I feel free to be a woman. Intelligent, desirable, sophisticated...ageless."

"Weren't you all those things before Garrett?" asked Dixie with quiet sincerity.

"Perhaps...Yes, I guess I was," confirmed Nadine. "But his eyes, Dix, they're like a mirror. I see myself, Dixie. I see the best of myself. You know I'm not one of those women who just wants a man around to validate her femininity."

"I know," said Dixie with a smile. "I know."

"And I was hell-bent on never falling in love ever again since Evander's death."

"True. True."

"But with Garrett," Nadine's eyes lit-up, "I realize God had something different in mind for me. Garrett and I connect on a level aside from just physical attraction. We both wanted to reach out, you know, to find real purpose. We reached out and found each other. Can't you understand that?"

Dixie tapped at the corners of her mouth with her napkin.

"I'm sorry for berating Garrett, Nadine. It sounds like real love." She reached for her handbag and whipped out her platinum credit card. "But I'm still scared for you."

Dixie looked up just in time to see Nadine's face shadowed with worry.

"Oh, Naddy," asked Dixie as if she already knew the answer, "you haven't told him yet how you feel, have you?"

Nadine shook her head. "Nope. Too scared. But it feels great being in love."

"I tell you what," said Dixie reaching for Nadine's hand, "you keep floating on the wave of love, sugar." Dixie raised the girl scout's hand signal. "And I'll be an objective, hawk-eyed friend committed to your best interest. Deal?"

Nadine relaxed and smiled. "Deal."

***

"Hey, Garrett," said Carl the waiter from behind the juice bar at the museum gallery.

"Carl, man, what's up?" He and Garrett slapped hands.

"Oh, a little of this and a little of that," said Carl.

"Is uh, Ms. Manhassette around?" asked Garrett. "She's expecting me."

"She went on her monthly lunch date with that science-experiment-gone-really-wrong. You know," continued Carl wiping down the counter, "Dixie Price. The one always hangin' around asking dumb questions."

Garrett laughed remembering his first impression of the socialite. "Okay, man. What time do you expect her back?"

"Oh, in about an hour," said Carl checking his watch. "You wanna wait for her?"

"Yeah," said Garrett taking a seat at the juice bar. "I think I will."

"What can I get for you? The Mango Juice Rumba is *my* specialty."

"I'll take one," said Garrett removing his overcoat and tossing it on the stool. "Sounds good."

"Alright."

Garrett glanced into the gallery. The smile drained from his face as he recognized a familiar black trench coat. As if in a trance, he walked into the brightly lit space. "What are you doin' here, Desmond?" asked Garrett pointedly.

Detective Desmond looked up from scrutinizing a bronze statue. "Oh, Garrett Hunter."

Garrett clenched his teeth. "I said what are *you* doin' here, man?"

Desmond smiled and pointed his scrolled museum

guide at Garrett. "I've got family in New York, too."

"You're followin' me, man." Garrett's nostrils flared. "There's got to be some law against this."

"I know you're guilty of something, Hunter," said Detective Desmond confidently. "And it's just a matter of time before I find it out."

"Am I guilty because I'm Black?" asked Garrett politely. "Or because I'm actually guilty? You know, with evidence? Isn't that what you police officers usually use?"

Desmond smiled. "It's nice to know you've played this game before. So, what, now you'll probably call your lawyer uh... Ingrid what's-her-name, huh?"

"Naw, man," said Garrett feeling adrenaline pump into his abdomen readying him for battle. "It wouldn't take but a few seconds to have you on the floor beggin' me to stop chokin' your–"

"I might enjoy the challenge," said the detective opening his trench coat and exposing his gun. "I might enjoy it at that."

"Look, man," said Garrett trying to keep himself under control, "Cat Fuller is dead. There's nothing anybody can do about that. Not you. Not me. So why don't you just take your ridiculous self back to Baltimore, okay?"

"Every since that day in the hospital, I knew you had a little mad streak in you, Garrett." Detective Desmond's blue eyes sparkled confidently. "I was right. Which leads me to believe I'm right about other things, too.

"Now, the way I figure," he said nonchalantly glancing about the gallery, "there are only two people left who know what really happened in that car; you and God. And last I checked, God's on the side of truth. *My* side. I intend to find out the truth."

"I ain't gonna dance with you, man," said Garrett pointing in his face. "But you, you better watch your step."

Detective Desmond ignored Garrett's threat. "You know, I'm really disappointed with my tour of New York." He shoved his museum guide into this coat pocket. "I thought the Black & White Museum Gallery was an old police car museum. See you around, Gingerbread Man."

"What did you say?" Garrett was flabbergasted. "How did you–"

"So it is true." Desmond nodded with satisfaction. "Listen, if you wanna find out more about yourself, log onto–aw, never mind. The look on your face was worth the trip."

Garrett racked his brain trying to figure out how the Baltimore detective knew something so significantly personal.

"Carl," said Garrett grabbing his coat from the juice bar stool, "don't tell Ms. Manhassette I came by, okay, man?"

"Yeah," said Carl holding his completed masterpiece, "okay."

Garrett arrived at his aunt and uncle's house still bewildered as to how Detective Desmond knew of his and Blake's secret.

He got out of his sports car and ambled up to the front door. The house was filled with shouting.

"Vivi, you trippin', girl!" shouted Blake bursting from the kitchen door.

"I'm trippin'?" she asked on his heels. "You're the one who's trippin'! And you're gonna pay Blake Hunter! You're my baby's daddy and you're gonna pay!"

"I've been sendin' you money every month for the past year!" explained Blake finally noticing Garrett. "What more you want? Blood!?"

Vivi crossed her arms and rolled her eyes. "My baby needs a daddy!"

"Then go get one!"

Vivi's eyes turned red. She turned quickly and looked Garrett up and down. "Lady killer."

The color drained from Garrett's face. His knees knocked.

"God don't like ugly, Blake," she hissed pushing past Garrett to get out the door.

"Then God must not like you!" shouted Blake as the door slammed.

"Blake," said Garrett, "what's goin' on, man?"

"That crazy witch gonna come up in here tellin' me she's takin' her case to the District Attorney! All because she thinks I'm messin' around! But we ain't even together no more."

"You said you've been sendin' her money, man," reasoned Garrett. "So, what's the problem all of a sudden?"

"The Gingerbread Men," said Blake shaking his head. "She's on this kick about the Gingerbread Men, G. I've never once mentioned it to her. But somehow she knew, man. But how?"

"Wait," said Garrett tightening his gaze on his cousin. "Did you say she mentioned the words *Gingerbread Men* to *you*? She actually said those words?"

"Yeah, man," said Blake flopping into a chair and resting

his hand on his eyes. "She actually said those words. She's crazy if she thinks me and her are gonna get back together, man! If I didn't know any better, I'd swear you told her or somethin'. But you're my boy. I know you wouldn't snitch on me like that, would you, man?"

Blake looked up and out the open door just in time to see Garrett peeling rubber down the quiet residential street.

Chapter Seven
The Substance of Things Hoped For

Sheets of rain fell relentlessly on the boulevards of New York. Garrett skillfully maneuvered his speeding sports car through the slippery streets and tangled traffic.

His mind was fixed uneasily on antagonistic questions that plagued him. Ugly possibilities bombarded him and sent him on vengeful, mental tangents.

He arrived at Nadine's townhouse and rapped on the door.

She looked out to find Garrett soaked from head to toe. "Come in here, Garrett," she said opening the door and then rushing to get a towel and blanket.

"You'll catch your death," she said tossing the wool blanket over his shoulders. "What are you doing without a coat on?"

"Nadine," he said putting her soft hand to his cheek, "I've got to know how you feel about me. Things have to be in place for me..."

"Garrett," she said pulling gently away. "Let me get a pot of coffee started. Then we can talk."

Garrett crouched down in front of the brown marble-framed fireplace and watched the flames lick at the air.

Nadine returned with a steaming cup of coffee and handed it to him. She knelt next to him and used the towel to dry his face.

Gingerbread Men

"Do you love me, Nadine?" he asked desperately.

"Garrett," she said peering into his eyes, "I get the feeling there's something you're not telling me."

He turned away. "...I don't know."

"*Is* there something you're not telling me?" she asked remembering Dixie's accusation at the restaurant. "This wouldn't have anything to do with Cat Fuller, would it?"

"I don't know," said Garrett shaking his head. "I don't know what's wrong or, or how..." Garrett held her hands. "I've got to go back to Baltimore. I don't know when I'll get back to New York. But as soon as I can, I'll get back to you. I just need to know if you love me."

"What do you mean you've got to go back?" asked Nadine recoiling. "For what? A job or something?"

"No, Nadine," said Garrett looking at the floor. "It's personal."

"Personal? Oh, I see. It must involve some woman."

"Nadine, you've got me all wrong," explained Garrett. "Something's happening. I don't know what it is. But I don't want to drag you into anything that would hurt you. Do you understand?"

"Garrett, you show up and my door this morning raving about how you've received salvation. Then you miss our coffee date at the gallery. And now you show up at my door like some wet puppy trying to find out if I'm in love with you before you leave for Baltimore? I have no claim to you, Garrett. You're free to do or go where you please!"

"You don't know how much of my heart you really own, girl," said Garrett irreversibly. "It has been one insane day. And if there was more to tell you, believe me, I would. I just need to know that everything really important in my life will be here when I get back."

Nadine was flattered and incensed at the same time. "I do...I can't allow myself to fall in love with you, Garrett." Nadine got up from the cozy fireplace scene and flopped onto the sofa.

"Why, Nadine?" asked Garrett moving over to her.

"For just this reason!" she shouted refusing to look at him. "You're going away! I barely know you, Garrett." She closed her eyes. "I can't do this."

"Why can't you, Nadine? Is it because of him?"

"No, Garrett...yes. Yes, Garrett. It's because of Evander." Nadine massaged her neck. "He rescued me. My parents were abusive physically and mentally. They disowned me when I decided to marry Evander. And not just them but my sister and two brothers. Evander's love made me a lady. It gave me dignity. Evander was the love of my life and that's something you'd never understand. You're leaving without explanation and I'm already suspicious! This isn't fair to either of us."

"So, all love makes you into something, huh?" Garrett sat back against the wrought iron and glass coffee table and thought aloud. "The love of God makes you blessed. Evander's love made you a lady. You're probably wondering what can this 28-year-old man's love do for you, right? My love, Nadine, can only make you happy. You've just got to trust me."

"Don't, Garrett..." She stood up and faced the townhouse view of a delicately lit garden outside her window.

"Oh, I don't want to replace him, Nadine," said Garrett. "I know I can't. If you say you don't love me, I give you my word, I'll leave and never see you again. I'll go away and try to forget about you. But most importantly, I'll leave you intact with every part of your life in place. Just the way I found it."

The prospect of her life being left as it was frightened Nadine to her core. "I love you, Garrett." She threw her arms around him. "But, but I just don't know."

"You said you loved me, Nadine!" Garrett jumped to his feet.

"Quiet, Garrett!" said Nadine shushing him. "Stop jumping around!"

"Don't you see, Nadine?" He grabbed her shoulders. "You said you loved me. *This* is love," he said spinning her around. "*I* can make it, girl. *We* can make it. I promise I'll come back. And all this stuff will be over with!"

"Oh, God," said Nadine finishing a twirl and landing against the back of the sofa. "Tell me I'm not bein' some silly old woman."

"What?" He felt a portion of his strength, happiness and will to fight return.

"Garrett, look at me!"

"Why are you hollering, Nadine?" he asked.

"I want you to take a good look at me!" she shouted finding little cause to celebrate. "I'm not twenty-four, Garrett," she explained carefully. "I'm not thirty four either. I'm forty-four. I can't have any babies for you. And I'm too old to be made a fool of. I won't be made a fool of, Garrett!"

"If love makes me a fool," said Garrett soberly, "then so be it, Nadine. Once you were brave enough to declare love, Nadine, against all odds. Love folks made fun of and couldn't understand."

Nadine softened and nodded. "...Evander used to call me Princess."

"Then I'll call you Queen." Garrett opened his arms to her.

Nadine smiled and nuzzled her face against the warmth of his neck. "No. Call me *girl*," she said allowing the rest of herself to fall into his arms for a passionate kiss.

***

Garrett pulled up to a small park in a quaint suburb in Baltimore. He spotted a warmly dressed blond sitting alone with a book. Garrett started over to her when he noticed two small children run to her. She distributed tender kisses and slices of apple from a sandwich bag. Satisfied with their treats, they ran off to resume their folly.

"Thanks for agreeing to see me, Andy," said Garrett.

She smiled politely and offered him a seat next to her on the bench. "I have to admit, Garrett," she began in a whisper, "I was a little upset that you didn't make it to the funeral. Then I found out you were in a coma. I'm sorry things happened this way for all of us."

"Cat was special," said Garrett remembering the good times.

"That she was," said Andy as tears stung at her eyes. "She was my best friend. More like a sister."

"Andy," said Garrett gently, "I'm sorry, I don't' have a lot of time. I didn't come here to reminisce about Cat. I came here to ask you some questions."

"What?" asked Andy pulling herself together.

"Did a detective by the name of Desmond come around to ask you any questions?"

"Yeah," answered Andy. "Blue eyes, bald head, black trench coat. Sure, he asked me lots of questions."

"About what?"

"Mostly about you, Garrett."

"What did you tell him?"

"What I knew," said Andy.

"C'mon, Andy," encouraged Garrett trying to curtail his anxiousness. "This means my life here."

"Okay, okay," she said with a sigh. "He asked me about you and Cat's relationship mostly. I thought it was strange that he would ask such things; I mean if they suspected that you..." Andy shook her head. "Garrett, it's still very hard for me. Some days I just can't believe that Cat is gone. She was so alive, so–"

"Andy, I know you miss her," said Garrett, "but what else

did Desmond ask you?"

"He asked me if I thought you were capable of murder or at least planning one."

"What did you tell him?"

"I told him no," said Andy as if there was no other possible answer. "Despite yours and Cat's obvious differences, I thought you were best for Cat. Not like the other guys she dated. Most of 'em rich and married but–"

"Andy, thanks,"

"Garrett, wait," said Andy grabbing a handful of his leather jacket. "I've got to know from you, Garrett. You wouldn't hurt Cat would you?"

"I know Cat must've shared things with you about us," began Garrett with his head hung low. "There've been a lot of women between our break-ups. It was no secret." Garrett looked Andy straight in the eyes. "But I never intentionally hurt Cat, Andy."

"She uh," Andy began as if she already knew the answer, "she wouldn't hurt herself, would she, Garrett?"

Garrett had finally found opportunity to tell the truth but this truth promised to damage the unstable Andy. "It was an accident, Andy," Garrett told her. "Just an unfortunate accident."

***

Garrett rang the doorbell of Cat's apartment.

There was no answer. He could here the operatic mantra of *La Femme Daphne*.

Garrett banged on the door. "Trevor! It's me Garrett. Open up! I know you're in there!"

The music went mute and a frail little man confined to a wheelchair opened the door. "What do you want, Garrett?"

"I need to talk to you," said Garrett waiting to be asked in to Cat's once beautiful apartment.

"Men," huffed Trevor who waited rudely blocking the door with his chair.

Garrett poked his head in and looked around the apartment. He noticed the blue glare of Trevor's computer in the dining room. "Aren't you gonna let me in?"

Trevor rolled his eyes.

"Look, Trevor," said Garrett with a sigh, "we may not have a lot of things in common. But we do have Cat Fuller in common, right?"

"To some degree," said Trevor batting his eyelashes and puckering his thin lips. "But only one of us truly respected the fine, decent person she was. One of us deeply loved and cared for her."

"Trevor," said Garrett shaking his head, "we're getting no where."

"Men," snapped Trevor giving Garrett the evil-eye. "I still refuse to invite you in."

"Fine, Trevor," said Garrett now frustrated. "I just need to know if anybody from Baltimore P.D. came here and went through Cat's personal things, that's all."

"Of course they did," spat Trevor. "What else do the police do in a murder investigation?"

"Trevor," said Garrett wanting to hurt the little invalid. "Trevor, did a Detective Desmond ask you questions about me and Cat?"

"Lots of men asked me questions," said Trevor. "I don't happen to remember their names."

"What did you tell them?"

"I told them that you were extremely violent with Cat often resulting in forced sex and blackened eyes."

"Trevor!" yelled Garrett. "Man, that ain't true!"

"I know, Garrett," said Trevor pleased with the rise he got out of him. "That's not what I really told them. But it may as well have been true! You hurt Cat more times than either of us could count! You used her up until there was nothing left of her but a miserable shell!

"Oh, the things that must've been going through her mind at the last possible moment!" Trevor laid his hand, complete with blood red nails, over his heart and dramatized a weak female. "*Will he love me? Does he love me? Can he ever love me?* I'm a firm believer in free love and I was rarely unsupportive of her choices in men. But you, Garrett Hunter, you broke the bank, baby!"

Garrett was speechless.

"Now if you'll excuse me," said Trevor backing his motorized chair up, "I've got work to do." He slammed the door.

***

Feeling no closer to solving the mystery called his life, Garrett drove back to New York at break neck speed. His mind flooded with scenes from the accident. Cat's venom-green eyes flashed before him. He could hear the shrill in her voice as she accused and cursed him.

Nadine's sweetness crept into his mind periodically and calmed him. Aunt Lena and Uncle Tyrone's devotion reminded him that he was part of something bigger, something stronger than himself. Family.

The tender thread that drew him back to New York along the lonely highway also included Blake's prejudice of Garrett's infamous womanizing.

"Lord," prayed Garrett aloud, "I don't feel saved. My life is in the same mess it was in before I accepted you. Could Reverend Freidman have made a mistake? Could it be that I'm not the one who even deserves Your love? I know You love everybody. But I didn't do anything wrong! I'm locked up just like thousands of other Black men. The only difference is, I get to drive around! I feel like I'm the only one in the world who's goin' through this. Help me, please..."

Garrett turned the radio on in his car and surfed the dial. His ears tuned into a sermon already in progress.

"*This man* who stole another man's wife and had the husband murdered just so he could have her? *This man* who loved God with all his heart? *This man* who began his career as a lonely shepherd boy, musician, warrior and then king of God's beloved Israel? Could *this man* be the apple of God's eye? Could a man such as him find favor with God Himself?"

Garrett slowed his car and turned up the broadcast. He didn't notice the determined headlights gaining ground from behind.

"Saints, I implore your open-mindedness!" continued the preacher. "The answer is yes! *This man* was David! A shepherd boy, musician to King Saul, a warrior and then yes, King. A womanizing, conniving man who had Israel in one pocket and the mercy of the living God in the other!

"Now some of you are asking today is it possible for God to love me despite the horrible, unspeakable things I've done. The answer is yes, again! The secret, my friends, is repentance! Repent daily! Repent moment by moment! Your repentance puts God on the throne of your heart, saints!

"David wrote many of the chapters of Psalms. And in each he gave glory to God!" The preacher chuckled. "There's a candidness about these chapters of Psalms. Even when angry and spiritually, mentally and physically desolate, David put God on the throne of his heart. He acknowledged God and gave Him glory! Even when his life was in a vile, stinking, unrecognizable shambles! And God, Saints, in His almighty understanding of human frailties helped him cope. Oh yeah! We serve a God who can get all the way down to our level and understand us! Give the Lord some praise!"

The congregation exploded in praise.

Garrett's eyes swelled with tears. He pulled onto the

soft shoulder and tuned into the rest of the message.

"Turn with me to Psalms 38," said the preacher, "And the Word of the Lord says:

O Lord, do not rebuke me in your anger or discipline me in your wrath. For your arrows have pierced me, and your hand has come down upon me–"

There was a tap on his window. "You're makin' this too easy for me, Hunter," said Desmond smiling viciously at Garrett.

"What the–" Garrett looked around. "You've been followin' me!"

"That's right," said Desmond unapologetically. He drew his gun and pointed it at Garrett. "Step out of the car."

"*My guilt has overwhelmed me,*" continued the preacher on the radio as Garrett gripped the steering wheel and closed his eyes, "*like a burden too heavy to bear. My wounds fester and are loathsome because of my sinful folly. I am bowed down and brought very low; all day long I go about mourning.*"

"Out of the car, Hunter!" screamed Desmond.

"Look, man," said Garrett, "Why don't you just–"

"I said out of the car, *boy!*"

"*Those who seek my life,*" said the preacher, "*set their traps, those who would harm me talk of my ruin; all day long they plot deception. I have become like a man who does not hear, whose mouth can offer no reply.*"

Garrett unlatched his seat belt and stood from his sports car leaving the door open.. "What did you call me?"

Desmond's eye twitched. "Got that mad streak stirred up in you, didn't I, boy?"

Garrett tightened his fists at his sides.

"If I remember correctly, you said something about choking me back at the gallery," said Desmond.

"*I wait for you,*" declared the preacher. "*O Lord; you will answer, O Lord my God. For I said, "Do not let them gloat or exalt themselves over me when my foot slips!*"

"You're a cop, Desmond," Garrett stated. "If I throw one punch, I'm goin' down. Maybe in prison for the rest of my life."

Desmond lowered his gun and tossed it safely away near his car. He removed his badge and tossed aside also.

The preacher's climactic oration quickened something in Garrett.

"*I confess my iniquity; I am troubled by my sin. Many are those who are my vigorous enemies; those who hate me without reason are numerous. Those who repay my good with evil slander me when I pursue what is good.*

"Lord, do not forsake me: be not far from me, O my God. Come quickly to help me, O Lord my savior!"

"I'm not a cop now. Let's go at it," said Desmond waving his fingers, "before I kill your Black–"

Garrett punched Desmond across the chin. Desmond recovered and slugged Garrett in the stomach.

Their bodies slammed against the car. Blood flew from their mouths and wounds as the congregation shouted praise unto the Lord.

The men tussled on the ground getting the better of each other. Each man fought his sanctioned demon.

Garrett got to his feet and side-kicked Desmond in the chin sending him to the ground like a feather. He stood over the unconscious cop.

"Do you love God today?" asked the preacher. *"Do you love Him and trust Him with all your heart?"*

Garrett backed away from Desmond, hopped in his car, turned off the radio and sped away.

Garrett walked into his childhood home and made his way up the stairs. He was exhausted.

He passed by Blake's room and noticed the door ajar. "Blake," said Garrett. Clothes were tossed all over the room. "Are you goin' somewhere, man?"

Blake shoved his silk boxers and dress socks into a suitcase. He glared at Garrett. "Get outta my face, man. What happened to you, man?"

"Long story, man," said Garrett stepping into the room. "What's goin' on?"

"Vivi said she found out about our little secret on the Internet!"

"Internet?" asked Garrett.

"Yeah, somethin' called the *Rovert Report* specializing in non-celebrity gossip."

"No..." said Garrett falling against the doorframe for support.

"Vivi said the whole deal about you and Cat's accident is in there," continued Blake. "Why'd you have to go and get mixed up with a white girl, man? This proves it! They ain't nothin' but trouble!"

"Blake, man, that's not how it is."

"If I was you, man," said Blake pointing at Garrett, "I'd

disappear, too."

"Impossible...how?"

"All I know," said Blake slamming drawers as he emptied them, "is that she said she's gonna make my life as difficult as possible starting with the sum of $20,000 dollars for back child support!" Blake grabbed his few remaining beers and tossed them into his suitcase. "I'm 'bout to get ghost for a while."

"Blake, man, stand up for yourself!" shouted Garrett. "Be a man! Do what's right. God'll see you through."

Blake stood erect over his hastily packed suitcase.

"You really believe that?" he asked. "You think God is gonna rescue you?" Blake laughed. "G., we ain't been nothin' but players since before we hit 13, man. We stole stuff together. Smoked weed together. We've had women, one right after the other. Sometimes two at a time! Women, man. Money! God don't just forget what you've done and start bein' your best friend!"

Garrett shook his head.

"Yes He does, Blake. If you tell Him you're sorry. Yes, He does."

"But what's goin' on right now, G.," said Blake, "it don't just go away 'cause you tell God you're sorry."

"Yes it will, B.," said Garrett. "If you put it in His hands. Yes, it will."

Blake shook his head and laughed.

"And I thought all gingerbread men looked alike and tasted the same."

"Enough about that gingerbread man stuff, B.," said Garrett waving his hand. "This is your son we're talkin' about. He's a gift from God no matter how he got here!"

"Look don't start pullin' that holier-than-thou crap on me, Garrett! You walkin' around here spoutin' *repent, repent ye sinners* just 'cause you're whipped by old lady Nadine Manhassette!"

Garrett lunged forward and punched his cousin in the nose. "She don't have me whipped!" he hollered as his cousin fell to the floor. "And she ain't no old lady!"

"My nose, man!" cried Blake as his hand filled with blood. "What did you do to my nose!"

"Blake, man," said Garrett as he realized what he'd done, "I'm sorry..."

"You're a gingerbread man, Garrett!" stated Blake snatching away from Garrett's help. "That's all you'll ever be!

We're manufactured from freshly pressed church suits and Sunday school lessons. But they don't know we're men! They don't wanna know!" Blake laughed hysterically at the blood on his hands. "Nobody can catch us. You can't catch me, I'm the Gingerbread Man!"

Garrett backed away from the insanity and raced out the door to Nadine.

Chapter Eight
How the Mighty Have Fallen

Garrett's car screeched to a halt at the curb of Nadine's townhouse. He ran up to her door and banged on it. "Nadine! Nadine!"

There was no answer. He walked around the side and shouted up to her bedroom window. "Nadine! You home? I need to talk to you!"

Still there was no response.

Garrett felt crazy as only bits and pieces of the current enigma fell into place for him. He knew the source of the gossip but wondered who would master mind such a slanderous thing. And he wondered if the lascivious details had reached his beloved.

He heard a police siren in the distance. He looked around to find Nadine's neighbors peeking through their blinds. Garrett hopped in his car and sped away.

***

Across town, Nadine rang Dixie's doorbell.

Dixie swung her door open and practically snatched Nadine into the vast dwelling. "Oh, sugar," said Dixie belting down the last swallow of bourbon, "you're not gonna like this." Dixie pointed to the computer in the other room.

Nadine removed her knit scarf and cap. "What's that on your nose, Dix?"

"Huh?" asked Dixie groping her nose. "Oh, this? One of those stop snoring strips and if you mention it to anyone, they'll never find your body! Now come on."

"Dixie," said Nadine following her slowly, "what are you talking about? You call me in hysterics from a sound sleep. And you tell me this couldn't be discussed on the phone. Now you're showing me your computer?"

"I'm not *showing* you my computer, Nadine," said Dixie trying to collect her thoughts. "It's what's on the computer screen."

Nadine read the screen. "Dixie, you didn't get me to come all the way across town to show me the *Rovert Report*, did you?"

"It's an underground web site, Nadine," explained Dixie. "Not everyone can get it. Forty-five minutes. It's only available for forty-five minutes on certain nights at certain times. After that, it moves." Dixie grabbed Nadine by her shoulders and sat her down in front of the screen. "Now read, sugar. Read."

"Ho-hum," sighed Nadine lazily looking at the screen, "The *Rovert Report*. The Stories Behind the News." Nadine looked over at the nervous Dixie. "Cute title...yadda, yadda, yadda....oh, like I really need to know that Senator Peterson got breast implants!"

"Not him, Nadine!" shouted Dixie lighting a cigarette and putting it to her lips. "Read!"

"...The only other story is an update on the Gingerbread Man and his Cat?" Nadine turned to Dixie. "Fairy tales, Dix? What gives?"

Dixie clicked the mouse and turned to the next page of the site. "Read."

Nadine's eyes fell on an airbrushed picture of a strikingly beautiful woman. "...Cat's Diary." She scrolled down. "Who Did She Love?...yadda, yadda–Garrett Hunter." Nadine's breath escaped her. "...Murder...car accident...lovers?" Nadine looked up from the horror slowly. "No, Dix."

"I'm afraid so, sugar," whispered Dixie with pouting lips.

Nadine clicked the mouse and went into the mock trial. To her dread, an artistic likeness of Garrett experienced torturous punishment. He was hung by the neck and had various parts of his body sliced off and fed to rabid dogs.

"I can't look at any more, Dix," said Nadine slowly rising from the chair.

"Naddy," said Dixie, "there's more."

"More?" Nadine shook her head. "Dixie, there's nothing left."

Dixie pointed at her friend. "You're mentioned this time,

Naddy."

"Me?" asked Nadine in shock. "This time? You mean, you knew?"

"Real names aren't always given," explained Dixie in a hurry. "Remember at Diamond's Bistro I told you about Trinket? Well, I'd been reading about the Gingerbread Man. But I never expected that it was Garrett."

"Trinket?" Nadine laughed. "The Gingerbread Man? C'mon on, Dixie." Nadine's anger showed. "Who am I according to the *Rovert Report*?"

Dixie shook her head and turned away. "I can't say, Nadine. Just take my advice and stay away from him." She took a puff from her cigarette. "You could hide out here for a while if–"

"My name, Dixie!" demanded Nadine

Dixie took a long, nervous drag from her cigarette "...Old Mother Hubbard."

Nadine discharged into laughter. "How could I be such a fool!"

"Now, Naddy, calm down," said Dixie. "I'll get my lawyer on this."

"Who is this *Rovert Reporter* to publicize the private goings on of ordinary people, huh!"

Dixie was silent. She ran her hand through her blond tresses.

"It's my life!" shouted Nadine her eyes welling up with tears. "My privacy! What's this world coming to if you can't fall in love without the whole world being free to put it up to ridicule? And Garrett, Garrett, Garrett...why couldn't I see through him, Dixie?!"

"My lawyer will–"

"You do that, Dixie!" shouted Nadine snatching her scarf and cap from the hall tree. "You get your lawyer to defend my good name! But, Dixie, who's gonna defend my heart?" Nadine ran out the door in tears.

***

"Cat Fuller, Garrett," said Nadine from the kitchen. "You never told me it was Cat Fuller!"

"Now hold on, Nadine!" said Garrett. "I told you all about Cat–"

"But what you didn't tell me is that she was red-haired, green-eyed and white!"

"Since when do you have anything against white people? Dixie's white. She's your best friend!"

Nadine laughed and put her hands on her hips. "Don't you know? White female victim with Black boyfriend automatically spells twenty to life. Or did you miss the whole O.J. thing?"

"Nadine, I had nothing to do with her death," he explained. "She, she was out of control that night. I think she wanted to kill herself!"

"You didn't tell me that she kept a diary and that graphic descriptions of your lovemaking is all over it!" She pushed past Garrett.

"What?" he asked. "A diary?"

"Don't tell me you haven't heard of the *Rovert Report* web page mania that is sweeping the eastern seaboard! And you," she said pointing at him, "you're the Gingerbread Man; dark, sweet and irresistible!"

Garrett turned a few shades of purple. "...Nadine, how could you possibly know–"

"It's in her diary, Garrett. She's implicated you and your cousin Blake! Not to mention a dozen other high profile often married men!"

"Gingerbread men...we were kids, Nadine," said Garrett taking a seat on the sofa. "Blake and I made that up to score with chicks."

"Church chicks, Garrett." Nadine crossed her arms. "Or did you forget where we met? How do I know you're not up to your old tricks?!"

Garrett grabbed his head. "Listen to me, Nadine. Cat and I had a thing. It started in college. We were young. We laughed at the world. We thought it was a joke that I was so dark and she was so white." Garrett chuckled a bit.

Nadine didn't find it funny.

"Okay," he told her, "so we were off and on for years. We both had a church background. I told her about what me and Blake made up. She even called me the Gingerbread Man every now and again. When we broke up, for the last and final time, she wanted immediately to pick-up where we left off. By then I'd already made up my mind to seek the Lord. I realized no relationship could survive on novelty."

"Thanks, Garrett," she said heading for the door.

"For what?" he asked following her.

"That's the first sane thing I've heard you say," said Nadine opening the door. "No relationship can survive on novelty."

"It's not novelty with us, Nadine!" he shouted slamming it.

Gingerbread Men

"How do I know that I'm not another one of your conquests, Gingerbread Man?"

"Don't call me that, Nadine," said Garrett firmly. "You've got to believe me. I love you. I was honest with you from the start."

"No," corrected Nadine pacing the floor. "If my memory fails me, all you told me was Cat's name. Catherine, you said. Never *who* she was. Never that you were a suspect in a wrongful death suit!"

"It didn't matter anymore, Nadine," reasoned Garrett. "Not after you came into my life. All the things that seem so important now—well, my name wasn't splashed all over the internet then!"

"Yeah, right," countered Nadine. "The concussion. The moment of clarity. Packed up. Sold your condo. Moved back to your roots!" Nadine laughed madly. "I fell for it hook, line and sinker...Oh, God, Garrett, I fell for you. This is crazy!"

"C'mon, Nadine, please!" He grabbed her shoulders. "Cat wanted me back but it was over, really over, as far as I was concerned. I knew I needed something more."

"Thanks again, Garrett." She turned her back to him so he wouldn't see her cry.

"Nadine, wait–"

"Dixie was right." Nadine snatched the front door open. "I am too old for this. I don't need this! Goodbye, Garrett."

Garrett dragged his defeated body and soul from Nadine's townhouse. He felt the slammed door only inches from his backside.

***

Days went by.

Weeks followed.

No one had heard from Blake. Aunt Lena and Uncle Tyrone were starting to hear snippets of the scandalous tale that surrounded their nephew.

Clad in dark glasses and a running suit, Garrett perched himself daily in a coffee shop less than a block from the Black & White Museum Gallery. He got privileged glimpses of Nadine who uncharacteristically rushed into the museum at 8 a.m. and didn't leave until well after 6 p.m.

Garrett got the attention of a homeless man who happened by one day. "Hey, man,"

"You talkin' to me?" asked the homeless man. He was missing teeth and smelling of garbage.

"Yeah, man," said Garrett, "you wanna make $10?"

Valorie M. Taylor

"What do I gotta do for it?"

"Just deliver this letter," he said pulling it from his pocket, "to the first employee you see at the Black & White Museum Gallery down the street."

"That ain't no letter bomb, is it?" he asked scrutinizing it.

"No, man," said Garrett. "Look, it's not even sealed."

"Well, let me see the money," said the homeless man.

Garrett showed him a ten-dollar bill and shoved it into his hand.

"Okay," said the homeless man with the money and the letter. "I'll deliver it."

Garrett settled back into his booth at the little coffee shop and began reading the paper.

A few minutes later, the homeless man returned with Garrett's letter.

"What are you doin' back here, man?"

"Returning this," he said holding the letter out to Garrett. "I gave it to the curator."

"Brown-skinned lady," asked Garrett describing Nadine, "about so high and really pretty?"

"Yep, that was the one."

"Well, what happened? Why'd you bring the letter back?"

"She took one look at it and didn't even open it. She gave me $20 bucks to return it to you." The homeless man dropped the letter on Garrett's table and walked away laughing. "That's the easiest $30 bucks I ever made! Wee-hee! And all because modern folks with all this technology still don't know how to communicate with each other."

"Hey, Alice!" shouted one of the patrons stuffing his face with a sub sandwich, "Alice, honey, your hair looks fine," he told her as she primped in a mirror.

"What do you want, Sal?" she asked popping her gum.

"Turn the TV up, doll, will ya'?"

"Today on East Coast Live," said the female announcer, "we'll talk with recently demoted morals committee chairman Jeff Hargrove about his alleged affair with Cat Fuller.

"We'll also be talking with a webmaster who runs an underground website much like the *Rovert Report* that has many of the east coast's political figures shaking in their boots. Is it really the story behind the news? Or is it a blatant invasion of the privacy of private citizens? Find out today on East Coast Live with me, your host, Morgan Davis Day."

The entire coffee shop commented. Garrett sat frozen in his seat.

Gingerbread Men

"Chairman Hargrove," said the masculine-looking Morgan Davis, "the television audience is waiting to know the truth from you. This alleged affair with lobbyist Cat Fuller, was it just a friendship that was somehow mistaken for something else?"

"I wouldn't call it a friendship, Debra," said the demoted chairman. "Ms. Fuller and I worked briefly together on a charitable fund raiser back in '94. I was happily married at the time. The only contact between Ms. Fuller and me was that we presented awards to recipients together. And the entire presentation is on video tape."

"But according to excerpts we obtained from the *Rovert Report*," said Debra, "Ms. Fuller describes in detail trips to the west coast, dinner at popular night spots and a more intimate relationship."

"Ms. Fuller is a liar!"

"We understand your anger, Chairman. Hargrove," soothed Debra. "The Baltimore Times quoted you as saying '...*using a slimy source of information such as The Rovert Report to demote a morals officer is a cheap way to get my seat...*" end quote. Are you saying that there were underlying reasons to have you removed from your post of over 15 years?"

"That's exactly what I'm saying, Debra," he answered confidently. "It's no secret that I am vocally opposed to selling condoms in student restrooms and legalized abortion for teenagers. Some of my constituents made their disdain clear. I suppose linking me to a young woman who died a tragic and unfortunate death was the ultimate way of getting me out of a position of authority."

"So, the authenticity of Cat Fuller's diary pages are in question, is that it?"

"Debra," he said, "the question has been answered. There should no longer be a question in the minds of the American public. If Ms. Fuller actually believed there was an affair transpiring between her and I after one brief meeting, then it was going on inside her head or somebody has found a way to ruin lives and make a little change in the process!"

"Thank you, Chairman Hargrove," said Debra. "Next we'll talk with a webmaster who believes his underground website is actually doing some good in the eyes of the public. Back after this."

Garrett sat nervously during the commercials never removing his sun glasses and pretending to read the newspaper.

"Hello, we're back," said Debra. "In this segment, we'll talk with an underground webmaster who says his story behind the news take on life is actually more informative than traditional investigative news programs. Meet Webmaster X."

A shadowed figure appeared on the screen.

"Webmaster X," said Debra, "how does your e-news website inform without defaming ordinary citizens?"

He laughed. "That's a twisted question, Debra. Okay, well, I guess the best way to explain it is that we are the paparazzi of news. We get it where we can, you know what I mean?"

"But innocent citizens such as the Gingerbread Men, who have no political ties or celebrity, are plowed under this paparazzi-style, as you call it. What about them?"

"In the wrong place at the wrong time, I guess."

"You don't sound remorseful at all, Webmaster X."

"I'm not," he said with a shrug. "Debra, you're only focusing on some of the more high profile pieces we've done. But what about the contaminated water issues and uncovering gambling schemes in suburbia, huh? What about that?"

"But isn't that how you make your money, Mr. X?" asked Chairman Hargrove. "Selling lies."

"Hey, you can't say that about our web site on TV!" returned Webmaster X.

"Oh, yes I can!" said Hargrove coming out of his seat and hollering at the screen. "It's little pip-squeaks like you with your heads up your behinds that ruin the lives of decent, hard working Americans!"

"This is Morgan Davis for East Coast Live," said Debra. "Thank you for tuning in!"

The credits rolled.

The coffee-shop crowd roared.

A disclaimer appeared on the screen amidst the mayhem:

The committee for safe Internet Use does not endorse such underground websites such as the *Rovert Report*.

Garrett glanced up at the screen ready to make his escape. He happened to face the mirror angled next to the TV. and saw the reflected disclaimer. The only word, that made any sense jumped out at him; Trevor.

Garrett's heart skipped a beat. "Rovert *is* Trevor." Suddenly it all made sense to him.

That night, Garrett's dreams were filled with retaliation.

Oh, how he could break the frail little degenerate in half with his bare hands, he fantasized. And what a service it would be to the private citizens who own their own life, their own privacy.

Schemes such as this kept Garrett up all night. He even considered murder but sufficed to simply injure, maim and frighten his nemesis. But left alive, Trevor could point the finger at him. Garrett didn't like the idea of prison.

He turned to God for help. After a brief plea for help, he pored over the Psalms of David for an answer and comfort.

Garrett's uncle pulled the squeaky ironing board from its wall holder and heated up the iron.

"Aunt Lena still won't iron your stuff for you, huh, Uncle T.?" asked Garrett.

Uncle Tyrone spun around with his fists up ready to defend himself. He eased into normal posture noticing Garrett sitting in the shadows of the breakfast nook. "Boy, you scared me. You liable to get your teeth rearranged messin' with me at this time of mornin'. What you doin' up at 4:30 anyway?"

"Couldn't sleep, man," said Garrett. "Too many things goin' through my head."

"Well, like what?"

"This internet mess, man," said Garrett. "Can't get any answers from the Lord. Nadine doesn't want to see me anymore. She won't return my calls. Aw, man! Just when I was tryin' to get my life together, all this junk blows up in my face!"

Uncle Tyrone laughed and laid his work pants out on the ironing board. "Congratulations."

Garrett huffed. "For what?"

"Well," said Uncle T., "you're being falsely accused, right?"

"Yeah."

"Your name being drug through the mud?" he asked. "Can't seem figure out a way to legally vindicate yourself?"

"That's right," answered Garrett

"Well, you've just joined the ranks of some pretty heavy hitters. Like Daniel, Paul, Peter, David, and the one and only, Jesus Christ."

Garrett thought about his uncle's observation.

"It's an elite group, Garrett," he said pressing the iron to his work pants. "Not everybody can get in. But these men set out to do good, just like you. They wanted to bring a sense of purpose to their lives and to the lives of others all the while serving the Big Man upstairs. They were pretty good jugglers, too. But they got chased out of town, beat-up, jailed."

Garrett closed his eyes on that word.

"But they all did one thing," explained Uncle Tyrone. "And you'll have to do it, too."

"What's that?" asked Garrett.

Uncle Tyrone turned from his ironing. "They faced their accusers. Him, her, it; you've gotta be ready for a showdown."

"Yeah," said Garrett his mind fused with images of war and revenge as he stood to his feet. "Okay," he said punching his palm, "then what?"

"Well, these jugglers, as I call 'em, who earned their stripes getting' their faces pounded because of the truth–"

"Yeah," said Garrett anxiously, "yeah. Go on."

"These mighty men of valor who sacrificed money, career and family to bring the truth to the world–"

"Alright, now!" shouted Garrett. "What'd they do?"

"They prayed for a miracle," said Garrett's uncle. "They prayed for guidance."

"Uncle T.," said Garrett shaking his head, "you're talkin' in riddles, man."

"Go ahead," said Garrett's uncle, "look it up in your Bible."

"Okay, okay. But God knows what happened in the car that night with me and Cat. He knows I didn't cause that accident. He knows she was out of her mind to do what she did. Isn't God a fair God? A defender of the wrongfully accused and all that?"

"He is," said Uncle Tyrone. "But he's also a God of war. Oh, His love is free. Salvation is free. But favor you have to earn, son. You can only get it by fighting on your knees."

Uncle Tyrone raised the squeaking ironing board and headed up the stairs leaving Garrett alone in the kitchen with his thoughts.

The telephone rang.

Garrett reached for it. "Hello."

"Garrett," whispered a familiar voice, "is that you?"

"Who is this?"

"It's me, Ingrid."

"What's goin' on?" he asked. "Why are you whispering?"

"Garrett, you never got this call from me. Understand?"

"Yeah."

"Detective Larry Desmond is allegedly linked to a white supremacy group here in Baltimore."

"What!" asked Garrett remembering the road-side brawl.

"They're a nasty bunch, too," said Ingrid.

"Look, I'm not afraid of–"

"Garrett, I looked into his wife's involvement with a Black man fitting your description a number of years ago. Similar fatal car accident involving Desmond's wife and daughter. Only the man survived. Desmond said the guy committed suicide. But the coroner's report clearly stated foul play because the angle of the gun shot could not have been self-inflicted."

"Ingrid, I..."

"Run, Garrett," said Ingrid. "Get as far away as you can. Do you hear me?"

"Ingrid," said Garrett. "I won't run."

"Garrett, don't be a fool!" she shouted. "You're not some street punk!"

"Even street punks need to know the love of God."

"You're insane, Garrett," said an exasperated Ingrid.

"If God doesn't love me enough to vindicate me," staring blankly at the scriptures, "then I'm a dead man."

"Garrett will you listen to reason? I can arrange for a name change and–"

"No, Ingrid," said Garrett. "My defense is in His hands."

Garrett hung up the phone on Ingrid's rebuttal.

Chapter Nine
Fulfillment

Garrett's racy sports car crept along like a big cat on the prowl. The black, wet streets of Baltimore glistened under faint boulevard lights illuminating his path of destruction.

Vicious, angry whispers hissed at him from vacant dwellings. He consumed their violent energy in gulps relishing the burning sensation that resulted in the pit his belly.

Garrett's hands became hammer, chisel, knife, even gun at his command. He imagined killing Trevor slowly, ever so slowly. His goal to make the little wimp suffer the same number of days he himself had suffered was a delight too delicious to fathom. But he would take his time, nonetheless.

A key appeared in his hand as he reached Cat's apartment door. He used it without hesitation.

Inside was Trevor.

Trevor, singing the horrible operetta, dressed as a female viking.

Trevor dressed in drag and dancing a gypsy-jig with a tambourine. Trevor dressed as Zeke. Trevor dressed as Desmond. Trevor impersonating Reverend Freidman ridiculously shouting "save me! Oh, Lord, save me!"

Garrett turned to the mirror as the disguised crowd taunted and laughed at him. In the dining room, sat Trevor, confined to a wheelchair, at his computer.

Garrett's hands shifted from one style of weapon to another as he took bold, hammer-footed steps toward his nemesis.

Gingerbread Men

Beside Trevor on the table were torn, tear-stained pages of Cat's diary. Garrett picked them up but couldn't read them clearly. Then he noticed a platter of gingerbread man cookies with their heads bitten off.

Trevor was guilty. Garrett was aroused by the fury that warmed him. He alone was judge and jury. Trevor's trial was over.

With his hand now formed into a knife, Garrett stepped back and whacked at the back of Trevor's neck. "This is for Nadine!"

"Humph..." said Trevor unscathed by the fatal puncture. He casually bit the head of another gingerbread man. "Men."

A chain appeared in Garrett's hand. He wrapped it around Trevor's skinny neck and pulled until he heard a snap.

"Men..." said Trevor unharmed as he leaned forward to tap on the keyboard.

Garrett backed away in exhaustion and confusion. "I'm gonna stop you, Trevor!"

"Stop me?" he asked spinning around in his chair. "Stop me?" He laughed. "I am rumor. I am the untamed tongue. I am the stuff the blanks are filled in with. Don't you know it's what you believe? As long as it's negative, people believe it."

"No," mumbled Garrett moving back to the living room door. Garrett's eyes fell on the massacred bodies of the Trevor look-alikes. Every way he'd attempted to hurt Trevor, he'd astoundingly hurt them. They lay moaning and wailing in pools of blood.

"You hurt me," said Trevor confidently standing from his wheel chair, "you hurt them. You hurt them, you hurt you."

Garrett scrambled to the door.

"Tsk, tsk," said Trevor shaking his head pitifully at the gruesome sight while *La Femme Daphne* sounded in. "Men."

Garrett twisted and then bolted from his pillow drenched in a cold sweat. His breath clamored through his lungs. His heart thumped around in his chest as if it had been injected with rhino adrenaline.

Wiping the sweat from his brow, Garrett rested on his pillow glad to be surrounded by the familiar trappings of the spare bedroom.

"My baby! My baby!" he heard Aunt Lena shouting from down stairs.

Garrett snatched a t-shirt onto his bare chest and raced down the stairs.

To his surprise, there stood Blake wrapped in his

mother's embrace with Uncle Tyrone proudly looking on.

"B.," said Garrett with a smile. "You came back, man."

"Yeah," said Blake kissing his mother gently on her forehead. "I came back."

"Where'd you go?" asked Garrett taking a seat at the kitchen table. "You didn't call or anything."

Blake touched his healed nose. "Yeah, well, Garrett, you've got a pretty effective left hook. Changed my mind about a lot of things."

"Hey, man," said Garrett, "sorry. I know I'm at fault for what happened with the D.A. and all."

"Naw, man," said Blake taking a seat. "I was just sayin' to my mom and dad that it's time I started takin' responsibility for myself, you know what I mean? I saw Vivi. She's mixed up with this dude." Blake shook his head hopelessly. "He ain't no good for her, man. He's a player."

Aunt Lena looked directly at Blake. "Takes one to know one, huh, son?"

"Now, Lena," scolded her husband. "C'mon, let the boy become the man he should be.""Alright, Mom," said Blake shaking his head, "maybe I deserved that. But now we're talkin' 'bout my son here. He don't need to see his mama bein' dogged like that by some dude that all he wants is to get wit' her. Vivi won't listen to reason either. But this dude don't care nothin' 'bout her. And he really don't care nothin' 'bout little Blake. That boy needs a man around."

"So, you tryin' to get back with her, man?" asked Garrett.

"I thought about it," said Blake honestly. "You know, for the sake of the boy. But ain't nothin' there, man. I guess I hurt her too much playin' the Gingerbread Man role. But I made a decision. Me and Vivi agreed. We're gonna share custody of little Blake."

"You mean," asked Aunt Lena with nervous excitement, "I'm actually gonna have my grandson around?".

"Yeah, Mom," said Blake nodding kindly.

"Thank you, Lord," said Aunt Lena wrapping her arms around her son. "Thank you, son. You're a good man."

Blake rubbed her arm. "I'm gonna start back in church, too, Mom."

"Oh, hallelujah!" shouted Blake's mother as she melted into praise. "Jesus!" she cried falling onto her husband. "Jesus!"

"Little Blake's got to know what bein' a real church man is all about," said Blake to Garrett with a little grin. "Not gonna deny him a father no more," said Blake battling a tear.

Gingerbread Men

"I had the best example, man," said Blake to his father. "There's no excuse, you know? Right or wrong, I'm his daddy, man."

Blake stood and faced his father.

"Welcome to manhood, son," said Blake's father, his soul full with family pride.

Garrett nodded approvingly.

***

Garrett found himself alone in his bedroom still clad in his pajamas even at 2 o'clock in the afternoon.

The details of the dream chased and taunted his righteousness around the hollow caverns of his mind. The ease in which he could consider murder on a subconscious level disturbed Garrett greatly.

Unshowered and unshaven, Garrett balanced a small Bible on his leg during respites of introspection. He closed his eyes and tried desperately to connect with his God; to recapture that pure, refreshing feeling he experienced as Reverend Freidman offered him salvation.

But his thoughts made a u-turn to the dream, its meaning, its purpose.

"I know who it is, Lord," he prayed quietly. "Why won't You let me confront him? It's the dream, isn't it? In the dream he said if I hurt him, I'd hurt the people who are expecting the best of me, huh?

"But it's not fair, Lord," said Garrett. "You let Israelites battle for their respect, why not me? Everything that I have is slipping through my fingers while I wait..."

In the quiet recesses of Garrett's prayer closet, he heard a voice of deliverance and instruction.

"*The peace that passes all understanding shall guard your heart and mine through Christ Jesus, Garrett. Not your fists. Not your strength. Why do you fight a battle that is not yours? Don't worry about things you cannot change. The peace that passes all understanding shall guard your heart and mine through Christ Jesus, Garrett.*"

Garrett opened his eyes slowly feeling renewed and ready.

***

Exactly three days later, Garrett sat glued to the television screen as the bright picture box illuminated the dark room of the otherwise silent Hunter home.

Aunt Lena crept in carrying her two year-old grandson on her hip. She joined her husband on the couch. She clutched his hand and gave him a knowing, faith-believing look.

"You think this show will clear everything up, G.?" asked Blake offering his cousin a soda.

"I'm prayin' it will, man," answered Garrett never taking his eyes off the screen. "It's got to," he whispered. "It's got to..."

Blake set the soda next to him and took a seat on the couch.

"Now, Blake," began Uncle Tyrone, "are you sure they said they're gonna mention the *Rovert Report* tonight?"

"Yeah, Dad," said Blake belching. "Excuse me. Vivi said she saw the preview this morning."

"Oh, Lord," prayed Aunt Lena, "Garrett needs Your help tonight."

"Sshh!" said Garrett. "It's coming on."

The program announcer's voice reverberated into the room. "Featured tonight on America's View; the scandalous information feeding frenzy that threatens the privacy of average Americans. Is what happens in *your* backyard newsworthy? We've got some underground information peddlers who say it is. But first, your host, Dr. Zoe Queenan talks candidly with the parents of the infamous web-celeb, Cat Fuller, about this act some are calling info-piracy. Is this the wave of the future?"

Garrett's heart beat out of control.

Dr. Queenan's deep blue eyes and dark black hair glistened under the studio lights as she spoke. "Good evening," she said with a quick nod. "Thank you, America, for tuning in. I'm Dr. Zoe Queenan. In the studio this evening, we have surprise guests. Sue and Otis Fuller, parents of Cat Fuller, a young woman who died tragically in a car crash this winter. Ms. Fuller's death differs from other deaths this year because a mysterious information-peddler and publisher of the *Rovert Report*, has somehow seized Ms. Fuller's diary. He or she has used the diary to ruin the lives of prominent as well as private citizens. The *Rovert Report* web-page has profited by selling limited and numbered copies of excerpts from Ms. Fuller's diary."

The disarming doctor turned to the plainly dressed couple. "Why have you come here today, Mr. & Mrs. Fuller?"

"We want the internet madness to end concerning our daughter," said Otis looking directly into the camera.

"I have to ask you this," said Dr. Queenan, "has anyone approached you about appearing on In Defense? Anyone perhaps named in Cat's diary? Anyone From America's View?"

"No," said the couple solemnly. "We've come here by the leading of the Lord," said Otis taking his wife's hand. "We just felt too many people's lives were getting messed up over something intended to be private in the first place."

"It's hard for any mother to admit that her daughter had problems," said Sue dabbing at her eyes with a wrinkled lace-hanky. "But Catherine had emotional problems." Pain shuddered through Sue's body. "We raised her in a good Christian home to the best of our ability."

Otis rubbed her back soothingly.

"I understand that Cat was often suicidal," said Dr. Queenan gently. "Is that true?"

"Yes," said Otis looking at the floor as he shook his head. "She tried to kill herself a few times. Always over some boy. Catherine was a pretty girl," said the old man with quivering lips. "Guys flocked to her. That doesn't mean she bedded everyone of 'em," he defended. "And the published portions of the diary suggest that she was the kind of woman who only dated married men! But it's not true. I tell ya', Catherine wasn't that kind of girl."

"Dr. Queenan," said Sue speaking-up boldly, "we want to end this but we also want America to know what it has taken to come here today." Sue's eyes gushed tears. "We lost our daughter tragically. Nothing we say here will bring her back." Sue became silent and then braved the remainder of her comment. "But the *Rovert Report* web page and the buying and selling of a young woman's fears and dreams is not what Catherine would have wanted. We simply do not understand why anyone would want to ruin the lives of so many people."

Dr. Queenan was at a loss for words and handed Sue a tissue.

"I don't believe her diary was written to some day hurt the reputations of prominent people," said Sue taking a deep breath. "Catherine liked to feel important and be around important people. That's no crime. But what's happening on the Internet concerning *my* daughter's good name ought to be a crime."

"So, let me see if I understand this correctly," said Dr. Queenan referring to hurried notes she had jotted down, "you don't believe The Gingerbread Man had anything to do with her death?"

"It was an accident, Dr. Queenan," said Sue. "An unfortunate, untimely accident. We've known Garrett as long as

Catherine had known him," Sue explained. "They were an item briefly in college."

"He sat at my table many times," said Otis obviously remembering Garrett fondly. "And he'd be welcomed there today if we knew where he was."

"He's a good man," agreed Sue. "We even went to the hospital and prayed for him while he was in a coma."

"*You* visited the Gingerbread–I mean, Garrett Hunter?" asked Dr. Queenan trying to mask her shock.

Garrett's heart skipped a beat as he faintly remembered warm hands on his chest and faithful prayers that filled his hospital room.

"Yes, we did," confirmed Sue. "He was always a gentlemen. He was a young man focused on his career. He'd never hurt Catherine, Dr. Queenan. Never."

Dr. Queenan turned away in disbelief.

"Doctor," began Sue, "we don't believe Garrett is guilty of anything. We're sorry his name is being drug through the mud based on innuendo and conjecture. Anybody whose career or life is suffering from this invasion and exploitation of privacy and this twisting of facts, well, we hope that our coming here today will put an end to it."

"You mentioned emotional problems, Mrs. Fuller," asked the doctor. "Did Cat ever seek professional help?"

"Catherine spent some time in a mental institution learning to cope with her anxiety and depression," confessed Sue uneasily. "...She was an only child. And because of her problems, we were extremely close."

"Doc.," said Otis, "we're not ashamed of our daughter. She was a grown woman who made her own decisions. We miss her. There are times me and Sue lay awake at night wondering if we should have raised her differently. That's normal, I guess. But we don't endorse or encourage the misuse of her diary for profit. And we're urging anyone who has participated in perpetuating this sick act to shake themselves and just, just stop."

"Mr. and Mrs. Fuller," asked Dr. Queenan, "do either of you have any clue as to who might want to profit from your daughter's private thoughts?"

"Honestly," said Sue, "we don't know anyone who'd want to hurt Cat by publishing such lies. Everyone she came in contact with instantly liked her."

Garrett closed his eyes and recalled her red hair blowing fiercely in the wind.

"The Bible says not to bear false witness against your neighbor!" interjected Otis.

"So there you have it, America," said Dr. Queenan turning to the camera for her close-up, "Sue and Otis Fuller, mother and father of Cat Fuller, speaking out for justice against their daughters' exploiters."

Sue put her finger up sheepishly. "May I just say, Dr. Queenan, that rumor and gossip are like viruses waiting to distort, dismantle and weaken the defenses. And we never really know how far it reaches until someone's life or career, their hopes and dreams are destroyed."

Blake ran his finger over his sleeping son's cheek.

Camera one focused on the middle-aged woman's sincere face.

"Whoever is responsible for this false truth peddling," said Sue as a tear trickled down her sallow cheek, "Otis and I are praying that you'll be brought to justice. And that lives that are so desperately in need of repair because of this unfortunate thing can find peace and fulfillment as Our Maker intended."

The doctor leaned into the couple and held their hands reassuringly. "I know this must have been extremely difficult for the two of you. Thank you, Mr. and Mrs. Fuller. Thank you. You're brave to be guests on America's View," she turned to the camera, "the prime time news hour bringing you the truth at any cost."

"Father," said Garrett dropping to his knees and putting his hands on the TV screen, "You said You would be the one to bring Trevor to justice, Lord. You said my fists would be useless in my defense. The Fuller's plea isn't enough. Please, Lord, please..."

This just in," said Zoe Queenan intently listening to her earpiece. *"Trevor Hellman of Baltimore, Maryland, who cleverly spelled his first name backwards to avoid suspicion while publishing the Rovert Report, was arrested at the beginning of this broadcast.*

Garrett sunk to the floor and let out a victorious yell as he watched a clip of Trevor being led from his apartment in his wheelchair.

"The confessed information peddler pled guilty at the time of the arrest to enhancing various portions of Cat Fuller's diary for profit and for defamation. Trevor Hellmore, as you can see in

this clip, is a disabled veteran whom former lobbyist Cat Fuller had given a home to while working with disabled and homeless vets two years ago. Hellmore faces the possibility of 10 years in prison and many defamation of character suits.

"And it appears that the Rovert Report fiasco has reached the Baltimore police department, as well,"

Garrett could hardly believe his ears.

"Detective Larry Desmond," she said reading from her papers, "has alleged ties to A.C.E., a white supremacy organization. Desmond is being sought for questioning in the 1993 murder of Roger Langston, a man with whom Desmond's deceased wife was romantically involved. More on that at 10 this evening."

A single tear raced down Garrett's clenched jaw.

Uncle Tyrone and Blake embraced happily. They praised the Lord so loudly, they woke the baby.

Uncle Tyrone put his hand on Garrett's shoulder. "...It's over now, son. It's over now."

Garrett looked up to Heaven and closed his eyes. "No. It's just begun," he said smiling. "The Lord did this, Uncle T. God alone." Garrett turned to his uncle. "I prayed for a miracle; vindication for me and for Nadine." Garrett stood up and pointed to the screen. "He gave me both."

"Hallelujah," sang Aunt Lena as her hands went up in praise. "...Hallelujah."

The doorbell rang.

Aunt Lena opened the door wiping her tears. Her hands went to her mouth as she gasped. "I'm so glad you're here." Aunt Lena gladly stepped aside.

Breathless, Nadine spoke. "Garrett."

He closed his eyes and turned to her not believing that he would ever hear her voice again. But there she stood; shocked, relieved, happy.

"I prayed, Garrett," she said amazed at what the Lord had done. "...He actually answered *my* prayer."

"What prayer, Nadine," asked Aunt Lena.

"I've been so stubborn," she admitted. "But I was sure that I loved Garrett, Mrs. Hunter."

Nadine stepped languidly to the man she was certain the Lord had chosen for her. "So I said the only thing that would prove to me beyond a shadow of a doubt that you and I are to be together is if someone confirmed Cat's mental state." Nadine broke down in tears. "I hated her, Garrett. I hated you, too. But when her parents said those things about her, I felt so sorry for her."

"It's okay," whispered Garrett, stoking her hair.

She closed her eyes and took a deep breath. "I prayed every single day since I said I never wanted to see you again. Crazy, huh?" She wiped her tears with her whole hand. "The Lord did all this for us, Garrett. You and me."

He held her sweet face in his hands and studied it with loving, appreciative eyes. Garrett felt rewarded with the depth of her brown eyes. He took his time relishing her alluring scent and the soft touch of her skin beneath his fingertips; all the things he'd missed and belabored to forget. He pulled her petite body into his kissing her gently on the mouth.

Nadine wrapped her arms around him and laid her head against his chest.

They both breathed an arduous sigh of relief.

"Thank you, Lord," they said in unison and drew each other in closer.

Valorie M. Taylor